Praise for Erin Dutton

Wavering Convictions

"The two women have great chemistry together. The romance is sweet…This is my first book by Erin Dutton, and I will be looking for more books to read by her."—*Rainbow Reflections*

Landing Zone

"Erin Dutton is great at writing relatable characters, and Kim and Lauren are no exception. These are two interesting, strong women who have a lot to figure out if they're going to be together, and I enjoyed joining them for their journey. The romance is also done well, giving that satisfying push and pull that often comes in enemies-to-lovers pairings."—*Lesbian Review*

Planning for Love

"*Planning for Love* has an engaging style that kept me hooked from the first page to the last. While I can't really call it an enemies-to-lovers romance, there's definitely a hate-to-love aspect that's so well done that it's delicious.…Erin Dutton knows what's up when it comes to writing romance, and she did a fabulous job with Planning for Love. It's sexy, sweet, and well worth checking out. I'll be reading this one again!"
—*Lesbian Review*

Capturing Forever

"While there is fire and passion, [*Capturing Forever*] is a thoughtful romance, well written and well paced, it brings to life the reality of adult experiences and the strength of family despite the mistakes we all make."—*Lesbian Reading Room*

"This story had so much depth and Erin Dutton managed to show how fragile relationships are and how they can be destroyed through careless words and stubbornness. The love scenes in the book were beautiful and emotionally charged. They were about deep love and were so vital to the story. I want to go back and re-r   in it and didn't want it to end."—*Kitt*

"The book is written very well and w   to finish…I found myself cheering for

This is one of those books I will reread someday, and that is how you really know that it is a book worth talking about."—*Amanda's Reviews*

Dutton "takes you deep into the heart of both these women…The story flows like a river, smooth on the surface, beneath, a current pulling you away."—*Lunar Rainbow Reviewz*

Officer Down

"This book is a true romance…I liked seeing the characters grow, expand their horizons, and become, in Olivia's case, the woman she so desperately wants to be."—*Prism Book Alliance*

"The story was fast-paced and I enjoyed reading about how the relationship between Olivia and Hillary developed from being work acquaintances to much more."—*Bookaholism.com*

For the Love of Cake

"Thoroughly enjoyable reading. If you like a good romance this will hit the buttons, and if you like reality cooking shows you will have a double winner. As many others will probably say – it has hot women and cake, what else could it possibly need?"—*Curve*

"In Dutton's highly entertaining contemporary, well-drawn characters Shannon Hayes and Maya Vaughn discover romance behind reality TV…Dutton's love story never loses momentum."—*Publishers Weekly*

Point of Ignition

"Erin Dutton has given her fans another fast paced story of fire, with both buildings and emotions burning hotly. *Point of Ignition* is a story told well that will touch its readers."—*Just About Write*

"Erin Dutton has written more than seven lesbian romance titles for Bold Strokes Books, and boy can she write."—*The Bright List*

Designed for Love

"*Designed for Love* is…rich in love, romance, and sex. Dutton gives her readers a roller coaster ride filled with sexual thrills and chills. *Designed for Love* is the perfect book to curl up with on a cold winter's day."—*Just About Write*

A Place to Rest

"If you like romances with characters who could live next door to you and the element of family interaction and dynamics, *A Place to Rest* is for you. It's charming, moving, and emotionally satisfying."—*Lesbian Review*

Fully Involved

"Dutton literally fills the pages with smoke as she vividly describes the scene. She is equally skilled at showing her readers Reid's feelings of guilt and rage at the loss of her best friend. Fully Involved explores the emotional depths of these two very different women. Each woman struggles with loss, change, and the magnetic attraction they have for each other. Their relationship sizzles, flames, and ignites with a page-turning intensity. This is an exciting read about two very intriguing women."—*Just About Write*

"Dutton's studied evocation of the macho world of firefighting gives the story extra oomph—and happily ever after is what a good romance is all about, right?"—*Q Syndicate*

Sequestered Hearts

"*Sequestered Hearts* is packed with raw emotion, but filled with tender moments too. The author writes with sophistication that one would expect from a veteran author....A romance is about more than just plot and character development. It's about passion, physical intimacy, and connection between the characters. The reader should have a visceral reaction to what is going on within the pages for the novel to succeed. Dutton's words match perfectly with the emotion she has created. *Sequestered Hearts* is one book that cannot be overlooked. It is romance at its finest."—*L-word Literature.com*

"*Sequestered Hearts* by first time novelist Erin Dutton is everything a romance should be. It is teeming with longing, heartbreak, and of course, love....as pure romances go, it is one of the best in print today."—*Just About Write*

By the Author

Sequestered Hearts

Fully Involved

A Place to Rest

Designed for Love

Point of Ignition

A Perfect Match

Reluctant Hope

More than Friends

For the Love of Cake

Officer Down

Capturing Forever

Planning for Love

Landing Zone

Wavering Convictions

Three Alarm Response

Visit us at www.boldstrokesbooks.com

THREE ALARM RESPONSE

by

Erin Dutton

2020

THREE ALARM RESPONSE
© 2020 By Erin Dutton. All Rights Reserved.

ISBN 13: 978-1-63555-592-9

This Trade Paperback Original Is Published By
Bold Strokes Books, Inc.
P.O. Box 249
Valley Falls, NY 12185

First Edition: June 2020

Credits
Editor: Shelley Thrasher
Production Design: Stacia Seaman
Cover Design by Tammy Seidick

Acknowledgments

I'm writing these acknowledgments only days after a devastating tornado hit Nashville. The news covers the devastation, broadcasting pictures and interviews and even drone footage that really brings home the vast damage. It's amazing to watch a community put aside all other differences and come together to help their neighbors. There's another side to tragedies like this, or like the event I wrote about in this book: the dedication of the first responders who help during the emergency and the aftermath. I know, it's their job, that's what they signed up for, your tax dollars, etc. I get it.

But this week, I stood in the dispatch center with the 9-1-1 call takers and dispatchers. I heard the voices of the officers, firefighters, and paramedics in the field. In the Emergency Operations Center, representatives from many departments in city government, police, fire, various utilities, public works, etc. all come together to get the city back on its feet. Their personal schedules and the needs of their own families are temporarily suspended while they give up days off and pull twelve-hour shifts, sometime longer, often with little regard to how what they see affects them personally. So with that, I want to express gratitude for all those who serve the safety and well-being of the public in every capacity.

As always, thanks as well to the staff at Bold Strokes Books for helping me bring these stories to life. Dr. Shelley Thrasher has been with me since book two, and this one makes number fifteen. Her editing makes my work stronger. I can't mention Shelley without also thinking about Connie. Connie, from my first GCLS conference when I was a new author without even a book out yet, you have made me feel welcome and a little less socially awkward. Your friendship is so special to me.

Thanks to you, the reader, holding this book (or ebook). Your time is valuable and I'm thrilled that you have shared it with me. Every new box of books is just as exciting as the first, and you're the reason I get to keep doing this.

For the First Responders

Contents

Rescued

CHAPTER ONE

Claire Willows jerked upright in her bed, her alarm having ripped her from sleep. But it was still dark, and the rhythmic pulsing squeal wasn't her usual wake-up tone. She glanced toward the nightstand, expecting, but not finding, the glow from her cell-phone screen. Not her alarm. Something tickled her throat, and she coughed, pulling in an acrid odor as she inhaled. Smoke!

Panic propelled her out of bed, grabbing for her phone as she went. She fleetingly thought of dialing 9-1-1, but when she realized Stu wasn't in the dog bed where he usually slept, her focus shifted.

"Stu, come." She coughed, then tried again. She couldn't leave without him, but the smoke was growing thicker. She knelt and swept her arm under the bed to feel for him while calling his name.

Her eyes burned, and every inhalation made her cough. Able to make out the shape of the door in the ambient light from her open blinds, she stumbled in that direction. Maybe if she left, Stu would follow. Suddenly remembering a nugget from elementary school, she dropped to her hands and knees. Smoke rises; get down low. She could breathe a little easier as she crawled toward the front of her apartment.

By the time she made it to the living room, she still hadn't found Stu. She couldn't leave him. She'd just turned to go back inside when someone pounded on the front door, then called in a muffled voice. She tried to answer, but she was already hoarse and doubted anyone could hear her response. The door burst open with a crack, and the hulking figure of a firefighter filled the frame. When he reached for Claire, she staggered back.

"Ma'am, you need to evacuate the building." A mask obscured his face and muffled his voice, but she could make out the words.

Before she could argue, he'd wrapped one thick-gloved hand around her arm and pulled her toward the breezeway.

❖

Britt Everett jumped down off her fire truck, feeling a tiny twinge in her right knee on impact. That was new. But so were a lot of the aches and pains she'd discovered in the past year. She wasn't worried, though. Several days a week in the firehouse gym had ensured she was still in better shape than most forty-year-olds she knew.

Her crew had been dispatched to the scene as part of a third-alarm response, which in a college town the size of Bellbrook, Indiana, meant almost every piece of equipment in the department was now on scene. Usually, the tone echoing through the hall at three a.m. would have pulled her from her bunk. But she'd been awake listening to the call-outs on the radio for the other companies, knowing that eventually her crew would be needed.

Fire had consumed one of the six multi-unit apartment buildings and spread to two others. Flames crackled as they licked out from under the eaves. The hypnotic orange glow competed with the aggressively flashing strobes from a dozen different vehicles.

She stepped over a charged hose as she made her way to the battalion chief in command of the scene. Firefighters from several engine companies saturated the exterior walls of the nearby buildings in order to minimize further damage, but the two involved structures would be a total loss.

When Britt reached the chief's side, she waited while he issued orders into the radio microphone clipped to the front of his jacket. Chief Jeff Cooper had been just two years ahead of her in high school, and they had run with some of the same crowd. As a rookie firefighter, she'd worked alongside him for a time on an engine crew before he started up the promotional ladder.

"Chief, Truck Seven is here and ready to go."

"Have your guys stand by for a few, Everett. I've got two other truck companies pulling residents out of the surrounding apartments. Once we get the fire under control, I'll need fresh crews to go in."

"Got it." She nodded toward the crowd at the edge of the scene, still too close to the action. Judging by their varying styles of sleepwear and their dazed expressions, most of them were residents of the complex. "Is PD coming for crowd control?"

He shrugged, but his attention never left the scene in front of him. He was a good incident commander, constantly assessing where resources were being used and anticipating where they might be needed next. "I requested them. But someone robbed the gas station down the street, so they're kind of tied up."

"We'll handle that until they get here, or until you need us for something else."

"Thanks."

As she crossed the parking lot, she gestured for the two men on her crew to head over to the group of onlookers. Families huddled together, parents draping their arms around their blanket-wrapped children. Some looked to be in shock, while others seemed already defeated by the damage to their building. None would be left adrift for the night. The Red Cross would be called to assist those that didn't have family or friends to shelter them. But they would all deal with the aftermath for weeks or even months to come.

Watching flames consume your home was traumatic enough, but even those who lived in apartments on the edge of the active fire would deal with loss as well. That kind of smoke left a cloying odor that permeated the soft surfaces of furniture, bedding, and clothing, not to mention the damage that thousands of gallons of high-pressure water caused.

As Britt approached, she scanned the crowd for any onlooker who appeared a little too interested in the firefighters' efforts. She hadn't heard anything on the radio about what caused the blaze, and they likely wouldn't know for hours, after the investigators got to work. But she'd learned long ago that trying to recall details from the scene later on was easier if she made a conscious effort to observe them now. And for whatever reason, arsonists liked to admire their own work.

Raised voices at the edge of the group caught Britt's attention, and she detoured in that direction. A female resident had engaged Anderson, one of her guys, in a heated conversation, and judging by her flailing arms and his exasperated expression, she wasn't backing down.

"What's the problem?" Britt asked as she reached them.

"This lady wants to go inside," Anderson blurted, talking over whatever the woman was trying to say. He seemed ready to hand off his problem to Britt, and the woman appeared as willing to be done with him. She immediately turned her attention to Britt, determination warring with the plea in her eyes.

If she sought an ally, she needed to look elsewhere. Britt's primary concern was always safety, of both her fellow firefighters and the public she served. And she wouldn't risk either for whatever memento this woman hoped to retrieve—not even for the chance to transform the distressed expression on her beautiful face.

"I'm sorry, ma'am. We can't let you go back in there." Britt held her arm out loosely, expecting the woman to obey her command, surprised when the woman surged forward, practically stumbling into her arms. Her palms landed on Britt's upper arms, clapping against the thick fabric of her turnout coat. Britt instinctively grasped her waist to steady her.

"No. I have to—Stu is in there." Tears filled her eyes, reflecting the glow of flames brightly against the cool tone of her pale complexion.

Suddenly on alert, Britt met the woman's eyes. Someone was still trapped inside. "Where is he?"

"In my apartment." She closed her eyes and shook her head as if fighting through her panic. "Apartment 225. He won't be able to get out." When she tilted her head back and met Britt's eyes again, her expression had changed, as if relieved that someone was finally listening to her.

"How old is he?"

The woman blinked. "He's seven. What does that matter? We're wasting time."

Britt grabbed her radio and engaged the mic. "Truck Seven to Command. We've got someone still inside, a seven-year-old boy."

"Boy? What? No. Stu is my dog." The woman still clutched a handful of Britt's jacket.

"Your what?"

"He's my dog. I couldn't find him as I was leaving. But he hides when he's scared. Sometimes in the space between the couch and the wall, or under the bed."

Britt sighed. "False alarm, Chief. It's a dog." She grasped the woman's arm and tried to lead her away. "Ma'am, I need you to go over there with the other residents."

"Are you going in to get him?"

"We'll do what we can."

Her eyes went cold, and she yanked her arm free. "I don't believe you."

Britt glanced over her shoulder. She was wasting time trying to sort out this conflict, though she had real work to do. "I'm not going to argue with you. Go wait over there until the scene is safe." She nudged the woman toward all the other residents still clustered together.

Much stealthier than expected, the woman slipped past Britt and sprinted toward the building. After a second of disbelief, Britt took off after her, but with her heavy gear and her helmet bouncing in her face at every step, she was no match for the woman's surprising speed. As the woman pulled away from her, panic built in her chest. This idiot would run into a burning building and get herself killed, and it would be Britt's fault.

Just as the woman reached the building, another firefighter emerged from the breezeway. Britt shouted, "Stop her."

The firefighter, his SCBA mask obscuring his face so Britt couldn't easily identify him, reacted to Britt's words and wrapped his arms around the woman, abandoning any concern of propriety or personal space in favor of safety. The woman struggled, then started to cough, both from her efforts and from the haze of smoke inside the hot zone.

"Let me go."

As soon as Britt reached them, the other firefighter shoved the woman into her arms, obviously more comfortable with Britt restraining her. Close up, she recognized him as one of the guys assigned to Engine Two.

The woman struggled, and Britt pulled her more tightly to her. "It's not safe."

"He's still in there. You can't let him die."

She didn't tell the woman that the chances for her dog were already not very good.

"You're not going in there. Don't make me call one of those police officers over to detain you." Britt tossed her head in the direction of two officers who'd arrived and were now stringing up yellow tape in front of the crowd. "They've already got enough to do."

"You'd have me arrested?"

"More like temporarily in custody. For your own safety."

She lifted her chin and glared. "Do what you have to do. But if you release me, I'm going in after Stu."

Britt stared at her, taken aback by the defiance burning in her eyes. She'd willingly run into that building for a *dog*? She was the bravest or the stupidest woman Britt had ever met. She sighed and turned to the firefighter still standing nearby. "Do we still have anyone searching for stragglers?"

He nodded. "Two of my crew are inside."

"See if someone can check apartment 225 for a dog. It's probably hiding behind the couch or under a bed."

"You got it." He turned back toward the building.

"Satisfied?" She loosened her grasp, testing whether the woman would make a move toward the building anyway. When she didn't feel any sudden motion, she released her more fully. A harsh cough interrupted the woman's nod. "Now go wait back over there before we have to take you out of here on a stretcher."

Not trusting her not to dart again, Britt followed her until she ducked under the crime-scene tape. She straightened and spun around to face Britt, her expression filled with so much defiance that Britt had to fight her own admiration. The woman's long, blond, sleep-tousled curls formed a halo of chaos around her head, and her pale eyes flashed with anger.

Britt turned and strode several paces away. At the edge of the police barricade, she paused beside officer Traci Sam.

"What the hell was all that?" Sam grinned, no doubt because she hadn't had to deal with the situation.

"Some crazy woman who values her dog's life more than her own."

"Lotta them around. She's cute, though." Sam rested her wrists over some of the gear on her duty belt.

"Sam." Despite her warning tone, she glanced at the woman again.

Sam winked. "Maybe I'll go comfort her, you know, sympathize about what hard-asses you firefighters are."

"Ha. You won't stand a chance after a firefighter rescues her dog. That hero worship comes on real quick with the straight girls."

"Just the straight ones? Well, at least I know I won't be losing out to you, friend. Your fate with that chick is sealed."

"True story." She walked away, resisting the urge to glance back at the woman.

Less than five minutes later, a firefighter carried a medium-sized brown dog out of the building. In Britt's peripheral vision, she saw the woman rush forward, past the officers, to meet him and take the dog. Despite her small stature, she held him securely against her chest, and the dog appeared comfortable in her arms.

❖

As Claire rejoined her neighbors behind the yellow tape, Stu began to struggle in her arms. At first, he'd been scared enough to be docile, but he'd never liked to be lifted off the ground. At thirty-two pounds of lean muscle, when he wanted to be let down, Claire couldn't contain him. As she set him on the ground, she grabbed his collar and kept him close to her leg.

"Ma'am, will this help? Maybe you could make a leash of sorts." One of the firefighters held out a piece of rope a few feet long. Claire had heard one of the other firefighters address him as "Chief."

"Thank you." Claire took the rope and bent to pass it through Stu's collar. After she tied as secure a knot as she could, the chief inspected her work.

"If he's not a puller, that should hold."

"He's used to a leash, so he won't try to go anywhere now." She patted Stu's back, and he pressed against her calf in response.

"When will we be able to go in to get our stuff?" Mr. Thomas, Claire's upstairs neighbor, shouted in the chief's direction.

"I'm sorry. You won't be allowed inside until the fire marshal has finished his investigation." He gave them all a sympathetic look, but it felt practiced, as if years of placating victims had ingrained the movements into his muscle memory. "You should plan to stay someplace else for a few days at least, maybe more."

"I don't know anyone's number, and my phone was inside." Mr. Thomas shoved past several other residents to get closer, as if that would change the chief's response.

Claire didn't have her phone either. Where was it? She remembered grabbing it as she left her bedroom, but by the time she got outside, she'd been so panicked about Stu that she hadn't realized she no longer had it. Maybe she'd dropped it as the firefighter dragged her from her apartment.

Had she lost everything but this pair of pajamas? If she'd known that after tonight she would have only one pair of shoes, she might have chosen more carefully before shoving her feet into the bright-green sneakers she'd left by the dresser. But that wasn't likely since she didn't even remember putting them on. She almost laughed at the image of herself carefully picking out the one outfit she wanted to save before fleeing her smoke-filled apartment.

"What do we do now?" Claire didn't realize she'd spoken aloud until the chief turned back toward her.

"The Red Cross has people coming to help the displaced."

Claire nodded. That's what she was now. Displaced. She didn't have her purse, but maybe she'd get it back. Until then, she had no money, no identification, and no place to go. Who could she call at this hour anyway? The rising sun had just started to paint the sky behind the smoldering apartment building in shades of pink, yellow, and light blue.

"If you need to use my phone to call someone…" The offer came from the firefighter who'd prevented her from going in after Stu. Her gentle tone didn't quell Claire's anger about their earlier exchange. She glared up at the woman, momentarily caught by her genuinely concerned expression. She'd taken off her helmet, and her short, dark hair stood up in messy, damp spikes. Her brown eyes were gentle, and Claire's irritation surged forward again.

"I don't need anything from you."

The firefighter pressed her lips together as if smothering a response. "Look, lady. I'm just trying to be nice here." If that's what came out, what had she been holding back?

"You weren't trying very hard earlier." Claire matched her candor, and by the look of surprise on the firefighter's face, she'd expected a little more hero worship and a lot less honesty.

"I was distracted—with trying to save your life."

"I should thank you for simply doing your job?" Claire walked away without waiting for a reply. She'd kind of been a bitch, but she didn't care. She didn't have time for someone who had no regard for a dog's life.

She had no idea what to do next. But she wasn't depending on any firefighters to help her figure it out. The Red Cross was coming. She hadn't even known that they helped out after a fire. They would probably establish some kind of temporary shelter for her and her neighbors, but would she be able to take Stu?

She kept a change of clothes and some toiletries in her office, since she never knew when a rambunctious pup would plant a set of muddy paws on her. If she could find a ride there, Stu would be safe there with her until she figured out where they could stay.

CHAPTER TWO

H ey, Captain. Come check this out. You made the news."

"Very funny, Anderson." Britt glanced across the open expanse of the fire station's living quarters. Mason sat with the crew from the engine at the long, industrial-style dining table eating some version of breakfast. Anderson drank his coffee while lounging on one of the couches and watching the morning news. Britt had just poured her own cup and doctored it to her liking.

"I'm not kidding. I mean, they didn't say your name, but that's definitely you holding that crazy chick from the scene this morning."

"What?" Stirring her coffee, she crossed to the couch. On the screen, a female reporter stood in front of the burning apartments. Her baseball cap and jacket with the station logo were probably meant to help her blend in, but the dyed blond hair poking out under the brim and her heavy makeup contrasted against the darkened scene behind her. Given the lack of flames and the color of the smoke still billowing from the building, the video had obviously been shot as they'd gotten the fire under control.

The dog-lover stood next to her, nervously glancing between the reporter and the camera. Now removed from the adrenaline of the scene, Britt could assess the woman more accurately. Her hair appeared as disheveled as Britt remembered. As if hearing Britt's thoughts, she reached up and shoved one side behind her ear. Around her shoulders, a drab, gray blanket, the kind the Red Cross usually provided, mostly obscured her printed-pajama top. Unable to make out the pattern on her shirt, Britt struggled to recall it from the scene. She remembered the feel of the woman in her arms, slight in stature yet surprisingly strong, but she hadn't focused on what she was wearing.

The caption across the bottom of the screen identified the woman as Claire Willows, adoption/foster coordinator at Release the Hounds Rescue.

"Ms. Willows, how's little Stu doing now?" The reporter glanced at Claire but kept her body angled toward the camera.

"He's okay now. No thanks to that firefighter." The camera followed her as she bent and patted the dog pressed close to her lower leg. "She acted like Stu was just another of my belongings."

They cut to a cell-phone video of Britt restraining Claire. Taken by itself, the video didn't look that bad. Surely, the viewers could have figured out that Britt's only concern was Claire's safety. But the next clip showed the dog being carried out and Claire rushing to him. Putting the dog on camera was a game-changer.

"Are you fucking kidding me?" Britt slid onto the arm of the couch, bumping her hip against Anderson's shoulder. She had no idea how much fallout would come from this interview, but it wouldn't be good.

"Don't worry about it, Captain. The brass will back you up," Mason said.

"Oh, you rookie." Anderson scoffed.

"She didn't do anything wrong." Mason was the most junior member of their crew, less than a year into his career, and didn't understand the politics of the department yet. His naiveté matched his fresh-faced appearance. At twenty-one he didn't look more than seventeen, especially compared to Anderson's weathered face, receding hairline, and full mustache.

"Officially, she followed policy. But the animal lovers are a sympathetic bunch. And in this town there's not a lot of news bigger than an apartment fire."

Even as the university had grown, swelling the population to about eighty thousand, Bellbrook retained a small-town feel in a lot of ways. Folks had only just started locking their doors when crime reportedly went up a few years ago, but even then, everyone blamed the college kids.

"HQ doesn't like it when the department looks bad," Anderson said.

Mason shook his head, his expression so bewildered Britt felt bad for him. "She did what we're supposed to."

"You're right, Mason. We trust our procedures and do our jobs, and people stay safe. That's the way it's gotta be," Britt said. "Sometimes, a situation is more complicated than that. But whatever happens, I'll handle it."

"That's why they pay her a captain's salary." Anderson patted Britt's knee and settled further into the couch.

"Just turn that shit off. Or at least find something better to watch."

He laughed as he switched the channel to one of the morning talk shows. She wasn't usually a fan of those either, but she'd take anything over that news report.

"There's our local celebrity."

Britt cringed at Jeff Cooper's voice from behind her and turned around. "Hey, Chief."

"I saw you on the news, Everett. Unfortunately, I'm not the only one who did. My office has been receiving calls all day. Sarah doesn't like answering the phone."

"I'm aware." Three years ago, Britt had briefly dated Jeff's long-time assistant. Sarah had complained that she spent so much time on the phone at work, she insisted on text-only communications in her personal life.

Jeff scowled at the reminder of Britt's history. He'd dealt with Sarah's moods for a time after the relationship ended. Actually, the whole thing had been his wife's fault for playing matchmaker between Britt and Sarah to begin with. Sarah eventually moved on, and the ban on Britt visiting his office was lifted. Since then she'd vowed not to get involved with anyone else in the department, a practice that eventually evolved into not really dating at all. Most of the time, she didn't even miss the mental drama of trying to figure out what another person wanted from her. But she did sometimes wish she had someone to go home to after shift.

"The department doesn't need any bad press right now." Jeff planted his hands on his hips and thrust his chest out—a move he'd picked up after his promotion. At five foot seven, with a lanky build that no amount of weightlifting could bulk up, he was smaller than a lot of the other firefighters.

"Understood, sir."

The city had just settled a civil lawsuit filed against the fire department after an engine hit a car at an intersection while responding to an emergency scene. The driver of the car had survived but sustained serious injuries that left him unable to return to his job as a licensed plumber.

"You're going to fix this."

"Absolutely. I can call her and apologize." When he shook his head, she rushed on. "Or find out where she's staying and talk to her in person."

"Apparently, this woman runs some kind of animal shelter. Your crew will volunteer there on Tuesday."

"We're off shift Tuesday."

"Exactly."

Anderson spoke up. "We all have to give up our day off because Everett tried to kill this lady's dog?"

"I didn't—"

"Yes, Anderson, because you succeed and fail as a unit. That's the way this works." He paused, but no one offered any further argument. "I'll email you the name of the place. You will all be there at zero seven thirty."

She rolled her eyes at his back before turning to her crew. "Guys, I'll figure out a way to pay you back."

"You bet you will," Anderson said. "And I can't wait to see how."

Claire jerked awake as a door closed someplace else in the building. That nice chief had arranged for a taxi to bring her to the rescue, and she'd dozed restlessly on the sofa in her office for a few hours, but she might have been just as rested having not slept at all. The sofa would've been long enough for an adult, if Stu hadn't claimed the end cushion as well as lying on top of her feet.

She stared at the ceiling, contemplating whether to try for a thirty-minute power nap before things got hectic. While she was deciding, a quiet knock sounded at her office door, and then it opened. Lila Cantori, the shelter director, hurried inside and closed the door behind her. Lila always seemed to be in a rush to get where she was going—partly because she was busy, and partly because she took very quick strides when she walked to make up for her short stature.

"Hey. I saw you on the news this morning. Are you okay? Was there damage to your apartment? Is that why you're sleeping here?"

Claire eased her feet from under Stu and sat up. He stood, turned in a circle, and settled close to her thigh. She rubbed her fingers under her eye, fighting the fog of stress combined with not enough sleep.

"I don't know what the state of my apartment is right now. I'm sure there's smoke damage, but the fire department wouldn't let us back in."

"You could have called. You know you and Stu can stay with me." Lila looked maddeningly refreshed with her flawless makeup, flowing blouse, and black capris. She always managed to tame her wavy hair into the smoothest bun.

"It was late—or early. I didn't want to bother anyone. I decided to grab a couple of hours here and figure it out today."

"You're coming home with me this afternoon. I won't take no for an answer."

She stretched her arms over her head, and her shoulders popped loudly. She smiled. "I guess I can't try to lie and say how comfortable this couch is."

"Do you need anything else?"

"Would you keep an eye on Stu this afternoon while I run out and grab some essentials?"

"Absolutely." Lila crouched and patted her thighs. Stu hopped down and ran over to her, eagerly tilting his head into some ear-rubbing. "I love hanging out with my favorite guy, don't I? But don't tell the others," she cooed. "What the hell happened anyway?"

Claire relayed the story, trying to sound braver than she felt when she recalled waking up disoriented and panicked. Then, not knowing where Stu was—looking back it could only have been a matter of minutes or so—but she'd been terrified. She'd have blamed herself forever if they'd been too late to save him. Nausea churned in her stomach at the thought of Stu trapped inside a burning building, and she'd been trying very hard not to think about any of her neighbors' pets as well.

Judging by the impassive response of that female firefighter, she hadn't understood why Claire had panicked so much over a dog. But Stu was so much more. He was her family, and aside from Lila and the others at the shelter, he was her only family. From the first day she'd met him, she'd known they were supposed to rescue each other.

"Oh, honey, that sounds scary. But at least you're both okay. After that news coverage, if you don't get a call from someone high up in the fire department, I'd be surprised."

"I don't know if that would change my opinion of the whole experience. I thought firefighters were supposed to run into fire to save lives. This bitch basically refused to do her job." The criticism sounded harsh even to her, but enough anger still lingered to justify the edge in her voice.

"Exactly. They should make her apologize personally."

"I won't hold my breath." Claire stood and circled her desk. "Instead of passing out from lack of oxygen, I think I'll try to get some work done. I've got a lot to do before this weekend's adoption fair."

"That reminds me. I've convinced that new barbecue place on Fifth to cater the adoption fair at half price." She'd secured a shaved-ice truck last week—the operator, a previous adopter from Release the Hounds, had agreed to donate his time as well as the product.

"Half price? That's great, but isn't that still going to be more than we can afford?"

Lila shrugged. "People have to eat, Claire. And unless you've suddenly learned how to cook—"

"I can cook."

"We can't cater the event with grilled cheese sandwiches and frozen French fries."

"Snob."

❖

At seven a.m. Tuesday morning, Britt parked her car in the small parking lot outside Release the Hounds Rescue. She chose the farthest spot from the front door so she wouldn't interfere with anyone coming to do actual business. The one-story building wasn't large, but it was well cared for. The neutral beige Hardie-board exterior and white trim appeared recently painted. A small sign next to a landscaped bed full of color asked that dogs be kept out of the flowers and pointed to a grassy area to the right of the building for them to do their business.

Inside, the empty lobby appeared clean and welcoming. On one wall a bulletin board touted "success stories," with photographs of dogs and cats being held by smiling adopters—singles, couples, and families with kids sporting huge grins. A separate board advertised other businesses in town offering pet services, such as grooming and boarding. Several flyers made impassioned pleas to be on the lookout for a lost dog.

She scanned the reception desk, searching for a bell or buzzer of some sort. She hadn't considered that no one would be here to greet her this early. But the front door had been unlocked.

"Hello." She angled slightly over the counter to look down the short hallway behind it.

"How can I help you?" As the woman came out of one of the offices, a look of recognition crossed her face, followed by confusion. Britt was used to that reaction while out of her turnout gear and helmet. She knew she'd seen Britt before but couldn't place where.

"We didn't formally meet the other day. I'm Britt Everett." She stuck out her hand, waiting until the woman took it before adding, "Firefighter."

"Claire Willows."

Britt had to respect how quickly she masked her flicker of irritation. By the time she gave Britt's hand two firm pumps and released it, she was all polite professionalism again. Today, she seemed much more put together than when they'd last met. The blond curls Britt had thought unruly were now tamed in an updo. She was dressed casually, in blue jeans and a teal V-neck T-shirt, but anything more than pajamas was formal compared to the last time they spoke. Light makeup, applied in a way Britt had never mastered and had long ago given up on, enhanced the blue of her eyes.

She might be stunning, but she was also trouble. She'd already proved that during her interview with that reporter—spouting off without even having the facts about fire-department policy or the safety concerns associated with entering an active fire.

"Come to my office. I'm just finishing up a few things. I wasn't expecting you until seven thirty." She led Britt around the reception desk to a surprisingly spacious office.

"I'm sorry. I came a bit early to get a read on things before the guys got here. I didn't think about how that would affect your schedule."

"It's no problem. As long as you don't mind me multitasking while we talk." She indicated a chair opposite her desk, as she dropped into one on her own side. She immediately woke up her computer with a few quick keystrokes.

As Britt entered the office behind Claire, a brown dog—the same one from the night of the fire, she thought—lifted his head from where he lay curled up in a dog bed by the desk. When he realized Claire wasn't alone, he stood and trotted over. As he approached, Britt stopped and took a step back.

"He's friendly. Have a seat." Claire focused on the monitor in front of her, seemingly unconcerned with Britt's comfort level. And why would she be? She probably didn't care if her dog took a big bite of Britt's leg after the way Britt had treated her.

Deciding to ignore the dog and hope he left her alone, Britt chose one of the two chairs on the opposite side of the desk—the one nearest the door. But as the dog still stood there eyeing her, she felt foolish. It wasn't as if she could outrun him if he decided to make a move on her.

As soon as she sat down, he advanced, and she tensed but didn't move. He laid his head on her knee and looked up at her with golden eyes. Only a white swath covering his chest, some black around his muzzle, and a black slash over each eye that moved like eyebrows as he peered up at her interrupted the smooth brown of his short coat.

"Relax. He doesn't bite." Claire barely glanced up from trying to find something on her desk, though Britt didn't know how she hoped to. The piles of papers situated around a couple of picture frames, a cup holding a bunch of pens, and a dog leash didn't appear to be organized in any particular way.

"I'm not really a dog person." She shifted uncomfortably in the chair.

"A cat person, then. Well, I won't hold that against you." Claire continued shuffling through the stacks on the surface around her, then stopped and held up a piece of paper, triumph painted across her lovely features. She pinned the page to the desk with one hand while she scrawled her signature across the bottom.

"God, no. Cats freak me out."

Claire lifted her gaze, and Britt felt her judgment. *What kind of person seemingly doesn't like any animals?*

"I don't—hate them or anything. But if I wanted to share my house with something that had little or no use for me beyond food, I'd get a girlfriend."

Claire's unexpected smile came quickly and transformed her expression. Until now, Britt had seen her only worried, angry, or coolly polite. And even then, she'd had no doubts about Claire's beauty. But happy-Claire was absolutely radiant.

"So, what is this place? Are you a private rescue or run by the city?"

"Both, actually. The city used to operate the animal shelter. But as the rescue culture evolved, the government didn't keep up. They started getting pressure to transition to a no-kill operation, but they didn't have the funding to do so. Eventually, rather than increase the budget, they contracted out the city animal-control services to our rescue."

"And you had the funding they didn't to make it work?"

Claire tilted her head and shrugged one shoulder. "We had a solid donor base, and adding the government funding helped. With the additional staffing needed to care for more animals and handle the emergency callouts, we still have some lean months. But somehow we always manage to keep things rolling."

From the hallway, Britt heard an influx of masculine voices—familiar ones.

"It sounds like my guys are here."

"If you'd like to join them in the lobby, I'll collect you all in a couple of minutes and give you a tour before we get to work." Claire focused on her computer again, clearly dismissing her.

CHAPTER THREE

A s Britt entered the hallway and called out a greeting to her crew, Claire inhaled deeply, then released her breath slowly. She could have followed Britt and introduced herself right away, but she needed a moment to compose herself. Since Lila had told her about the call from the fire chief offering a crew to do volunteer work, Claire had been preparing to face the insufferable firefighter. Seeing Britt had reminded her that she could have lost Stu that night, yet she'd handled her anger and remained professional, if not a little standoffish.

But she had a million things to do more important than babysitting a bunch of firefighters who probably didn't want to be here either. She refused to listen to them complain. If they did, she'd just remind them to thank Ms. Everett for their current circumstances.

She'd cleared her morning to give the firefighters a tour and get them started on a fence-repair project so she could salvage the rest of her day. Why should she give up a full day's work because the fire department needed to atone?

She went to the lobby, where Britt made introductions. She'd brought Anderson, a man in his fifties, with gray hair and a weathered face, and Mason, who seemed barely out of high school. Since they referred to Britt as Everett, she figured those others were last names as well.

She led the group through the hallway, pointing out administrative offices as they passed, and out the back door.

"We ask that you always come and go through the main building. And if you have to use one of the gates leading to the parking lot, please check the latch behind you. We rarely have very many dogs out here at once, but we like to give the dog-friendly ones a bit of play time and socialization." Two other buildings sat behind the main one, and with the chain-link fences connecting them, they formed a sort of triangle. The area inside the fence served as both play yard and training grounds. Another smaller fence behind one of the buildings allowed for more intense training with the dogs who didn't yet deal well with distractions.

"Do you get many that aren't good with other dogs?" Mason asked.

Claire nodded. "Some just need time to build the confidence to be around other dogs. But a few never do. So we make sure those go to a suitable home and give them plenty of one-on-one love while they're here."

"Can we play with one of those dogs today?"

"You're here to work, Mason." Britt answered before Claire could say anything. "If you want to play with dogs, come back on your own time."

"Actually, that's a great idea. We always need dog walkers and playmates." Claire rushed to soften the edges of Britt's rebuke. "In fact, we're having an adoption fair this weekend, and you're welcome to come help out with the animals. I'll personally make sure you get to play with some of them. Maybe we can even talk you into taking one home with you."

"I'd love to adopt a dog someday." He seemed to avoid looking at Britt while he gave her a warm smile.

"Yeah. Do you think your mom will let you?" Anderson asked.

"I'm getting a place of my own—soon." Mason's objection brought a round of good-humored laughter from the other two.

Claire chuckled, too. "Keep us in mind for when you do and you need a companion. Here we are at what's affectionately called the cat house." She led the men inside, but Britt paused at the door.

"I'm good here."

"My mistake. When you said you didn't like cats, I didn't realize you meant you were afraid of them." She released the door and turned to head in, but she wasn't surprised when it didn't close behind her. She didn't have to look back to know that Britt had followed her inside.

"I'm not afraid of them."

Claire laughed and adopted a condescending tone. "Of course not. You're a big, strong firefighter."

❖

By the time they finished the tour, Britt was itching to get to work. She didn't need to know all the inner workings of the rescue in order to complete her atonement. And Mason was annoying her. Usually an introvert, he was becoming downright chatty.

Britt shared an eye roll with Anderson behind Mason's back, and if Claire noticed, Britt couldn't tell. She kept giving Mason details about the rescue operations. Britt did admire Claire's passion for her work and the way she seemed to take pride in some aspects of the facilities while simultaneously acknowledging where they had to let things go that should be fixed. She had a good grasp on maximizing what funds they had. When she talked again about the saving grace of volunteers, Britt jumped on her chance to steer them back to the purpose of their visit.

"Hey, you don't want to waste a minute of this good labor you earned with your publicity stunt."

Claire ignored the jab, but her jaw tightened, as if her silence took some effort.

"We're here. Give my guys a chance to flex their muscles. What do you have lined up for us?"

When Britt threw in her comment about their muscles, Mason blushed and glanced at Claire. Good Lord, the kid was obvious. She guessed Claire to be mid-to-late thirties, but maybe Mason was into older women. She didn't blame him, of course. Claire was beautiful— not unattainably so, but in a wholesome, genuinely approachable way, though she hadn't seemed very approachable back in her office. But maybe she reserved her disdain for firefighters she didn't like.

"Several sections of the chain link fence need repair. I purchased the supplies last week but haven't gotten around to working on it."

"Sure. We can knock that out," Britt said.

"Great. And this afternoon, the owner of the pet store in town wants to drop off some large bags of dog food. They constantly have bags that accidentally open while being moved around the stockroom or put out on the sales floor. Since they can't sell them, she tapes them and brings them to us. It'd be great if one of you could help her unload them."

"We'll keep an eye out for her. So where are the fence supplies?"

They followed Claire to the side of one of the buildings, where a bunch of new fence posts and rolls of chain link had been neatly stored.

"You'll find any tools that we have in a supply closet just inside that door. If you don't have what you need, I can usually borrow it from our neighbor. He's a DIY-er and has tools that I wouldn't even know how to use properly."

"Will do. Anderson keeps a bunch of tools in his truck, too. I'm sure we can figure it out."

Claire's smile carried an unexpected mix of gratitude and relief, and Britt very much liked feeling as if she'd helped lighten her burden. Claire hesitated, her expression softening, then walked away. Britt caught herself trying to analyze the moment when she felt the smile on her own lips. Perhaps that's what had inspired the change.

She didn't have long to focus on what that meant—they had work to do, and she didn't want to get caught watching Claire walking away, by her crew or by Claire. As she joined the guys sorting out the fence supplies, she glanced at each of them, but no one seemed to have noticed her distraction.

While they worked, her mind kept wandering back to Claire, beginning with the feisty yet annoying woman who'd challenged her on that fire scene. When had she gone from describing Claire as "bitchy" to "feisty"? Earlier, in Claire's office, Claire had started to open up but then shifted to cool dismissal so quickly that Britt thought she might have imagined the thaw. And Britt had resorted to snark, seeking some reaction. Maybe Claire reserved her warmth for animals, because otherwise she seemed far too stuck-up for Britt to waste any more time on.

She settled into a routine with the guys as they moved quickly through the fence repairs. When she heard a loud diesel motor rumble up out front, she sent Mason to help unload the dog food, because his young back could handle slinging fifty-pound bags. She got in her workouts at the firehouse between calls, so she didn't need to challenge her strength in her free time.

With their one-day-on shift, then two-days-off schedule, a lot of firefighters had a side hustle as electricians, plumbers, general contractors, and other trades. She preferred more low-key activities on her off days. She could spend hours lost in a good book or bingeing a variety of movie genres. When it came to anything other than fighting fire, she was downright lazy.

Two hours later, Claire reemerged from the main building looking very cool compared to the sweat dampening the back of Britt's neck and the collar of her shirt. Resentment surged again. She basically had to act as forced labor while Claire enjoyed her desk job, all because she'd put Claire's safety above that of some dog.

"I just came out to check on you."

Britt didn't respond, but it sounded like Claire meant to "check *up* on" them.

"And to bring you some water. It's hot, and you're working hard out here."

Mason pulled the hem of his shirt up to wipe perspiration from his face, displaying a set of abs that would impress many women. As he accepted a bottled water, he gave Claire a friendly smile, and she returned it. Either Mason's attention or the heat had flushed Claire's otherwise pale complexion.

When she turned away, Britt gave her a knowing smile. Claire shoved a bottled water in her direction and stalked away. She didn't try to hide her chuckle and saw Claire's back stiffen, but she kept walking toward the office.

"Pretty sure you're barking up the wrong tree there, rookie," Anderson said.

"What do you mean?" Mason asked.

"She plays for Everett's team."

"What?" Britt had been trying to ignore their banter, but Anderson had her attention now. "What makes you think that?" Sure, she'd wondered, but after Claire's interactions with Mason she wasn't sure. Maybe she was bi. Either way, hearing Anderson's comment made it even more real.

"She's been friendly with him but carefully polite. Most women fall for his bashful-firefighter routine."

"Hey, I'm—"

"Yeah, yeah, I know. It's the genuine article, not a play for women. But still, it works. And I guess you didn't catch the way she gave Everett the once-over when she thought no one was looking."

"Come on. If she did, it was just—you saw that news interview. She doesn't even like me." She shifted her weight from one foot to the other and back. She didn't hide the fact that she was a lesbian, but she also didn't talk about her personal life with her crew.

"Oh, I know that. The woman can't stand you."

"So then why would she be checking me out?"

He shrugged. "Maybe she didn't realize she did it."

"Like it's some kind of ingrained lesbian instinct?" Britt laughed, but Anderson appeared to give the idea careful consideration before nodding.

"Exactly."

"Even if you're right, we aren't all attracted to each other just because we're lesbian. The woman is arrogant, too much of a do-gooder for me."

"God, you're right. Why would you be interested in a hot woman who cares so much about animals she dedicates her life to saving them? If you swap out animals for people, you guys are pretty much the same." Mason grinned and ignored her annoyed look.

Anderson tapped her shoulder with his fist. "Look at that. Mason thinks you're hot, too. Maybe his problem getting women is really that he's attracted to lesbians."

"I don't have a problem getting women. And I don't think you're—" He glanced at Britt, flushing bright red. "I mean, it's not that you're not good-looking. I just don't think of you that way. You're my captain and old enough to—" Now he looked downright horrified.

"Okay. Well, I think that's about enough chitchat." Britt set her bottle down next to a roll of fencing.

"I bet he was going to say, be his older sister." Anderson chuckled.

"Back to work," Britt said more sternly.

Claire glanced at the clock, then out her office window. The firefighters were cleaning up the remnants of the fence supplies, having served their agreed-upon sentence. Initially, she'd thought this assignment would be a waste of time, expecting them to drag their feet because they resented being there. But they'd accomplished more in several hours than she could have in a couple of days. She owed them a bit of respect.

Satisfied, she headed back outside, holding the door for Stu to follow, now that the fence work was finished. As they crossed the yard, Stu spotted the guys and gave a little whine, asking for permission to meet them. He stayed at her side until, with a wave of her hand, she sent him forward. He galloped closer, and Mason bent as if expecting to have to catch the ball of energy. But Stu stopped just a couple paces away and sat down.

Mason glanced up at Claire. "He friendly?"

She nodded. "He's trained to sit and wait until you greet him. He was a jumper, but I finally broke him of that habit. So every time he does this is a victory."

Mason held out a hand and stepped closer, letting Stu sniff him. Stu gave his hand a quick lick. Then when Mason began petting him in earnest, he moved farther into the embrace, his love for a good snuggle taking over.

"He's adorable," Mason said.

"He isn't available. In fact, that dog is the reason you're out here today," Britt said. "Still in love with him?"

"Yes. Yes, I am. How could I not love you?" Mason cooed to Stu instead of answering Britt directly.

"It's good to know someone sees the value in a canine life." Claire looked at Mason, because she didn't think she could keep her composure if she addressed Britt directly.

"Forgive me for not giving that life more value than yours."

She could—forgive her—she realized, because she understood that not everyone felt the way she did about animals. Not everyone could look in the soulful eyes of a dog that had never had a bit of attention and, oftentimes, had even been denied its basic needs and see its pure desire for one thing—love. Claire could relate. Her dating history had been a disaster. Then when she'd finally given in to Lila's pressure to try online dating, things had become almost comedic. After a string of really bad dates, and one woman who completely stood her up, she'd decided she preferred Stu's company and gave up altogether.

She took another breath before she spoke, still determined to be the bigger person and prepared to admit her faults.

"Thanks, guys. We appreciate all the help." She glanced at Britt, holding her gaze for a moment before encompassing the rest of them. "I just wanted to say, the night of the fire, I was scared and stressed, and you were just trying to do your jobs. In hindsight, talking to that reporter was maybe not the best way to handle my frustration. So, thank you for what you do, and for giving up your day off today to come see what we do." That was good enough for an apology. At least she didn't have to say the actual words, *I'm sorry.*

Relieved they were leaving, she walked them toward the front of the main building. Aside from her general snarkiness and obvious resentment about being at the rescue, something about Britt unsettled Claire. She'd just managed to herd them toward the door. In fact, the guys had already exited and congregated on the sidewalk outside, when Lila came down the hall from her office. Britt turned away from the door at Lila's greeting.

Claire also angled herself so she could introduce them. "Britt Everett, this is Lila Cantori, director of Release the Hounds."

"It's nice to meet you." Britt extended a hand. "I'm—"

"Oh, I've heard all about you." Lila winked at Claire, and heat rushed to her cheeks.

"This is where everyone always says 'all good things, I hope,' but since I can guess where your info came from, I'm quite certain none of it was good."

"In my defense, you weren't very nice to me the first time we met," Claire said.

"You mean when I was concerned for your life and safety?"

She wanted to throw out a biting response to match Britt's condescending tone but was far too aware of Lila's attention. And despite their friendship, Lila was still her boss and the director of the center, so as much as she hated to, she gave a polite smile.

"Thank you again for your time today."

Britt's answering grin hinted that she had a clue what Claire had to suppress to get the sentiment out. "You mentioned an adoption fair on Sunday. What is that? I mean, I guess it's pretty much what it sounds like, right? You're trying to get people to adopt one of the animals or to donate money?"

When Claire simply stared at her, wondering why she didn't just leave, Lila answered instead. "Yes. Of course, that's the goal. But we'd also like it to be a community event, where people come, hang out, get to know each other, and build a relationship with the rescue. Volunteers and fosters are just as important to what we do as donations."

"I'd like to come back. Help out—if you need it."

"That's really not necessary." Claire jumped in, attempting to avoid spending more time with Britt. "You fulfilled your duty."

"Actually, that would be great." Lila gave Claire a curious look. "We don't turn away volunteers. I'm sure we can put you to work doing something."

Britt smiled, and Claire wished even more that Lila hadn't been present for the offer. Claire had already apologized for her part in the press fiasco. She would be perfectly happy if they never had to see each other again.

"Great. What time should I be here?"

"Eight o'clock, if you can."

Britt nodded. "I get off shift at six, so that will give me time to grab a shower and get over here."

Claire ignored them while they exchanged phone numbers, "Just in case something comes up," Lila said with a flirty grin. Britt blushed, while Claire managed a polite good-bye and excused herself, mumbling something about needing to reply to an email. She hurried to her office, and though she didn't close the door, she avoided listening to whatever was happening in the lobby.

A few minutes later, Lila's heels sounded against the tile in the hallway, growing closer until they paused at the door to Claire's office. Claire kept her eyes on her computer screen, but she could feel Lila's expectant gaze and could picture her, leaned against the door jamb with her arms folded.

"How long are you going to make me stand here before you look at me?"

Claire grimaced, then met her eyes. "How long would you have waited before you went away?" She'd been wrong. Lila had one arm laid across her belly, her other elbow resting against it, and she cradled her chin in her hand. She appeared pensive but likely wasn't, since she always thought she knew what Claire was thinking.

"She's cute. Did you see that blush? Adorable." Lila winked.

"God, please, Lila, I'm begging you. Don't pursue her." Cute? Not Claire's first choice of words. Confident? Irritatingly so. Strong? As someone who'd been physically restrained by Britt, Claire had to admit that she was indeed strong. Butch? Yes—just the right amount of butch. If Claire was prone to clichés, she might say tall, dark, and handsome. It was unfortunate that Britt also had an insufferable need to be right and a clear God complex.

Lila flounced into the room and dropped into Claire's chair. "That's not a fair ask. She's a firefighter, for Christ's sake. A woman in a uniform trumps whatever weird loyalty thing you're about to pull out."

"She wasn't in uniform today." Though she had worn a T-shirt with the Bellbrook Fire Department seal over her left breast.

"Oh, you didn't see that? Maybe it was only when I closed my eyes." Lila grinned. "Okay. I'll make a deal. I can't ignore her. But I won't give her the full-Lila press."

"Deal." It was the best she was going to get.

"I'll have to let her fall for me the old-fashioned way."

Claire chalked up the twist in her stomach to the thought of having to spend more time around Britt, rather than the idea of her dating Lila.

"You have to admit, today wasn't as bad as you thought it'd be. They had pretty good attitudes and worked hard."

"I've already admitted to them that I misjudged. I don't think I owe that to you, too." It had been easy to hate Britt when she was a shadowy figure obscured by the weight of heavy firefighting equipment. But faced with seeing Britt as a real person—a fit, attractive woman whom Claire had tried very hard not to watch out her office window as she worked all afternoon—she had a more difficult time holding on to that hostility. Britt clearly wasn't happy about having to come to the rescue, but she'd worked hard, when a lesser person might have slacked off and sulked around, wasting time until she could leave.

"Are you about ready to head out?" Lila stood.

Since Claire and Stu had been staying in Lila's guest room, they'd all been commuting together in Claire's Subaru. She'd thanked her higher power daily for her tendency to park far from her apartment, at a spot on the end where no one ever parked near her. Many of the vehicles parked in the row closest to the building had sustained damage.

She'd lost all her furniture, her clothes, except the spare bags she kept both at work and in her car, and mementos from her past that she hadn't even begun to catalog in her head yet, but finding out that her slate-blue Crosstrek was a casualty as well might have broken her. As it was, she'd only had to go to the Subaru dealership and have another key made, as both sets had been in her apartment. Then she'd been able to reclaim at least a small piece of her life.

"I'm ready. This will all be here tomorrow." She locked her computer. When she picked up Stu's leash, he hopped out of his bed and trotted to the door.

"He's ready," Lila said.

"When we're here, he settles right in. But he's always excited to go—doesn't matter where." From the first day they'd met, Stu had been glued to her side. He'd come in to the rescue skinny and covered in ticks. She'd given him a bath and carefully removed every one, then assigned him a kennel at the far end of the row and left the one next to him empty so he wouldn't have the stress of unfamiliar neighbors, and still he'd cowered in the corner. That first night, she'd stayed at the rescue, intent only on being close if he needed her, but when she couldn't stop thinking about him, she ended up bringing him to her office. Lila had found them both curled up asleep together on the sofa in the morning.

For a few days, she'd pretended she could bear the thought of someone else adopting him. Over the years, she'd gotten good at resisting bringing home every stray that tugged at her heart—she had to, or she'd have been kicked out of her apartment long ago for hoarding pets. She dedicated herself to finding them all good homes and giving them tons of love while they stayed at Release the Hounds. But Stu's big sweet eyes and Velcro personality had gotten to her. So she'd filled out adoption paperwork, ignoring Lila's snarky comment about how she should appreciate being able to sleep in her own bed again instead of at the rescue.

CHAPTER FOUR

"Make it stop," Britt groaned as she dragged herself out of the single bed in the bunk room that she'd crawled into only—she glanced at her watch—twenty minutes ago.

"Radar didn't look promising earlier. There's another line of storms right behind this one." Two beds over, Anderson sat up, rubbing a hand over his shaved head.

Bellbrook had been hit with several rounds of thunderstorms with high winds during the last sixteen hours of their shift. Her day had been a blur of motor-vehicle accidents, downed power lines and trees, and one water rescue, when a creek rose over the road and an impatient driver didn't heed the detour signs set out by public works. She wasn't even counting the fire-alarm activations sprinkled in between, because most of them turned out to be false, caused by power surges and outages.

She hurried to the truck, grabbing her gear on the way. By the time she slung her turnout coat inside the open door and pulled herself in after it, Anderson already had the engine running. As they pulled into the street, Anderson flipped on the emergency equipment. Britt lifted her radio closer to her ear, to hear it over the screaming siren as she advised dispatch they were rolling.

"Truck Seven, you're responding to a report of a vehicle versus a pole with wires down on the car. The driver is inside."

She acknowledged the transmission, checking their location against the address of the incident. They were only a few minutes away, but the weather conditions slightly increased their response time. The heavy fire truck remained stable on all but the most treacherous roads, but Anderson needed to pay more attention to the motorists around them. Drivers whose inattention kept them from seeing the truck coming tended to make panicky moves once they did. On wet roads, those quick maneuvers could lead to additional traffic accidents. If they had to stop to assist in the event of a wreck, dispatch would have to send another truck to their original call, delaying response to their victim, who might desperately need help.

Anderson stopped the truck on the street, a safe distance away, angled to block any oncoming vehicles from approaching the incident. A small gray sedan appeared to have left the roadway and hit a pole, hard enough to crack the wood and bring a wire down to rest across the hood of the car. Several bystanders loitered about with cell phones out. Some were probably Good Samaritans calling 9-1-1, the others hoping for a photo and an interesting story for their social media. Either way, they were all now way too close to her scene.

"Everybody back up," she called as she jumped down from the truck. "Anderson, confirm that's a power line and not telephone or cable. Then make sure dispatch has called for a cut-off."

She got close enough to the car to see the driver behind the wheel while staying well clear of the power line.

"Sir, can you hear me?" She shouted to be heard through the closed window.

The man bobbed his head and closed his eyes, then popped them back open, obviously fighting for awareness of his situation. She called out to him again, and he turned a hazy gaze on her.

"You've been in an accident." When he reached for the door handle, she extended her hands, palms out, then pointed at the hood of his car. "No. Don't try to get out yet. There's a wire down on your car." When she was sure he understood those instructions, she went on. "Are you hurt?"

He clapped a hand against the opposite shoulder, where the seat belt slanted across his chest, then touched a cut on his forehead; blood ran down the side of his face. When he eased his hand back and stared at his fingers, he paled.

"That doesn't look too bad." Britt scanned the rest of him and didn't notice any obvious deformity, but she couldn't see his lower extremities clearly.

"Head wounds bleed a lot." He sounded like he was parroting something he'd been told rather than possessing genuine knowledge.

"Right. Just sit still and let us work, and we'll get you out of there in no time."

An ambulance rolled to a stop nearby, and two female paramedics, Jenna and Candace, climbed out, but they hung back, waiting for Britt's signal to come in. They were good friends of hers, and she was relieved she wouldn't have to worry about them. They'd responded on calls with her countless times and had always respected scene safety. She glanced once more at the driver, and then, assured he was staying put, she moved closer to the paramedics.

"He's got a laceration on his forehead and probably a bruise from the seat belt. Doesn't appear to be in any distress right now. As soon as we get the power shut off, he's all yours." She greeted them with a friendly smile but was all business about their patient. They could chat in their group text later.

Jenna nodded. "Just let us know. And if we can help in any way…"

"Sure. Let me check in with my guys."

She met Anderson over by the vehicle, glancing once more at the driver. He was on the phone, and whomever he was talking to didn't seem to be calming him down. He waved his free hand about wildly, pausing every so often to touch his forehead. The flow of blood from his wound appeared to have slowed, as she didn't see much fresh blood each time he pulled his fingers away.

"What's the ETA on utilities? Driver's getting antsy."

"You know they never give us one."

Somehow, the electric, water, and telephone companies had gotten on the same page and all refused to give ETAs. Britt could never get away with that. If someone came over the radio and asked how far away she was, she damn well better tell them.

As she turned for another glance at the driver, a small SUV with the logo for a local news station pulled in behind the fire truck. A man hopped out, already filming with his cell phone.

"Damn it." Britt strode toward him. Mason made a move to abandon crowd control in order to intercept him, but she waved him off. She stepped in front of the reporter, doing her best to obstruct his view of the vehicle. "Back up. We have live wires here."

He flashed her what she was certain he thought was a charming smile—his on-air smile, no doubt—full of perfectly aligned, bright-white teeth. "I'm just getting a quick shot."

"You can get it from over there." She flipped a hand toward the other side of the street. "What are you doing here anyway? This isn't exactly a big story. Even for Bellbrook."

He shrugged, his demeanor changing now that she'd made it clear they weren't going to be buddies. "I was out getting storm coverage when I heard it go out on the scanner. I figured this will do if I don't find something better."

"Better?" She sneered at his choice of words. She understood the media's job and could even respect those reporters who managed to do theirs while staying out of her way. But she was fresh off a black eye, courtesy of some prissy little reporter, and not feeling very generous toward the whole breed.

"You know what I mean."

"I do. Which is exactly the problem. So back off. And move your car. It's too close to my truck."

He dropped all pretense, and his expression twisted derisively. "Thanks for nothing." As he walked away, he muttered, "Bitch," just loud enough for her to hear.

She drew in a breath, suppressing a dizzying urge to snap back at him, but she suspected he'd never stopped recording. When the footage went to air, his curse would be edited out, but whatever she'd been about to say would have only dug her hole deeper with her chain of command.

Britt leaned against the jamb of the large overhead garage door, the truck ready behind her and, in front of her, a gray and sulfur-yellow sky casting an eerie, early morning glow over the town. The rhythm of a sprinkle of rain on the metal roof created a white noise that she found oddly comforting, given the electricity in the air.

Anderson joined her in the doorway carrying two mugs.

"Coffee?" He held one out to her.

"I don't know. How long until the next round is on us?"

He shrugged. "Thirty minutes. And by the looks of that sky, it's going to be active."

"Then I pass on the caffeine. But let me hold one of those mugs to warm up." Hours of running in and out of the rain had left her chilled so deep that even layering on a sweatshirt when they returned from that last run hadn't helped.

"Are you still going to that adoption thing today?"

She nodded. She'd hoped they would get relieved by the next shift before catching another run, but if bad weather churned up again, the chances were better that she'd get stuck out on a scene and be late getting back to the hall for relief. If the next crew took over in time, she could still grab a power nap and a hot shower first. Otherwise, she'd resort to loading up on caffeine to make it through the day. "It's forecast to clear up by then, so hopefully they'll still get a good turnout."

"I thought you didn't like animals. Is this about Ms. Willows?"

She shook her head too quickly to be believed.

"You never tell me the good stuff."

"There's a reason for that." She shot him a grin to soften the impact of her words. It wasn't that she didn't trust him. She did, mostly. But she refused to be the lesbian that the male firefighters gossiped about when she wasn't around. They probably did anyway, but she wouldn't add any kindling to their fires. "There's nothing to tell, man."

"She single?"

"Don't know." She didn't add—*don't care*—because she didn't think he'd believe her. She curled her fingers more tightly around the mug, clinging to the warmth still radiating through the ceramic. Was she pulling off casual? Anderson's suggestion that a different kind of tension might be brewing between them did things to her insides that she didn't like. She hadn't felt that flutter of attraction in a very long time, and experiencing it while thinking about Claire both excited and irritated her.

"Are you?"

She chuckled at his implication that she'd been hiding a girlfriend. In reality, she was just as lazy about relationships as she was about everything else that didn't have to do with firefighting. She couldn't say she was too busy to date or that she couldn't find Ms. Right. She just didn't care to try, when she'd rather spend time alone.

Typically, she'd go home after shift, grab some sleep if she needed it, and have a chill day. Her second day off, she took care of any errands she had. That time by herself recharged her for the next shift, when she had to spend twenty-four hours in a row around other people. She certainly didn't volunteer to go hang out at fund-raising events with someone who didn't like her very much at all.

She still didn't know why she'd done it. One minute she'd been trying for a civil good-bye, eager to escape the rescue, and the next she'd been asking about the fund-raiser. If she was being honest, she'd admit the fact that Claire so clearly didn't want her to attend played at least a small part in her desire to do so. She'd known Lila was flirting a bit, feeling her out. And Claire probably thought that's why she'd suddenly showed an interest in coming back. Lila was pretty and friendly, but Britt couldn't envision pursuing anything with her. She told herself it was because Lila and Claire worked together and she didn't want to spend any more time around Claire than she had to, but since she'd volunteered for the adoption event, that was clearly a lie.

Claire surveyed the guests starting to trickle into the yard from the main building, hoping the crowd would get bigger as the day continued. She'd done everything possible to promote the event, even accepting an interview on a local morning-television show, though she'd tried to talk Lila into taking her place.

Along the fence, a handful of vendors had set up booths under brightly colored pop-up canopies. She'd spent two days visiting local establishments and talking up the event, in the end securing attendance from several pet-related businesses and one woman who made and sold dog clothes.

The barbecue caterer and shaved-ice truck would set up in the parking lot, in order to keep anyone from bringing food inside the fenced area, where adoptable dogs might be roaming around. She'd set up a buffet-style table and some folding chairs nearby and posted a sign at each entrance asking guests to respect this rule for the safety of both the dogs and attendees.

Volunteers would rotate the available dogs into the yard throughout the morning, always loosely watching guest interactions. The dogs who weren't friendly with other pups or needed to be careful around small children could be visited inside the dog house under closer supervision.

Not to be left out, those looking to adopt a feline friend could stop by the cathouse, where volunteers waited to make a match.

Since she'd done the television interview, she'd made Lila agree to schmooze the VIP donors. Claire became nervous when she knew a lot of money was on the line, stuttering over the thought of how many animals they could help with a large donation. She would much rather leave the fund-raising to Lila while she coordinated the volunteers and helped with animal care. In fact, she'd volunteer to clean the dog runs and the cat rooms every day if she didn't have to beg for funds.

She stopped to check in at the adoption and foster sign-up table, making sure plenty of applications were available. As she turned away from the table, another cluster of people walked in. Claire's heart soared along with the attendance, then seemed to stumble in her chest as the group dispersed onto the grass, leaving Britt standing alone in front of the gate.

Britt looked freshly showered, her dark hair apparently free of product—soft and touchable. She wore comfortable clothes—navy knit shorts and a gray T-shirt with a faded logo on the front. She had said she'd basically be coming from work, and Claire blamed that knowledge for the fact that she suddenly could imagine Britt shrugging out of her suspenders and shoving her turnout pants down over her boots before stepping out of them.

As she drew her gaze up Britt's body and met Britt's eyes, she realized she'd been caught—if not full-on checking her out—looking far too long. Unexpectedly, Britt's expression reflected the interest swirling through her.

It was a moment—for sure. And if not for their history of animosity, she'd have called it a snapshot from her favorite rom-com. Across a crowded lawn—two women's eyes meet and—and what? How could she connect with a woman who took every opportunity to remind her of exactly what she thought of her career and life choices? She recalled the flickers of humor and humanity suggesting that a real woman lurked under the snark—a woman, in spite of everything, Claire wanted to know more about.

Britt broke the connection between them, scanning the grounds as she picked her way through the other guests. Claire used the time before Britt reached her to take a couple of steady breaths.

"Hi." Certainly, the full-morning sun had brought the flush to her cheeks.

Britt lifted her chin in greeting. "The guys on the engine said they saw you promoting the event on television. I'm sorry I missed it. I'm sure it was much more entertaining than the last interview you did."

Claire's foolish warmth frosted over. Did Britt really have to be such a jerk? She might have seen a hint of regret in Britt's expression, but no apology for the jab was forthcoming. Connect with her? Forget that.

"You look exhausted." Most women would have considered Claire's observation catty. And maybe she intended it that way—a little bit. But Britt appeared unfazed.

"Busy night. But on the upside, I got credit for activity during twenty-two of the last twenty-four hours." She held up her wrist, indicating her smart watch.

"You didn't have to come in. If you'd texted we would have understood." If she'd canceled, she wouldn't be here confusing Claire—er, spoiling her excitement for the event she'd worked so hard to plan.

Britt shook her head. "I made a commitment. Besides, I'm kind of used to operating on little sleep."

"You don't have to go in again tonight, do you?"

"No. I don't work again until Tuesday. I'll get some rest before then."

"Okay. Well, it's forecast to get warm quickly this morning. So drink plenty of water and get out of the sun when you need to." Claire regretted the words as soon as she spoke. Why was she babbling about the weather and staying hydrated?

"Don't worry. I have plenty of experience dealing with heat." Britt winked and headed across the lawn to greet Lila, leaving Claire standing there feeling foolish and, once more, turned around by Britt's hot-and-cold attitude.

CHAPTER FIVE

Britt sat down in the grass under the tree and opened her bottled water, watching people mill around in front of her. She'd been working alongside one of the rescue volunteers, a college kid who said he'd worked at the rescue since high school. They'd stocked a table with cases of water for volunteers and guests, filled large water bowls for the dogs roaming around the lawn, and then gone into the dog kennel building to tend to the animals there. Lila had joked about putting the firefighter on water duty as she'd hooked her up with the kid. But he was a nice guy and clearly possessed a selflessness she didn't often associate with his age group.

The event seemed to be exactly what Lila said she wanted, a picnic day of sorts for the community. In addition to the food vendors, a veterinarian had set up a table, offering special rates for anyone adopting a dog or cat that day. Britt had also wandered by booths for a doggie spa and a pet store.

Some of the older dogs had been taken back inside as the day warmed to a temperature uncomfortable for them. And even the more active pups had settled in temporary wire enclosures under one of the tents for an afternoon nap. She yawned, but she'd passed the point where a nap would be productive. Now she had to hold on until she could crash. In fact, even sitting down was dangerous.

She leaned against the tree, and the rough bark pressing into the center of her back made her just uncomfortable enough to stave off her fatigue. A breeze ruffled the leaves overhead, breaking the heat for an instant, then feathered away. Across the grass, several kids ran around the lounging dogs, trying and failing to motivate them to play and chase. The children's parents had sought out shade as well, standing in clusters talking about whatever parents gossiped about when they had a moment away from their offspring.

A trill of laughter from one of the smaller kids drew Britt's attention again. The girl, about four years old, giggled again as a large, furry dog—taller than she was—swiped its tongue across her face. The girl's dark pigtails reminded Britt of her niece, and she made a mental note to squeeze in a trip to her brother's place outside of Indianapolis. She enjoyed hanging out with her niece, especially since she'd been growing into the sassy personality she'd had since she was two. Britt had never felt the pull of motherhood, but she loved being the fun aunt.

She closed her eyes, letting the distant voices, the faint music playing from one of the vendor tents, and the tinkle of wind chimes hanging by the back door of the main building mingle in layers that pulled the stress of her busy shift from where it balled in her chest.

A tickle against her hand jerked her awake. She stared down at a midnight-black cat, who stood next to her thigh and unflinchingly met her gaze. Glancing around, she tried to figure out how long she'd been asleep, and if she'd gone fully under or just drifted momentarily.

"Hey there. Where did you come from? Shouldn't someone be missing you?" She hadn't noticed any of the cats roaming around today, but she'd seen lots of people going inside the cat building. Maybe one of them had accidentally let this one out.

The cat ducked its head under her arm and pressed close, settling against her side. When she held out her hand, it inspected her, nose twitching, eyes oddly steady. After a disrespectfully long time, it finally rubbed its head against her fingers.

"Seriously? What were you so unsure about?" She curled her fingers and scratched behind its ear. A steady purr vibrated against her hip. "Don't get attached, little dude. If you're looking for a new home, you're looking under the wrong tree."

The cat crawled over her legs to her other side and began batting at her empty water bottle. Britt knocked it over and rolled it a few inches away. Startled, the cat fell back a few steps, then recovered, dropping into a crouch, almost visibly coiling like a spring. Seconds later, it pounced, attacking the bottle with its front paws and teeth, crinkling the plastic.

"What's all the racket over here?" Claire leaned against the tree next to her, so close Britt had to tilt her head all the way back to see her clearly.

"It looks like someone escaped from the cathouse." Britt held up one hand and mimed pointing behind her palm at the cat with the other, as if hiding her gesture from the cat.

Claire shook her head. "Betty thinks she's a dog."

"Wait—Betty?"

Claire shrugged. "That's what I get for letting one of the volunteers' sons name her. He thought it was funny. But we had a deal that he could name the next one that came in and so—Betty, it is."

Britt shook her head sympathetically at the cat. "Such a shame. You're not a Betty at all, are you?"

As if in agreement, Betty sat down, lifted one leg, and began licking herself in a very indelicate manner. Britt looked away, giving her some privacy, but that left her looking into Claire's laughing blue eyes.

"She gets irritable if we make her spend too much time around the other cats. She used to sit and watch the dogs play outside and vocalize her discontent, so one day we tried letting her out with a couple of them. She followed them around for the entire afternoon."

"And she doesn't wander off?" She chanced a glance back at Betty, thankful she was done with her grooming.

Claire dropped to one knee next to Britt and stroked her hand over Betty's shoulders. Betty arched her back, leaning into the caress, and gave Britt a lazy look that clearly meant she was enjoying Claire's attention. Britt had never been jealous of a cat before.

"She's not even curious about what's outside the fence. She was rescued from an abandoned barn, along with a mama dog and her litter of puppies."

"So she's a feline with a chosen canine family." Britt smiled.

Claire tilted her head and lifted one side of her mouth in an amused half-smile. "You seem quite pleased with that idea."

"I am." Britt had often felt closer to those people she chose to surround herself with than with her biological family, first with her close friends in high school, then with her firefighter family, and especially with the lesbian-first-responders peer group she'd discovered early in her career. To this day, they got together at least once a month for a wine-and-themed-food night. "Do you rescue only dogs and cats? No horses or goats hanging around here?"

"We weren't set up for other livestock. And the cost to do so versus the number of animals just didn't make sense. So we partnered with a farmer down the road to rent barn and pasture space only when we need it. He even donates feed and helps take care of them."

Claire rubbed under Betty's chin, while Betty leaned into her touch yet didn't leave Britt's side. "You seem pretty comfortable with her. Ever think about adopting?"

"Remember when I said cats freak me out?"

"You're in luck. She's a dog."

She laughed. "Are you always working?"

Claire shrugged. "Maybe. You two do look cute together."

"I work twenty-four-hour shifts. Not exactly conducive to taking in a pet."

"Therein lies the beauty of cats. They kind of enjoy their alone time."

"Yes. But she's a dog."

"Dog, cat, what does it matter as long as she's self-sufficient and good company when you get home."

Britt narrowed her eyes and pointed at Claire. "Nice try. But I already know from experience that you'd say anything to get your way."

Claire's expression shut down immediately. Her eyes, previously sparkling as she teased Britt, shuttered like a beach house in a storm. She folded her arms across her chest as if trying to contain something—some reaction, or comment, or possibly her entire composure.

Before Britt could say she'd been joking—sort of—Claire planted her hands on her hips and thrust her shoulders back.

"I know you don't think animal rescue is a noble profession. But we can't all be superheroes. And what we do here matters to some people and to the animals we help. And to me personally."

"I don't—"

"Before I came to work here, I was killing myself in a mid-level corporate job, so stressed I started having anxiety attacks and almost daily migraines. I probably would have been dead by fifty. My doctor mandated me two weeks off work, and while I was convinced the company would fall apart without me there to push paper around, I did what he said. But I'm just not the sit-at-home type. So I came here to volunteer during that time. And this place changed my life. After a week back at work, the migraines started again, and I put in my notice.

"So, screw you and your snide comments, because they just make you sound like an asshole anyway." Before Britt could respond, she stalked away and, ignoring a curious look from Lila, headed for her office.

Claire returned to the event fifteen minutes later with no hint that she'd lost her composure. She stayed on the opposite side of the lawn from Britt, and if they did venture into the same space, Claire seemed to be making sure at least one other person was around. She needn't have worried, though. Even if Britt wanted to mention the blowup, she wouldn't know what to say. She had to apologize, that much was clear, but about what specifically, and what would she say?

❖

"Mama, I want to get him a green collar." The boy, about seven years old, wrapped his arms around the chest of a gorgeous Great Dane mix. The dog—named Duke, after Marmaduke—stood docilely in his embrace. The boy tilted his head to look at Claire. "Green's my favorite color. I think it's his, too."

"It's a great choice."

"It's my turn to hold the leash." A smaller girl tugged at their mother's arm.

"Let your sister hold it," the mother said without looking at either child, while she continued to fill out the paperwork Claire had given her.

The first time Claire had seen the mother and two children come in, she'd pegged them as searching for a tiny puppy, or maybe an adorable kitten. The kids seemed well behaved, but a bit high-energy, and Claire always cringed at matching small children with even smaller animals.

She'd found another cause for worry when the two kids had gravitated toward the larger dogs. They had several large breeds that were good with children, dog friendly, and one even liked cats. Still, she'd made sure to consult carefully with the mother about the needs and challenges of larger dogs. The woman seemed to understand, saying she'd grown up with them herself and was thrilled that her kids didn't want a yippie, moody little dog—her words.

Today was their third visit to Release the Hounds and the day they got to take Duke home. Claire's heart had swelled with irrational pride at his patience and even temperament each time she watched him play in the yard with those two kids. Typical of a dog his size, he somehow seemed clumsy and gentle at the same time.

She let herself get caught up in the kids' excitement about their new family member, partly so she wouldn't have to notice what Britt was doing on the other side of the lawn. The last time she'd looked, one of their most generous *and* most talkative donors had cornered Britt. When she caught a sly glance from Lila, she knew why. Though Lila didn't know the whole story, she must have picked up on enough of the tension between them to know Claire was madder than usual. She'd inflicted the donor on Britt—thereby both punishing Britt and keeping Lila from having to deal with the small talk.

"We already bought Duke a big, fluffy bed to sleep on, and Mama says he can stay in my room cause I'm the biggest."

Claire bent closer but spoke loudly enough for the mom to hear, too. "He kind of seems like a cuddler, so he might try to climb right into bed with you. Are you okay with that?"

The boy's eyes grew wide, and he nodded vigorously. "I like to cuddle, too."

You and me both, kid. As she straightened she glanced toward where she'd last seen Britt, surprised to find Britt's gaze. Did Britt like to snuggle in bed on a lazy morning, or maybe after a round of hot sex? How would it feel to lie in Britt's arms? She jerked her eyes away, hoping Britt couldn't have seen anything lustful in them, but felt even more guilty when she met a curious look from the kids' mom.

She gave the family a small tote bag containing treat samples, a coupon for vet care, and a pamphlet on dog training, making sure they had her contact information in case they needed anything. Her standard adoption contract included a clause stating that if any problems occurred, the adopter would return the dog to her rather than try to rehome it. Of course, she couldn't enforce that requirement, but she hoped all her adopters would honor it. Her worst fear was finding out that a pet she'd placed had been passed on to a less-than-desirable or even dangerous situation.

She gave Duke one more hug before she sent him off with his new family, and then she sought out Lila—who unfortunately was engaged in what appeared to be very easy conversation with Britt. Lila touched Britt's arm flirtatiously as she spoke, and Britt didn't seem to take issue with the contact. She smiled easily and appeared almost as relaxed as she had when Claire had seen her nearly asleep under the tree. And Claire was jealous—yes, she'd admit she was jealous. Her conversations with Britt never felt as effortless as this one. Just when she thought they were connecting, the tension surrounding the origin of their introduction would rise between them again. And Claire hated that tension, because without it, maybe they could have something meaningful.

But she'd thrown meaningful out the window when she'd basically told her off earlier. She hadn't set out to blow up. They'd actually been having a fun conversation about Betty when Britt made one more snide reference to the day of the fire. Suddenly the push and pull of this day— hell, of their entire relationship thus far—had felt overwhelming, and Claire couldn't contain herself.

The crowd had thinned, and she was tempted to ask Lila to wrap up the event so she wouldn't have to face Britt again. But the part of her that had been carefully cultivated—ironically, mostly by Lila—to think about the politics of running the rescue wouldn't let her be that rude. Britt had come here because of her, in a roundabout way, and her manners wouldn't let her disappear into her office, no matter how much she wanted to.

Choosing the cowardly way, she waited to approach until Britt was walking toward the gate with a group of people and addressed them all at once.

"Thank you all so much for coming and supporting Release the Hounds." She continued with her usual spiel, hoping none of these volunteers had heard it before. *We couldn't do what we do without you, yada, yada, yada.* She didn't have the focus to get more creative with Britt's eyes on her. And they were. Every time she scanned the group, Britt was looking at her—of course, since she was the one speaking. Though she fought not to linger on Britt's face, she couldn't miss the expectant expression, as if Britt wanted to say something to her.

She wrapped up her remarks, then hurried across the lawn without giving anyone time to corner her for conversation. She pulled out her cell phone, glanced at it, then held it up in a gesture toward Lila, as if indicating that she had to take a call. After waiting for Lila's nod, she beelined for the main building, letting out a small sigh only as the door swung shut behind her.

Inside her office, Stu lifted his head from his bed, then, seeing it was her, settled back down. She'd let him in when the afternoon grew hot, knowing he'd be napping anyway. She left her door open, expecting no one would disturb her, since they'd been keeping guests out of the main building during the event. Lila would find her way inside after seeing the stragglers out, but until then, Claire could answer some emails in peace.

❖

Britt eased the heavy back door to the main building closed with an audible click. She glanced down the hall toward Claire's office, sure Claire's ear was attuned to the sound of the door. She hadn't really thought she could sneak in here anyway.

When she saw that Claire was focused on the computer in front of her, she paused in the doorway for a long look. Claire's eyes were shuttered as she glanced between the screen and a paper to the side of the keyboard. As Claire had railed earlier about Britt's lack of respect for her job, passion had burned in her gaze, enhancing her beauty and lighting an answering fire inside Britt.

Stu's eyes were on her, the skin on the top of his head wrinkled slightly as he looked up, and she imagined he was judging her. But he stayed curled up in his dog bed, so maybe not.

"Are you just going to stand there? Or are you coming in to sit down?" Claire glanced up and said, "Oh," disappointment evident on her face.

"Thought I was someone else, huh?" Did Claire sense the bubble of hope in Britt when Claire had welcomed her?

"Lila."

Britt nodded. "She's finishing a last-minute adoption." Because she suspected Claire would want to know, she added, "I don't have a name, but it's a cute little black poodle."

Claire's small smile reflected genuine love. "Toby." When their eyes met, her grin fell away, and Britt wanted it back.

She could see why Claire was so good at her job. The energy around happy, fulfilled Claire was infectious, and if Britt hadn't already come in here to apologize, she would now. No matter what Britt thought, or didn't, about Claire's livelihood, this event made it clear that she was doing something meaningful—and in this moment her love for rescue radiated around the room. If Claire was the sunlight, Britt wanted to bask in it. If her words had dimmed that light for even a moment, she had to try to reverse their effect.

"You were right."

"I was?"

Britt sighed, and giving up on waiting for an invitation, she entered the office and sat on the couch against the wall rather than the chair opposite Claire.

"I'm an asshole." She gave her a half-smile. "Sometimes."

"Oh—well—thank you."

"I shouldn't keep making you feel bad for what happened when we met. And I'll definitely try to dial down the sarcasm. But maybe you're also a little sensitive about the situation? Can I never in the future of our friendship make a joke about it?"

"The future—our friendship."

"Sure. I'd like to have one." What the hell was she saying? She should have shut up after *I'm an asshole*. She didn't know what part of her was in charge of her mouth right now, but it certainly wasn't her brain.

"A friendship?"

Britt stumbled over her response. Claire seemed pleased—and surprised—about the idea of something between them. She should just agree. Say *yes, I think we should be friends. Maybe catch a movie or go to dinner—someplace nice and quiet where we can talk and get to know each other better.* Whoa. That was beginning to sound like more than friendship.

"A future." A vacuum followed her words—a heavy, almost unpalatable silence—that she perhaps should have tried to back out of, but what the hell? She was in this far already. Instead she let the phrase hang there, anxiously awaiting Claire's response.

"A—you want to have—a future—with me?" Claire's words ended on an awkwardly high note, not so much a question as a statement of disbelief.

She took an extra beat before answering, not because she was unsure, but so she could inject the confidence she felt inside. "Yes."

Keep it simple. "I mean—maybe. We'll see." So much for simple. She'd gotten out her shovel and started digging a hole.

"We'll see?"

Britt chuckled at the edge of annoyance in Claire's voice. "In spite of our rocky start, I like you." She shrugged, forcing nonchalance, but very aware of how vulnerable she sounded. "I'm up for seeing where things between us could go—if we can get past the animosity. In fact, I'll start by asking you to have dinner with me tomorrow night."

"I work until six."

"I'll make a reservation for seven."

"Make it six thirty. I tend to skip lunch, and I'm hungry by then. And pick me up here." Claire rested her elbows on her desk and folded her hands together, clearly assessing Britt's reaction to her assertiveness.

Contrary to Britt's professional need for obedience, she had no problem giving up some control in her personal life. In fact, under the right circumstances, she enjoyed it.

"Any food allergies or cuisine you just won't eat that I should know about?" She purposely didn't ask for a specific restaurant, letting Claire know that control went both ways. She would choose the place, but she'd do so with Claire's needs and desires in mind.

"None. I'm not picky about food."

"Good." She stood, sensing a good exit point, before Claire could change her mind.

Stu also rose and approached her. He slowed as he got close, as if sensing her unease around dogs. She almost chuckled. Here she was, a firefighter brave enough to run into fire, and this dog could tell he should be tentative with her.

She squatted down and held out a hand for him. Wasn't that how you approached unfamiliar dogs? He took an obligatory sniff, then stepped forward to rest his chin in her hand. When she didn't move, he tilted his head and nuzzled further into her touch. She stroked one ear and the side of his head.

"He's so warm."

"You should try sleeping next to him. He's like a furnace." Claire's face flushed. "I mean—he sleeps in the bed—my bed. I wasn't suggesting you should—oh, hell, I'm shutting up now."

Britt laughed. "I got it." Stu moved into the space between her knees, and she rubbed over his back and down his side. His hair was short and tight against his body, making him feel very smooth.

"He's pretty forgiving. He probably doesn't even remember that you were going to let him die in that fire."

"Now who has the snarky comments?"

Claire smiled. "I guess it's okay to joke a little."

"I'm sorry I didn't ask sooner. How are you doing—you know, after the fire? Do you need anything?"

"I'm adjusting. Getting a whole new wardrobe is proving more frustrating than I would have expected. I love shopping as much as any woman, but for a handful of items at a time, not everything I own. Just for this place alone I run the gambit from getting-dirty clothes to presentable-for-the-public ones."

"I can see where that would be stressful. I'd have it easy. A few uniforms and I'm set for work, then some super-casual stuff for my downtime."

"I bought enough to get by for a while, until I figure out what else I really need. I've been staying with Lila. The apartment manager says it's going to be weeks, maybe longer, before any of us can move back into our units. They're letting anyone who choses to opt out of their lease, so I may go that route and find a new place. I had renter's insurance so my belongings are covered. Some of my neighbors didn't."

Claire was much more calm than a lot of victims Britt had dealt with before, but given what she knew about her, she wasn't surprised. Claire had made a quick assessment about her career, then initiated a major change, something most people would labor over for a long time. Claire's practical nature and the value she placed on her work at the rescue probably helped her process her loss.

"That might be a good idea. Even for the units with smoke damage, restoration takes time. And with so many affected apartments over there, it's a matter of getting to them all."

The sound of the back door opening, then closing, alerted Britt that their time alone was limited. She straightened, but before she could make a smooth escape, Lila burst into the room.

"The guys are taking down the last of the canopies. That was one of our smoother events, don't you think?" She glanced back and forth between Claire and Britt, then gave an exaggerated grimace. "Sorry. I didn't know you had company."

"I don't really. Britt was just saying good-bye on her way out," Claire said.

"Right. And of course, I had to see this guy one more time." She gave Stu another pat between his shoulders. Because Claire clearly didn't want Lila to know the depth of their conversation, she glanced at Claire one more time, grinned, and then said, "I'll see you tomorrow."

She didn't even make it to the back door before she heard Lila ask, "What's tomorrow?"

She wanted to linger to catch Claire's response but remembered hearing the door earlier, and, if Claire was listening for that sound, she didn't want to get busted listening in. So she continued through it, trying not to think about just how much she was looking forward to dinner tomorrow, the first actual date she'd had in quite some time.

Chapter Six

Claire pulled on a beige sweater over the blue-and-beige floral skirt she'd borrowed from Lila's closet that morning. She wanted to give off the vibe that she'd definitely changed after work, without appearing that she'd tried too hard. She glanced at her phone, and seeing that Britt should arrive in less than ten minutes, she picked up her small makeup bag and hurried to the single-occupant restroom across the hall from her office.

She hated being late and didn't want to make Britt have to wait, but she'd gotten tied up on the phone with the nervous foster of one of their senior dogs right at six. She'd spent fifteen minutes helping the young woman decide whether to take the dog to the emergency vet or monitor her until tomorrow morning, then reassuring her that she was doing a great job. She'd had some concerns about pairing the woman with a senior dog, but she seemed passionate about making sure the older dog didn't have to spend another day in a shelter setting. And she'd been great every step of the way. Her instincts were spot-on, and Claire had only needed to give her a bit of confidence in her decision-making.

"What time is your suitor arriving?" Lila pushed open the door Claire had left half ajar.

"My what?" Claire laughed. "She's picking me up at six thirty. So get out of here. I need to get ready." She leaned toward the mirror and applied a light coat of mascara.

"Where are you going?"

"She didn't tell me."

"What's the big secret?"

Claire shrugged. "It's dinner. She texted me it would be close, since I told her I'm always hungry after work. It isn't like we have that many choices on this side of town. Thank you for taking Stu home." She'd considered leaving him at Lila's that morning, but he was so used to being at work with her, and Lila's was still unfamiliar to him.

"Not a problem. We're going to bond while you're gone. If I can't have your firefighter, I can at least try to steal the affection of your dog."

"She's not *my* anything—"

"Yet."

"And you're just jealous that she didn't fall for your charms."

Lila shrugged. "I told you I wasn't giving her the full treatment."

"That's right. I wouldn't have had a chance against that." She touched up her lip gloss, then smoothed a hand over her unruly curls. She'd tried to stay out of the wind today but couldn't resist an afternoon play session with some of the pups to calm her nerves. Now she wished she'd planned to meet Britt at the restaurant at seven and taken the extra thirty minutes to go home and freshen up properly. But this was who she was—sometimes frazzled because the animals took priority—no sense pretending otherwise.

Lila angled her upper body back into the hallway. "I think your date's here. I just saw a car pull into the parking lot."

"Damn it. Okay." She glanced one last time in the mirror, then hurried back to her office and grabbed her car keys, so when they got back she wouldn't have to come inside before heading home.

"Tell her to have you home before curfew. Stu and I'll be waiting up. Or should we not?" Lila gave an exaggerated wink.

"It's dinner. Nothing more," she said over her shoulder as she reached the front door. But what she saw on the other side made her wonder if she could stop at dinner.

Britt stood there, looking back at her through the glass, with her hand raised as if about to knock. She wore a light-blue button-down shirt under a navy vest and very nicely fitting dark jeans. She'd gotten a haircut since yesterday, and her hair looked neat and smooth as it swept back from her forehead.

Claire called a good-bye to Lila, then unlocked the door and stepped out quickly before Lila decided to come down the hallway.

"You look great." Britt gathered Claire close in a quick hug—just long enough for Claire to feel the press of her warmth and catch a hint of her perfume. She'd never been someone who could pick out specific aromatic notes, but Britt's scent made her think of fresh-cut grass and summer days.

When Britt released her, Claire stepped back and waved a hand in front of Britt. "I thought you said you wore only casual clothes during your downtime. I wasn't expecting this."

"Then I hope it's a nice surprise."

"Most definitely."

Britt led her to a late-model black SUV and opened the passenger door for her. The interior was spotless and smelled like leather.

"New car?" she asked as Britt slid behind the wheel.

"Yep. I've had it about three months. A new ride was a necessity after my old Explorer finally died, but I spoiled myself a little with the bells and whistles on this one."

"It's very nice." She gestured toward her Crosstrek at the far end of the parking lot. "My car is my one indulgence. We have only one van at the rescue, and I want to make sure it's free if one of the animals needs transport, so I use my own car for business a lot."

"I love that color."

"That was one of the selling points, too."

Britt navigated onto the street, and less than ten minutes later, she pulled into the only remaining spot in the small parking lot of a local gastropub.

"Is this okay? You said you're typically hungry after work. The service here is fast, and the food is good."

"I've never been here. But I've heard good things." The restaurant had been open less than a year, but the buzz was great. Several of her fosters loved the place, and they'd said the front patio was dog friendly, which went a long way in her crowd.

As they passed through the front door, she saw a stainless-steel water bowl near the patio gate, confirming what she'd heard. She liked this pub already, and as long as the food didn't disappoint, she was planning to bring Stu back sometime. Situations like this provided good socialization as well as training opportunities for him.

Despite the full parking lot, they were seated quickly. Dark wooden tables dotted the center of the dining room, but the hostess led them to one of the booths lining two walls. A huge chalkboard over the bar listed the offered beers and microbrews, as well as a handful of wine selections. Modern industrial light fixtures over each booth cast a glowing circle over the occupants, making their little space feel more intimate.

As she settled across from Britt, she picked up her menu, as much to figure out her order as to find something to look at other than Britt. She was incredibly handsome, and the vee where the collar of her shirt opened drew Claire's eyes like a magnet. She couldn't stop thinking about whether Britt's fresh summer scent would emanate from that spot and how warm the skin there would be under her lips.

"This is a nice place." Did her voice sound weird? And couldn't she think of anything more creative to say than that? Just then her mind latched onto something she could talk about. "I got a call from my apartment complex today. They have a couple of boxes of things the restoration company salvaged from my apartment that I can go pick up."

"That's good news. I've worked plenty of fires, but it's still hard for me to grasp how it must feel to lose so much—the irreplaceable things especially."

"It's all just stuff in the end, isn't it? I hope some special old photographs are still there, but the fire has really put everything else in perspective. There's something to be said for whittling your life down to what really matters, though I'd rather have done it voluntarily."

"Did you have a lot of family heirlooms?" Britt asked after they'd placed their orders and the waiter walked away with the menus.

"Not really. My parents were kind of hippies—and very nomadic. For a little while when I was growing up, we traveled and lived in our van, staying at one commune or another until it was time to move on. Even today, they live a very minimalistic lifestyle—all about having experiences rather than collecting physical items."

"Do they live close by?"

She shook her head. "They're in New Mexico—for the moment. I see them once a year when they pass through on the way to someplace else. What about you? Are you close to your family?"

Britt held out her palm and tilted it back and forth in a so-so gesture. "It's complicated. My parents weren't thrilled I wanted to be a firefighter because they both have fancy jobs with important titles. They were even less excited when I came out. We're still family, but we just don't have much in common anymore, so we're not super close. And I have a brother, but his wife isn't a fan, so I don't see him much."

"Wow. That's rough."

Britt shrugged. "He made his choice for his family, I guess. They have a daughter, and I make it a point to visit for her. But it's always kind of awkward between the adults, so I hang out with her for a bit, then take off."

"Wow. I'm sorry."

"I don't mean to bring down the conversation. I do have people in my life that I think of as family—firefighters and friends."

Claire nodded. "I'm thankful for the people I've surrounded myself with. My colleagues and I have shared goals, and we win and lose together."

"When you think about it, you've come full circle to a version of your parents' lives, without all the traveling."

She'd always considered herself very different from her parents, and she had been, until her career change. But looking back, she could see now that over the past few years, she'd migrated her life to one that modeled more of their values.

Their waiter delivered their meals—steak and garlic fries for Britt, and a burger topped with avocado and fried jalapeños for Claire. As they ate, their conversation turned to more casual topics, punctuated by awkward silences until one of them thought of something else to say. Still, for someone whose conversations with new people almost exclusively centered around animals, Claire was proud of her ability to carry on an adult, non-dog-themed exchange.

❖

Britt parked next to Claire's car, then got out and circled the SUV. She opened Claire's door and held out a hand to help her down.

"If I can't walk you to your front door, at least I can see you to your car." She didn't often adhere to conventional manners, because what was conventional about dating a woman? But, at least in this way, she felt it important to convey her respect and attentiveness to the woman she'd spent the evening with.

"Thank you. That's sweet."

As they stood next to Claire's car, she grappled with what to say next. They'd only had dinner—a good meal, with a mix of nice conversation and the kind of natural silences between two people just getting to know each other—but just dinner all the same. So why did the emotions tumbling through her feel so much deeper than first-date feelings? In the end, she endured a long silence, squeezing one of her hands with the other. Just when she'd decided to ignore the chaos, open Claire's door for her, and say good-night, Claire sandwiched one of Britt's hands between hers, stroking her extended fingers.

"Hey. Relax."

Damn. She wanted to be so much cooler than this. On the job, or with her friends, she had as much confidence as she needed, but these types of early relationship situations were always difficult for her. With Claire, she wanted to work through her awkwardness, so she opted for honesty. "I don't do this a lot. My job is my life, and I've been happy with that." Britt glanced at their hands, then Claire's face.

"So you want to know if I'm worth making a change in that routine?"

"Not exactly." Now Britt avoided looking directly at her, instead directing her attention to the ground near their feet. "I'm quite certain you're worth all that and more, which is scary. We've known each other less than two weeks, and we spent at least half that time not even liking each other."

"I agree."

Tension pulled at her shoulders, but she didn't look up. "You do?"

"Yes. I agree that I'm worth it. But in case you have any doubts…" Claire closed the distance between them and captured Britt's lips with hers.

Britt grasped her waist as their chins rose and what had begun as a tentative exploration became an honest-to-goodness, feel-it-to-your-toes kiss. And, as they eased apart, Britt wanted to do it again. So she did. She stroked her fingers against Claire's neck and up to cradle her jaw and guide her into another kiss.

"You're very good at that," Claire whispered as they drew slightly apart, seemingly making a unanimous decision to stay close, arms around each other.

"Me? I thought you totally carried that kiss."

"Maybe it was both of us together." Claire slipped her hands under the back of Britt's vest and curled her fingers into Britt's shirt. "Perhaps we'll need to test further."

"Definitely." Britt cupped a hand against the back of Claire's neck, beneath her hair, and kissed her cheek. The sound of crickets brought her back to where she was—the parking lot of the rescue. She stepped back, trying to contain her desire to sweep Claire into her arms again. "But maybe not here." She took a breath, not afraid to let Claire know that she wanted her. "We have time."

Claire nodded. "Luckily, we don't have too many nosy neighbors."

Britt opened Claire's driver's door. "All the same, I'm not going to push you up against the side of this car."

Claire bit her lip, and Britt wished the parking lot were more brightly lit. She wanted to watch the same arousal that was singing through her fly across Claire's expression.

"Maybe another time." Claire tossed her a flirty wink as she got into her own car.

CHAPTER SEVEN

Claire exited her favorite bakery, cradling a medium-sized box next to her with one arm, while she held Stu's leash in her other hand. The still-cool morning air made a long walk comfortable for both of them. Since the fire, she'd been lax in taking him to the park for their usual strolls. Lila's neighborhood was much more walkable than the area near her apartment complex, so she didn't have an excuse not to get some exercise, for herself and for Stu.

She'd been thinking more and more about opting out of her lease. This morning she'd seen a cute little cottage-style house for rent around the corner from Lila's house. Maybe she was ready for something more than a one-bedroom apartment, and though Stu got plenty of time in the yard at the rescue, it might be nice for him to have one of his own. She'd taken a picture of the for-rent sign and planned to call later to inquire about their pet policy.

When she turned the next corner, she could see Britt's fire station across the street and two blocks away. Suddenly, she had second thoughts about her idea to stop by with cookies for Britt and her crew. Maybe they didn't like drop-in guests. Was she being presumptuous after just one date? She almost turned around and walked back to Lila's house. But the box under her arm spurred her across the street. She didn't want to eat all those cookies by herself. Yes, her coworkers and the visitors to the rescue would devour them, but she'd bought them for the firefighters, and suddenly she really wanted to deliver them to their intended recipients.

Three large overhead doors spanned the front of the beige-brick building, over which *Bellbrook Fire Dept. Station 7* stood out in black-metal lettering. To the left of big bay doors, a sidewalk flanked by brightly colored flowers led to a pedestrian door that appeared to be the main entrance for the public.

As she approached, the door opened, and a firefighter exited with a cigarette in one hand and a lighter in the other—barely clearing the door before he lit up.

"Can I help you?"

"I'm looking for Britt Everett." Too late to back out now.

"Hold on." He balanced his cigarette on the edge of a planter to the right of the door and stepped back inside. A few seconds later, he reappeared with Britt behind him. He threw his thumb over his shoulder in case she didn't see her, then picked up his cigarette and walked around the corner.

"Sorry. Politeness goes out the window when it's time to head to the side patio for a smoke." Britt gave her a quick hug and bent to pat Stu between his shoulders. "This is a great surprise. I didn't expect to see you today." Britt's happy expression melted her doubts about whether she should have come by.

"Lila's place isn't far from here. Stu and I were walking in the neighborhood, so I thought I'd drop off some cookies from that bakery on the corner as a thank-you for volunteering last weekend and for dinner Monday night." She tilted her head toward the corner in question and handed over the light-blue box.

"I recognized the box."

"There's enough to share."

Britt raised the lid and peeked inside, then frowned at Claire. "Why do I have to share? None of those guys went to the adoption fair, and I know they weren't at dinner."

"Don't pout."

"Why not? It's adorable."

Claire smiled. "Yes, it kind of is. So stop it."

Britt matched her smile, then gestured toward the door. "Since you're here, do you want a tour?"

"I do, actually. I've always been curious if these places really do look like the ones on television."

"Um, not as fancy and probably not as clean, but otherwise—sure."

She glanced down. "Is Stu okay? I can't leave him out here."

Britt turned, waving a cupped hand as she went. "Bring him. Firehouses are notoriously dog friendly."

Claire clicked her tongue to get Stu's attention as Britt led them inside. Stu pranced through the door, his nose twitching in the air. They passed a room with several rows of tables and chairs, which Britt explained was where they conducted pre-shift briefings and also used as a conference room when needed. At the end of the hall, she pointed toward a closed door.

"Sleeping quarters and locker rooms are through there. We won't go in, though. The guys on the engine were out all night, so they're grabbing a nap while they can."

"Do you have a lot of those shifts where you don't get any sleep?"

"It varies. Bad weather, a big-event weekend at the university, a large-structure fire—things like that can mean we stay busy for most of the shift. But most of the time we can squeeze in a few hours here and there. We have more downtime on truck than the engine crew, because they go out with the paramedics on a lot of medical calls."

"Why would you need a fire engine on a medical call?"

"It's not as much the engine as the manpower. We have more engines in the city than ambulances, and all firefighters are EMTs. Some have paramedic-level training, too. We can get medical treatment to the patient faster sometimes with an engine. Plus, if it's a bad call, a firefighter can jump in and ride to the hospital to assist the paramedic in the back. Extra hands are always welcome if you're doing CPR."

They continued through to a large living area, decorated with a flat-screen television and two navy sofas. A long table against the far wall held two desktop computers, one of which was currently occupied by a man checking his social-media site. Claire glanced away, lest he think she was reading over his shoulder. The adjoining space held a large dining table surrounded by mismatched wooden chairs, as if they had been replaced one by one when they'd broken, with little thought for the design of the other chairs.

Britt led her past a kitchen with appliances that appeared to be commercial but were far from shiny and new. "Budget money mostly goes to update firefighting equipment. The house gets what's left over and what we can pool together as a group."

"Is it true that you guys cook big meals together? Like on television?"

Britt laughed. "Yeah. That's one thing TV gets right. But not every meal. We never know when we're going to be interrupted. We try to eat together one meal a shift, whether we cook or order in.

"We have plenty to do in our downtime. If we aren't on the street, we might be cleaning our house or the truck, or doing training exercises. Anderson and I have been around a while, but we need to keep our skills up. And Mason's a newer guy so he needs to build muscle memory so we can do things quickly when we get out there. We set up ladder drills and rope skills, things like that. Or we exercise and do strength training."

"So I can rest assured you're not sitting around wasting taxpayer dollars?"

"Exactly." Britt guided her through to the vehicle bay. "Then there's community outreach."

"Is that what this falls under?"

"Yes. You wouldn't believe how many beautiful women I have to give tours of the fire station to. It's a real hardship."

Claire gave Britt's shoulder a light shove. Stu's nose started twitching again as they entered the large open area where the fire apparatus were parked. Claire picked up a hint of exhaust, the smell of rubber, and maybe some kind of strong cleaning solution. She could only imagine the hundreds of odors Stu was inundated by. She gave him a little slack in his leash, and he sniffed around, inspecting a roll of hose, a pair of tall rubber boots, and some kind of heavy metal tool.

"He seems to like it here. Maybe he's got some Dalmatian in him."

"I don't know about that. But some kind of hunting dog is definitely in the mix. He loves new smells. Small animals get his attention right away, too."

The vehicles inside the bay seemed massive, all of them far taller than her and still not anywhere near the soaring ceilings of the room. Two large, gleaming red-and-chrome apparatuses were tethered to lines coming down from the rafters, which plugged into panels on the side with a number of dials and buttons.

"You have two fire engines here?"

"That one in the center bay is an engine. They have the primary responsibility for actually fighting the fire. It's loaded with hundreds of feet of hose and has a water tank that can be used until we can hook up to a hydrant. The other one, the truck, is the one I ride on. See the aerial ladder on top?"

Claire nodded.

"We handle the operations that support the work of the engine—ventilation, for example, and search and rescue. And the rig carries the ladders and power tools, stuff like that. The empty bay on the end is for the ambulance, or medic unit, as we call them. Ours is out on a call right now. They catch a lot more runs than we do, so they're gone a lot."

A loud series of tones and noises blared through the bay, and Claire jumped. Stu pressed against her leg, but he didn't appear overly stressed. A robotic female voice gave out an address and some other information that indicated some kind of emergency. Claire had trouble making out the details because of the echo in the cavernous room.

"Do you need to go?"

Britt shook her head. "That's for our engine and a medic from another station. Hold on to Stu, though. The crew will be coming through here in a hurry in a second."

Claire shortened Stu's leash, though she felt confident he wouldn't leave her side. Several firefighters rushed to the fire engine one bay over from where they stood. The overhead door hummed and clacked as it rolled up. Then the vehicle doors slammed, and the engine crept forward, pausing at the entrance to the street before turning right. As they surged away from the firehouse, the rev of the big diesel faded into the growing whine of the siren.

Stu flexed his back and let loose a howl—a gentle howl—no other word could describe the careful way he tilted his head back and bayed at the departing engine.

"Throw some hound dog into the recipe." Britt ruffled a hand over Stu's head.

Claire chuckled. "I've never heard him do that before. He's always perked up when he hears sirens but never howled."

"Up close they must hit just the right frequency for him."

"Maybe. "I'm keeping you from work. If you'll show me to the front again, I'll get out of your way."

"You're fine. We're okay to have visitors. But it's this way." Britt guided her into the building with a hand against her lower back.

When they paused in a hallway with rows of academy graduation photos hanging on the wall, Claire scanned them for Britt's face. But under the brims of their hat, the tiny faces looked remarkably alike. All the men were clean shaven, and the women looked just as stoic and strong in their uniforms.

"What year did you say you graduated the academy?"

Britt chuckled. "I didn't say." She moved to a photo halfway along a row. "But I'm in this one."

Claire skimmed the faces, and when she found her, she wondered how her gaze hadn't gravitated to her right away. Britt looked quite impressive in her light-blue dress shirt, navy tie, and navy jacket with two lines of shiny silver buttons down the front, but so did the rest of her class. Also, like them, she stood tall, her posture indicating pride, only the wide grin on her face distinguishing her from the others.

"You're the only one smiling."

"They told us to look solemn for the photo, but I just couldn't contain myself. I'd known I wanted to be a firefighter since I was six years old. And that right there," she gestured at the photo, her eyes glowing, "that was the moment, you know—when it all came together."

"You got your dream."

Britt nodded. "And I haven't stopped feeling like that every single day since."

Her passion was as intoxicating as the darkening of her eyes as she moved closer to Claire, slid her arm around Claire's waist, and pulled her in for a kiss. Claire ran her hands up the front of Britt's polo shirt until she linked them together behind her neck, melting into her. How could she have missed the taste and feel of Britt's mouth already?

When a door slammed nearby, Britt jerked back. Seconds later, one of the guys Claire recognized from Britt's crew strolled through the hallway.

"Everett. Ms. Willows, nice to see you again." Anderson clapped Britt on the shoulder as he passed.

"Sorry. I forgot where I was. I'll hear about that later," Britt said after he'd disappeared in the direction of the locker rooms. Her face had a slight flush, and Claire could feel an answering heat in her own cheeks, only her pale complexion didn't hide it as well.

"Are you—we didn't just out you, did we?"

"No. The guys know I'm gay. But contrary to firehouse tradition, I'm pretty private about my personal life, what there's been of it."

Claire turned back to the photo on the wall, taking the time to collect herself. She'd lost her head as well, thinking only about pressing closer to Britt. She hadn't even considered Britt's standing with her coworkers. In the photo, Britt's hair was smoothed back and secured somehow behind her head. "You had long hair."

"Yep. From kindergarten until about my first month out of the academy. My hair was always thick, and I soon learned that it absorbed smoke. After a structure fire, I had to wash it several times to get rid of the smell. So it wasn't a hard sell to cut it. Still, after a fire like the one at your apartments, I have to mix cider vinegar with my shampoo to help get it out."

"How long was it?"

Britt held up a finger while she pulled out her phone, then navigated to her social media. After a couple of touches and a scroll, she rotated the screen toward Claire. In the photo, Britt sat behind a birthday cake decorated with icing in the shape of a fire engine. Her hair parted in the center and fell almost to her shoulders.

"I posted this for one of those throwback Thursday things. My eighteenth birthday. And the day I became eligible to apply as a firefighter recruit."

"Eighteen? Wow. I would have guessed twenty-one."

"Many departments have a higher minimum, and they want you to have had some fire-science courses and at least your EMT license. Bellbrook Fire accepts applications at eighteen and then does most of their training in-house."

Britt appeared years younger than eighteen as she pointed at the cake with that same huge smile that would later survive the rigors of academy training and reappear on graduation day. Her eyes shone with what could only be absolute joy.

"You clearly love what you do."

"I can't see myself doing anything else. But you should know that you emit the same energy. If you hadn't told me about your past, I would never have pegged you doing anything else. Your commitment to the rescue is evident and admirable."

"Thank you." She was proud of her work, but she wasn't always comfortable with compliments about it. She loved the animals, but she got so much sanity and joy out of the rescue that she felt she did the work for selfish reasons, too. "I should let you get back to work."

As they turned toward the door, Britt brushed her hand down the outside of Claire's arm, and Claire felt the gentle contact in a shiver across the back of her neck. She wanted more of Britt, and she wanted her someplace they wouldn't be interrupted.

"When will I see you again?" She angled toward Britt as they reached the door, managing to control her urge to press closer and wrap her arms around Britt.

"I'm off tomorrow. I thought since you visited me at work, I could come see you at yours. Maybe bring you some lunch?"

"That sounds great." She leaned in enough to speak quietly so only Britt could hear her. "I really want to kiss you right now."

Britt glanced over her shoulder, then stole what was probably supposed to be a quick kiss, but it turned into more when Britt moaned against her mouth and gathered her closer. Claire ran one hand up the side of Britt's neck and threaded her fingers in her hair.

"You're dangerous." Britt grasped Claire's waist and created some separation between them.

"I think that was your fault. I'm very much looking forward to lunch tomorrow, but just so you know, we're going to need to be more alone than that, very soon."

Britt grasped her hand and squeezed. "I feel the same way. I just didn't want to rush this. I want you to be comfortable."

"I can safely say I am quite uncomfortable at the moment. But luckily, I know a solution to that problem. In fact, let's skip lunch, and you can pick me up at the end of the day instead."

CHAPTER EIGHT

Britt parked in the back of the lot at Release the Hounds and entered through the gate into the yard. The front lot was pretty full, and people were leaving the building with dogs of various sizes. She remembered Claire saying something about one of her foster meet-up groups, where fosters would bring in their dogs for socialization, both for the dogs and the people. They could discuss any training issues with Claire and let her know their progress so she could update the dog's adoption page on the website.

Britt had managed to fill her day with busywork, but she'd only been marking time until she could pick up Claire. Looking so forward to seeing Claire felt somewhat surreal, given that not very long ago she'd dreaded having to come here to pay penance. She didn't feel contrite about her actions the day of the fire and would do it all the same way today. Claire's life, a human life, was the most valuable thing Britt had sworn to protect. But she better understood Claire's actions that day. She hadn't been some spoiled woman trying to go back in to save her material things, and Britt had come across a few of those in her day. Stu was Claire's family.

As she entered the gate to the yard, Stu trotted over to greet her, his whole butt wiggling as his tail whipped back and forth. She paused to squat and greet him, rubbing his ears and down his back before continuing to the main building. He licked her hand, and when she straightened to head inside, he pranced along beside her, still seeking her attention. But after she opened the door, he retreated to the yard.

Claire looked up from her desk as Britt walked into her office.

"Hey. I'm almost ready to go. Would you mind letting Stu in for me while I grab my purse? Lila's going to take him home with her."

"Sure." She returned to the back door, but as soon as she stepped outside, she knew something was wrong.

Stu wasn't in the yard. She scanned along the fence near the doghouse, where it ran under the overhanging limbs of a large maple tree, thinking he might have sought some shade. But she didn't see any movement back there. She called his name and tried for a whistle, which came out as a lame lisping of air.

When she looked at the gate, dread unfolded in her gut. She'd closed it behind her, hadn't she? But the space—the Stu-sized width between the gate and the fence, indicated otherwise. She ran over and searched the area just outside the fence, and hearing the clack of the latch as she closed it made her think that she hadn't heard that sound as she pulled the handle when she entered. And now, Stu was out there somewhere and could get hurt. She was responsible for putting him in danger yet again. Claire was going to lose it when she found out.

"Hey. What's the holdup out here?" Claire exited the main building, and Britt spun around, seeing Claire visually sweeping the yard for Stu.

"The gate—I was sure I closed it when I came in." She hurried over to Claire, desperation churning bile in her stomach.

"Where's Stu?"

"I don't know. I'm so sorry. I looked outside the fence and didn't see him. But he's only been gone a matter of minutes. I came in, and you sent me right back out. I'm going to jump in my car and go look for him. Has he ever gotten out before? Is there anyplace he'd go?" Britt's limbs were weak with adrenaline, and panic drove her voice up an octave. What if she didn't find him? She couldn't forgive herself if anything happened to him.

"Okay. Slow down." Claire, surprisingly calm, grasped Britt's shoulders.

"I can't. Claire, if he's out there by himself—I can't think about—" She couldn't verbalize the images now starting to fill her head. And she couldn't get his face out of her mind either—the way he laid his head on her knee and looked up her with the most trusting eyes.

"I know. I know this feeling you have right now."

Britt took a deep breath, forcing oxygen to her racing brain. Claire did know this feeling, times ten, because she'd had the added fear and adrenaline of having just been pulled from sleep to find her apartment filled with smoke. She seemed to have been dealing with everything so succinctly that Britt sometimes forgot how scary that day must have been.

"Is the gate closed now?"

Britt nodded. "It's latched. I checked."

"Okay. Come with me." Claire took her hand and led her into the back door of the main building.

She resisted. "Shouldn't we go look for him?"

"We are." Inside, she continued through the hallway to the reception area, now empty of the foster crowd Britt had seen leaving earlier.

Through the glass of the front door, Britt saw Stu sitting on the welcome mat as if that was where he always waited to be let inside. Her legs actually felt weak as the fear left her body, replaced by a wave of relief so monstrous she wanted to cry.

"Are you going to let him in?" Claire's question, laced with humor, propelled her across the room, and she swung open the door and knelt.

"Hey, buddy. You scared the crap out of me." He moved into her open arms, greeting her with a wiggle and a swipe of his tongue against her chin. She cradled his face in her hands and kissed the top of his head, surprising even herself.

"He's gotten out before. And believe me, the first time, I went through all the panic, too. He doesn't go far. I don't know why he goes to the front door instead of returning to the gate. But for some reason, he's decided this is how he wants to come in."

"You could have said something when I was having a meltdown back there."

Claire shrugged.

"You enjoyed that, didn't you?"

"No. That would be mean. Okay—maybe a little. But I knew he wasn't in any danger." Claire held out a hand, and when Britt placed hers in it, she helped her up. "Are you ready to go?"

"Okay. But Stu's coming with us."

"He'll be okay with Lila."

"I'd planned to cook for you at my place anyway. If you have some food here you can bring for his dinner, he can hang out there with us."

"Are you sure?"

"Why not?" She tried to sound nonchalant, but she truly wanted Stu with them. After all, the cute little guy had essentially brought them together—indirectly.

Claire bit her lip and drew her eyebrows together, as if she wanted to say something more.

"What?"

"I didn't want to be presumptuous, but I did bring an overnight bag, just in case. Are you still okay with him coming with us?"

Britt's heart leapt, but she made a face, playing with her. "You said he sleeps in the bed, right?"

Claire pursed her lips and nodded slowly.

"The foot of the bed, at least?"

Claire shook her head.

She rolled her eyes. "Okay. But he's not sleeping on my pillow." When she glanced down at him, his forehead wrinkled and he raised his brows. "Puppy-dog eyes won't change my mind, dude. Let's go."

"I'll grab him some food and treats and meet you outside."

"We'll be waiting in the backyard. With the gate firmly shut."

❖

When Britt opened her front door, Stu paused on the threshold until Claire waved a hand to signal he could enter. He began checking out the living room, sniffing every corner carefully. Though Claire didn't initiate as thorough an inspection, she did look around at the modern, organized space. The leather sectional made her breathe a little easier about bringing Stu along; at least he wouldn't leave his short, needle-like hair stuck in the fabric of a sofa. He would stay off it if she told him to, but then he'd lie on the floor with his back pressed against it.

The living room opened to a kitchen gleaming with white Shaker cabinets and stainless-steel appliances. A light-gray backsplash brought out the vein of color in the expensive-looking stone countertops.

"That is a serious kitchen." Claire circled the island, drawing her hand along the cool, smooth countertop.

"Do you like to cook?"

She laughed. "Not really. But luckily, a person can actually live on grilled cheese. And if you put sliced tomato in there, it's practically gourmet."

"Do you like mushrooms?"

"I do."

"How does mushroom risotto sound for dinner?"

"I just told you I subsist on cheese and bread. I'm not going to turn my nose up at actual, good food."

"Great. I'll get started in here. Feel free to give yourself and Stu a tour."

She slid onto a stool at the edge of the counter. "If you don't mind, I'll keep you company. Then later you can show me the rest of your place." She heard the promise in her tone, and judging from the way Britt's gaze dipped to her mouth, then lower, she'd heard it, too.

"We could skip dinner and order a pizza—later."

"You can't promise a girl mushroom risotto, then try to substitute pizza."

"I was hoping what I was offering in the interim might be a satisfying alternative."

She grinned at the emphasis Britt put on *satisfying*. "What if I want it all?"

"Then you shall have it all." Britt's lopsided smile contradicted her serious tone, and Claire couldn't tell which was more real. But Britt bent and pulled a pan from a lower cabinet and placed it on the stovetop to heat. "One amazing risotto coming up."

Claire rinsed a plate and placed it in the dishwasher next to the others. In exchange for the meal, she'd insisted on cleaning up while Britt relaxed. As she straightened, she glanced over at Britt, sitting with Stu on the couch. Once given permission to get on the furniture, Stu had very few boundaries with regard to personal space. He sat right next to Britt and had one of his front paws planted on her collarbone. But she didn't appear bothered, as she stroked his head and spoke quietly to him.

"If you tell him to get down, he'll respect your rules. I know it doesn't seem that way right now." She walked closer, pausing to stand behind the opposite "L" of the sectional. Stu glanced at her, then turned back to Britt.

"He's okay." Britt grinned. "I kind of like the attention."

"Of course, until he punches you in the eye."

"What?"

"I'm sure you've noticed he uses his front feet like hands, but he's not always coordinated. I've caught more than one paw to the face."

Britt leaned a little closer to Stu. "You wouldn't hurt me, would you?"

Stu swiped a tongue from Britt's chin up the front of her face. Britt jerked back and Claire cringed. Britt surprised her by rolling her eyes and laughing out loud.

"Not exactly the answer I was looking for, pal." She rubbed his ear good-naturedly.

It wasn't the response Claire had expected either. For Britt, Claire figured doggie-kisses would be crossing a line.

"You really don't have to pretend—you've already told me you're not an animal person." She circled the couch and stopped in front of Britt. "And somehow I'm still into you." She dropped one knee onto the cushion next to Britt's thigh.

"I definitely want to explore that statement. But first, I promise I'm not kissing up to your dog to get to you—no pun intended after he snuck that one in." She grinned. "This guy won me over. I didn't realize it until I was losing my mind with worry."

Charmed by the sweet sincerity in Britt's eyes as she glanced at Stu, then back at her, she took Britt's hand and pulled her off the couch. As she tugged Britt toward her, she flashed Stu a quick hand signal, indicating he should stay where he was.

"As much as I love that you two are bonding, I believe I was promised a tour of the rest of the house—specifically, your bedroom."

Britt slid her hands around Claire's waist as she stood, and Claire marveled at how such a simple embrace could make her feel so secure—so cared for. She pointed in the direction she thought the bedroom might be and gave Britt a questioning look. Britt nodded, then, capturing Claire's hand, she led her that way.

Britt paused in the doorway and released Claire, then crossed to the nightstand and turned on a lamp. The room was decorated in varying shades of gray, and in the soft glow, Claire felt like she'd stepped into a black-and-white movie—one of those old romantic flicks, complete with Britt cast as the hunky hero.

She grasped a handful of the front of Britt's soft, gray T-shirt and stepped into her. When she kissed her, she made her intentions known. She wanted to feel Britt against her, and Britt complied, slipping the shirt up and over her head. Claire stroked Britt's firm stomach, then along the band of her white cotton bra.

"This, too, please. All of it."

"You, too."

They undressed and slid into bed, under the covers. Britt gathered Claire close and kissed her, unhurriedly, like they weren't naked in bed together. Claire, seeking progress, slipped her thigh between Britt's and moved over her. She took control, surprised and even more turned on when Britt didn't protest.

She mapped Britt with her hands—finding firm muscles underneath soft curves, lingering when Britt twitched and moaned under her touch. Britt's pleasure—and her submission—pulled Claire along with her as she spiraled into orgasm, and just seconds before Britt let go, Claire guided Britt's hand to her own center, and she tumbled over with her.

Claire awoke later than usual the next day. She rolled over, finding Britt still asleep with her back to her. She snuggled closer, pressing into the space between Britt's shoulder and the bed.

Britt chuckled and rolled onto her back. "You're a morning cuddler, huh?"

"Yep." When Britt stretched out her arm, Claire ducked under it and aligned herself against Britt's side, head on her chest. "Do you have any plans for today?"

"I don't. Maybe some light housecleaning and paying a couple of bills."

"I have *the most* exciting plans. Would you like to join me?"

"I feel I'm obligated to say yes to *the most* exciting plans."

"Don't you want to know what they are?"

"I'm still saying yes." Britt grabbed her hand and pulled her arm across her. Claire wove her hand under the covers until she found Britt's skin. "If I hate it, at worst, I get to spend the day with you. That's good enough for me."

"We'll see if you still feel that way when I tell you what it is." She played her fingertips against Britt's side. "We're going furniture shopping." She announced the plan as if offering a treat.

"Oh, wow. That sounds—"

Claire laughed. "Still think it's good enough?"

"Sure. Yes—what kind of furniture are we looking for?"

"All of it. I rented a house—around the corner from Lila's place."

"That's great. So you decided not to wait for your apartment to be ready?"

"I saw this place while out for a walk. It's a cute little house and already has a small fenced yard in the back. As it turns out, the owner is a donor at our rescue. He has no problem with Stu and is even waiving the security deposit. I can move there in two weeks."

"That's great. So we're furnishing a whole house."

"Maybe not all at once. The house already comes with appliances. Today, I'm shooting for a bedroom set and a couch. Maybe a coffee table, too. That'll keep me comfortable until I get the insurance money and figure out what else I need. So, are you in?"

"I'm in. But first, we should shower." Britt sat up and swung her legs over the edge of the bed.

"Together?" She levered up onto her knees and wrapped her arms around Britt from behind, resting her chin on Britt's shoulder.

"Yes, please."

CHAPTER NINE

Britt jumped down from the truck, her heavy gear shifting on her body from the impact. Because of the already congested area due to the music festival, they'd been able to get within only two blocks of the scene.

"Grab the med bag and what tools you can carry. We're on foot from here." She grabbed a battery-powered saw from the compartment closest to her. Once her crew was ready, they headed toward the scene.

They'd been dispatched to a motor-vehicle accident for a car that had driven through the barriers and into the music-festival area. No one could say for sure how many were injured at this point because the 9-1-1 center was flooded with calls.

At the perimeter of the festival, the chaos became apparent. Those who had fled the immediate area had stopped, lost and in obvious shock as to what to do next. Some were assessing their own injuries or those around them. Some had been contacted by first responders or festival employees and were being directed to the first-aid tent, where, Britt had heard over the radio, medical triage had been set up. People stood around holding cell phones, presumably calling either 9-1-1 or family and friends. Some even looked like they were texting or posting on social media already. This thing probably already had a hashtag.

Britt moved her team closer, and the car, crashed into one of the large event tents, came into view.

"Captain, this is—" Mason surveyed the bedlam in front of them.

She met his eyes and used a firm voice to combat the fear leaking into his eyes. "PD has secured the scene. All the paramedics in the county and two neighboring ones are on the way down here. We're assigned to rescue. Head for that wreckage and help anyone who may be trapped. Ambulatory patients can be directed to the triage area." She pointed toward the east side of the festival footprint.

"The driver of the car—" Mason glanced toward the vehicle.

"The police have him. He'll be going to the hospital, too. Mason." She drew his attention back to her. "People are panicking, and you need to be a calm voice in the chaos. Triage their injuries and tell them where to go. The police will probably want to talk to anyone who hadn't already left the area before we arrived."

Almost immediately, they came upon Traci Sam and a civilian tending to an injured teen. They weren't able to safely get him to triage because of the damaged tent structure around him. Britt cut away enough pieces to get a backboard in there just as paramedics arrived. Once they'd handed him off, she and Mason kept moving, looking for their next priority task.

She kept an eye on Mason as they worked through many of the walking wounded. A couple of times she spotted Anderson, who also seemed to be watching over the youngest member of their crew, but they didn't have time to exchange more than a passing glance.

Aside from the large number of festival-goers who'd been in the path of the car and either hit directly or with a glancing blow, many people were hurt in the flood of panic that followed. The stampeding crowd had knocked down anyone moving too slowly or those who hesitated amid the wave of pedestrian traffic. She saw sprains, bumps, bruises, and lacerations, but worse was the trauma in the eyes of the people she treated, many of whom had witnessed the initial incident.

The festival had boasted a large array of acts, from older artists with an established fan base to emerging stars, resulting in a wide age range in the attendees. Britt helped a woman in her early sixties to the triage area, fearing she'd broken her arm. She came upon two teen brothers who'd lost contact with their father during the melee. They displayed no adolescent bravado when they saw Britt. Instead, they clung to each other and to her with tears in their eyes as she escorted them through the scene. At triage, they learned that their father had been seriously injured and transported to a hospital. Britt hooked them up with the incident commander to secure them a ride in the next unit headed to the hospital. She later saw them climbing into the back of a patrol car as she brought in yet another non-critical injury.

Three hours later, Britt took one last glance at the festival grounds before climbing into the passenger seat of the fire truck. The police investigators would be on scene for hours still, taking photographs and measurements, and writing reports. But all the patients had been transported or had signed releases, and the scene was clear of safety hazards, so Fire and EMS were finished.

The city had gone dark while they worked, and the streets seemed more calm than usual, but it was barely ten p.m., and with eight hours left of her shift, she couldn't count on it staying that way for too long. The ride back to the station was quiet, while they all processed how someone could purposely mow people down with a car. When they got there, she dropped out of the truck, landing on muscles that had stiffened from fatigue during the short ride. She took a few steps, trying to loosen up, and saw Anderson and Mason walking just as gingerly.

"It's been a while since a scene beat me up like that." Anderson planted his hands on his lower back, moaning as he arched.

"Let's hope it's a long time until the next one, too," Britt said. "I don't know about you guys, but I'm going to grab a shower and some sleep before we get another run."

As soon as she got inside the locker room, Britt pulled out her cell phone and unlocked the screen. She navigated to recent calls and connected to the only person she wanted to speak to right now.

"Hey." Claire's voice was soft and filled with relief. "It's good to hear from you."

"Sorry it took a bit. But we just got back."

"No worries." She chuckled. "Okay. A few worries. I saw the news. It was hard to know you were out there and not be certain you were okay."

"It's the job."

"I know. I kept telling myself you can take care of yourself. But the reporter said someone from Bellbrook Fire was injured."

"Yeah. It was a paramedic, a friend, Jenna. You haven't met her yet."

"They said it might be critical?"

Britt nodded and pinched the bridge of her nose. "She's alive and fighting."

"Okay. Do you want me to go to the hospital? Can I do anything for her family?"

"It's sweet of you to offer. But the scene is wrapping up, and that place will already be packed with firefighters. We're about to grab some sleep, and if we don't get another call, I'll take the guys and go up there in a few hours to see her. Our chaplain will make sure her family has whatever they need." She paused a beat. "I just—after seeing—well, it was bad, and I really wanted to hear your voice."

The silence that followed told Britt that Claire understood what she was admitting. This was confirmation that she was all-in—and the idea made her happier than she could have imagined—or at least she would be if Claire felt the same way. How many seconds of silence had passed? It felt like too many. Maybe Claire didn't return her feelings.

"Me, too," Claire finally said, and then she chuckled. "I mean, I didn't see the scene, but I—it's good to hear from you."

Was that a "good to hear from you" in the way you thank a friend from high school for checking in after several years?

"In fact, I was hoping I'd get to see you after your shift, if you're not too tired."

She was exhausted, but despite what she'd told the guys, sleep probably wouldn't come soon. By morning, she'd be dead on her feet. "My place?"

"That sounds perfect. I'll meet you there."

As soon as Britt opened the door, Claire stepped into her and wrapped her arms around her. When Britt started to ease back, after the normal duration of a hug, Claire held on and even adjusted to a more intimate embrace.

"How are you?" she whispered next to Britt's ear.

Britt sighed. "I don't even know." The quiet confession didn't sound like much, but Claire suspected that with anyone else Britt would have brushed off the question or maybe offered an assurance that she was fine. For Britt, even admitting she was uncertain meant vulnerability.

"Did you sleep?"

She shook her head.

"Did you go to the hospital?"

"No. We caught two more calls and just got back from the last one as our shift ended. But I called Jenna's partner on my way home. She's stable."

Claire skimmed her lips along Britt's cheek as she released her, then captured her hand and tugged her toward the bedroom.

Britt resisted. "I won't be able to sleep."

"Let's just lie down for a minute. You can talk about it. Or you don't have to. I don't know what's best for you in these situations."

In the bedroom, she undressed Britt, while she stood passively, helping only when she needed to lift a foot to step out of her pants or sit down so Claire could remove her socks. After Claire finished, she helped Britt into a pair of knit shorts and a T-shirt, then guided her into bed. She quickly stripped down and put on similar clothing, then slid in next to her.

They lay quietly for several minutes, and she was hoping Britt might fall asleep but suspected too much was still going on in her head.

"Most of what we see is just another call, but every now and then we catch one that gets to me. Yet I don't have any experience letting anyone else in while I'm dealing with it, except other firefighters. And we tend to gloss over traumatic events so we don't let them affect the next run. Negative outcomes are part of the deal." She took Claire's hand. "I haven't wanted to share this part of me with anyone in a long time, but I want to with you. Can I let you know when I'm ready? It's still a lot to talk about right now."

"Sure." She wanted more. But she'd seen the news coverage, with photos and cell-phone videos from festival attendees. She couldn't imagine what it was like in the moment, so certainly, Britt would need time to decompress. And maybe the best thing Claire could do was be present if she needed her.

Claire didn't sleep, but Britt did eventually drift off. When it seemed she was deep enough that Claire wouldn't disturb her, she picked up her tablet off the nightstand and opened the e-book she'd started the night before. She read for a couple of hours while Britt dozed and had just finished her book when Britt began to stir.

Britt stretched and rubbed one hand through her hair, leaving it standing up in all directions. She turned onto her side and looked up at Claire, her gaze still hazy from sleep, and smiled.

"Thank you. I guess I needed that."

Claire kissed her head. "I'm here for whatever you need."

"This is perfect right now." Britt slipped her fingers between Claire's, holding her hand gently. "I'm glad I'm here with you."

"Me, too."

"Would you go to the hospital with me later? I want to see Jenna. Also, some of my friends will be there, and I'd like you to meet them."

"Yes. I will."

"Good." Britt nodded. "But let's stay here a bit longer." Britt closed her eyes again.

Claire held her, brushing her hair back from her forehead in a rhythmic motion to lull her back to sleep. She thought about the day they'd met and how little understanding she'd had of who Britt was. She'd judged her immediately as some arrogant asshole on a power trip. But she saw now the toll Britt's mission—because it was so much more than some job—could take on her. While *she* was still the person who would run into a burning building to save a dog, and Britt was still the firefighter who would try to stop her, they had found some very nice middle ground. In Britt, Claire had someone she could trust and—yes—someone she could love. What had happened today at that festival drove home the idea that she should tell Britt about that love as soon as possible. She wasn't promised tomorrow to do it.

She glanced at Britt's face, peaceful in sleep. Maybe she could wait until she woke up. She snuggled closer. Britt shifted in her sleep and wrapped an arm around Claire, anchoring her to her side, and Claire closed her own eyes as well.

PUSHED

CHAPTER ONE

The steady beep signaling an alarm on the portable metal detector had Officer Traci Sam turning toward the queue waiting to get into the Bellbrook Jams music festival. The man who had just walked through glanced around as if someone else might have set the thing off. Traci grabbed a handheld wand off the table beside her and directed him off to the side.

"Put your hands out to your sides and stand still." Once he'd formed a human "T" she began sweeping the wand. It signaled as she passed over his right, front pocket. "What do you have in this pocket?"

When he started to shove a hand in there, she grabbed his forearm to stop him.

"Whoa. Did I say to reach in there? I asked what you have."

"It's a flask."

"I'm going to remove it from your pocket. Do you have anything sharp in there that could stick me or otherwise hurt me?"

"Of course not."

Once she'd removed it and confirmed it was a flask, she held it out to him. "You can toss it, or you can take it back to your car. But it's not going inside."

He grumbled as he turned and threw it into a nearby trash can, then held out his arms as if daring her to scan him again. Despite the fact this was the fifth annual festival and the publicity included the rules for entry for several weeks leading up to it, attendees didn't pay attention to the warnings. Only two festival-goers later, she stopped a middle-aged woman carrying a bottle of water.

"Ma'am, you can't bring in outside beverages." She pointed at a sign posted next to a trash can several feet before the metal detectors.

"It's just water."

The woman started to brush past her, but Traci stuck her arm out. "The festival vendors have water for sale."

"For three times what I paid for this. What, do you get a cut or something? Is that why you're being such a hard-ass when all you have to do is look the other way?"

Traci didn't respond, but she kept her expression resolute. She'd learned early in her career that, as a short, female police officer, some people wouldn't take her seriously, so whenever in uniform, she maintained a strong, professional demeanor.

"Lady, you just saw her make that other guy throw his flask away." One of the young men waiting behind the woman had clearly grown impatient with all the delays.

"This is what I pay my taxes for?" the woman said as she dropped the bottle into the trash can and gave Traci a snide look.

Traci stepped aside, again without taking the bait. The "I pay your salary" line triggered many of her coworkers, but not her. She didn't care where her paycheck came from; her job was the same—protect the people. And by the way, she paid her own taxes, too.

"Enjoy the festival," she said politely, barely giving the woman another look before turning her attention to the rest of the queue.

A quick glance at her watch confirmed she had only thirty minutes left working the gate before she was relieved. Her next post was to patrol inside the festival, and she'd much prefer that assignment. She was glad to complete this one at the beginning of the event so she could spend some time inside the grounds. At least there, she could hear some good background music.

Her time at the gate flew by with no major incidents, unless she counted the kids trying to ride scooters through the entrance. She turned them around, ignoring their protests about having already bought tickets. She warned her relief in case they tried again and headed inside the festival.

She usually didn't like crowds and wouldn't sign up to work these special events. But she needed the overtime to pay off some charges run up by an ex she was foolish enough to give access to one of her credit cards. Unbeknownst to her, the ex had written down her credit-card number, and when Traci had tried to break it off, she'd gone on a shopping spree. She'd been able to get the amount she owed reduced, but she wanted the balance paid soon. It was bad enough being responsible for that mistake, but adding interest was rubbing salt in the wound.

The festival was one of Bellbrook's largest annual events, drawing attendees from hours away. The only events that came close in size were the county fair, the Fourth of July celebration, and the year the university basketball team made the NCAA playoffs. It was well known among Bellbrook PD's officers that the organizers paid their security staff very well. Their reputation for safe, family-friendly entertainment had been key to the growth of the event.

Traci had finished her regular patrol shift at three p.m., grabbed a quick sandwich at her favorite deli on Main Street, and then reported directly to the incident commander for assignment. She'd be exhausted tomorrow, but she had two days off to recover before she returned to work.

❖

Nicole Klein wandered along a row of food trucks parked near a curb on one border of the festival footprint. She slid her sunglasses from her hair down onto her face, making her feel more protected in the crowd of strangers, as well as blocking out the afternoon sun. Normally, she would never have come to an event like this by herself, but her favorite folk band was booked in a time slot later this evening. She'd stepped way out of her comfort zone to hear them live. After forking out the price for the ticket, she'd convinced herself she should come early to get her money's worth.

The food-truck fare smelled great, but nothing she saw on the menus could unlock her nervous appetite. She hated crowds, even more when she was immersed in them alone. She usually didn't go to the movies or out to eat alone. When she traveled for work, she barely left her hotel room during her downtime. Yet here she was, wandering among strangers with two hours left until the band she came to see appeared.

She'd be hungry later, and when the crowds picked up, the lines at the trucks would grow as well. Seeing several empty tables nearby, she decided on a gourmet grilled cheese and stood in the appropriate line. A few minutes later she carried a paper tray with her sandwich to one of the tables and sat down. Eating would kill some time. She pulled out her cell phone and checked her work email while she lingered over what would serve as her dinner.

It wasn't unusual for Nicole to work on the weekend. Being one of the top account managers at the most successful financial-advisory firm in town meant she had to be available at all times. She handled some of the largest portfolios in the company, and if her clients didn't feel like they got enough attention, they would quickly take their business elsewhere. She'd promised herself she wouldn't work this weekend, but then she'd amended that decision to not working today. And here she was checking email, but, she rationalized, reading a few emails on her phone wasn't really the same as going in to the office, or even logging in remotely on her computer. Maybe she wouldn't answer any emails, just read them. She scrolled, then paused on one from a very wealthy client. She could answer just this one. *No.* She chastised herself. *No work, for one evening.* Resolutely, she exited her email app and locked her phone.

She glanced down, realizing she'd barely eaten any of the sandwich and had let it go soggy. She gathered her trash and dropped it into a can as she stood to make a round through the vendor booths in the arts-and-crafts area. As she turned, she registered movement out of the corner of her eye seconds before she heard a loud crash. Everything happened so quickly after that. An older sedan had barreled through a temporary barrier and was still moving, next impacting a crowd of people standing nearby. People screamed and tried desperately to jump out of the way, but the big car knocked them down like crops in the path of a harvester. The vehicle finally came to a stop after colliding with one of the larger festival tents, bending the metal poles as if they were paperclips.

Suddenly, a crush of people trying to escape jostled Nicole, who stood frozen in place. They seemed to come from every direction. Someone crashed into her and shoved her hard into someone else, and she caught an elbow just below her eye, pain bursting through the side of her face like fireworks. She cupped a hand against her throbbing cheekbone, and after being pinballed for several seconds and almost knocked to the ground, she began to push back. She thrust out her arms, desperately driving for space and balance in the chaos. Realizing she wasn't making any forward progress, instead she tried to reach the edge of the crowd. Doing so pushed her out of the traffic flow, close to the car, and she could finally stand still without being dragged along by the crowd.

She stared at the driver's window and spotted the man behind the wheel slumped forward, unmoving. Around her people were yelling and crying, some just beginning to pick themselves up off the ground. It seemed like blood was on every person she saw.

Several police officers rushed past her toward the car, spurring her into action of her own, but she didn't know where to begin. What should she do? Who should she help first? She drew on her need to be in control and made a decision, focusing on two victims near her who appeared seriously injured.

Two uniformed women lay on the ground a couple of feet apart. Their gray polo shirts said EMS across the back and had yellow reflective stripes around the short sleeves. One woman lay facedown and didn't appear to be moving, while the other had already rolled to her side.

"Jenna?" The ambulatory paramedic scrambled to her knees and crawled closer to the other. The injured paramedic—the one she'd called Jenna—moaned louder as the other one grasped her shoulder.

"Wait. I don't think we should move her," Nicole blurted, then felt stupid for giving medical advice to a paramedic, but she looked pretty shaken up. "Should we?"

The paramedic stared at her for a moment, then seemed to snap out of it. "Not yet. Let me assess her injuries."

"It seemed like that shoulder hurt when you touched it."

"Okay. What's your name?" she asked while she carefully ran her hands over Jenna's shoulders and arms.

"Nicole."

"Nicole. Hi. I'm Candace." Candace pulled a radio from a clip on her belt and pressed a button on the side. When it appeared to be working, she issued a call for assistance, gave their location inside the festival, and, after glancing around, added the approximate number of injured in their immediate area.

After she finished, the radio continued to chatter with excited voices, and Nicole couldn't make out which belonged to the dispatcher, other first responders on scene, or those en route from other locations, but a lot of people already seemed to be involved.

❖

Traci sprinted toward the sound of the crash, weaving to avoid the people headed toward her. Some of them had blood on their clothes, but she didn't bother stopping to check on any of them. If they were able to flee, they didn't need her help as badly as whoever was in and around that car. She called out instructions as she passed, but she didn't think anyone could hear through their panic.

The car, a 1980s Cadillac, a tank really, had done major damage after hurtling through the temporary chain-link-fence panels that defined the festival border. A path of debris led to the car's resting place in the mangled remains of a huge event tent. She arrived just behind two other officers, blinking against the sting of gasoline mixed with rubber that burned her nose as she scanned for victims.

"A woman's under there." One of the officers crouched, peering under the front of the car. "I can't tell if she's breathing."

"If I can get my arm in there, I can check for a pulse." The other officer tried to scoot partway under the chassis. "We need FD to get in here and stabilize this car."

Confident they were doing what they could for that victim until EMS arrived, Traci leaned into the driver-side window, which was open—open, not broken. The driver's forehead rested against the steering wheel, and when Traci touched his shoulder, he moaned.

"Hey, buddy." He started to stir, and she tightened her hand. "Try not to move."

He rolled his neck back, and his head rapped against the headrest. Blood poured from a cut on his forehead down the front of his face. He looked to be in his thirties, specks of gray just starting in his black, military-style crew cut. The neat hairstyle contrasted with the scruff of a half-grown beard on his face.

"Hey. Take it easy. You could be hurt."

Traci's sergeant appeared in the open passenger window and met her eyes across the cabin space. "How is he?"

"I don't know, Sarge. He seems out of it."

"Paramedics are on the way."

The driver moaned again and rubbed at his temple. "How many did I get?"

"What?" His words were muffled by his hand scrubbing over his face, so Traci bent closer to hear him better. She didn't smell alcohol and was close enough that she should, if he'd been drinking. Maybe he had a medical condition or had fallen asleep behind the wheel.

"How many people did I hit?" Something felt off. He was asking about the victims, but Traci wasn't reading worry in his tone.

"I don't know for sure."

"I hope it was enough." When he met her eyes, the triumph there dropped a cold stone of dread into her stomach, and she clamped her mouth shut against the urge to vomit right there next to the car.

"Did he just say what I think he did?"

Traci stared through the car. "Yeah, Sarge. This was an intentional act, not an accident."

The first wave of paramedics and firefighters arrived, those that had been working extra duty at the event in the first-aid tent. They began tending to the woman under the car and several other victims it had directly struck. Dispatch would be sending as many ambulances as were available, but they were responding from other parts of town, and even neighboring jurisdictions, and would still be several minutes away or longer.

The sergeant grabbed the arm of a passing field-training officer and waylaid him from wherever he was headed. "I need you with the driver. When he goes to the hospital I want you in that ambulance. He's in police custody pending further investigation. Once he's freed from the vehicle and transported, have your rookie secure the car. Tell him Crime Scene can photograph the outside, but no one touches the inside until we have a search warrant."

"Yes, sir."

"Sam, you need to turn in a supplement and make yourself available to the detective when he gets here."

She nodded, knowing she was hours away from that conversation. First, the scene needed to be secured, patients treated, and witnesses interviewed. Then she'd add her statement to the mountain of reports the detective would use to obtain the necessary warrants.

CHAPTER TWO

"What can I do to help her?" Nicole asked as Candace bent over Jenna once more.

"She's unconscious, but she's breathing. So I don't want to move her until we get a cervical collar and backboard over here." Candace glanced around, her gaze snagging on a teenage boy half sitting and half lying among the wreckage of the tent. "We need to help him."

Given a task, Nicole nodded and rushed over, contorting under and around the bent tent pole. When she crouched in front of him, his glassy eyes didn't focus on her.

"What's your name?"

He didn't respond. She cast a look over her shoulder, but Candace was again bent over Jenna, who looked like she was in distress. Candace spoke rapidly again into her radio.

"What do I do?" she muttered, getting no help from her patient. His lack of response could indicate a head injury. She struggled to remember the first-aid training that had been part of her company-sponsored CPR class. Airway, breathing—his might be a little shallow. She was pretty sure he was in shock.

She scanned his body. Shit. His black jeans were soaked with blood around his left thigh. Instinctively, she slapped her hand over his leg where the fabric looked the most saturated. He jerked and cried out, but she persisted, trying to stop the bleeding.

"Ma'am, are you okay?" A police officer angled her head under the pole to make eye contact with her.

"I am. But this kid needs help." Blood pooled in the space between her fingers, and when she pressed harder, he screamed, then passed out. "I can't even tell where all this blood is coming from."

The officer glanced over her shoulder, then grabbed the microphone clipped there and spoke into it, but Nicole couldn't hear what she was saying through the chaos around them. The officer turned back to them and dropped her hand onto Nicole's shoulder.

"I'm going to try to get in there with you and see if I can help." She squeezed Nicole's shoulder. "Just try to relax and stay as still as you can so we don't jostle him."

"He's bleeding so badly. How are we even going to get him out of here? I can't sit here and watch him die." Panic edged her voice near shrill. She thought she saw his eyelids flicker at her words and immediately regretted letting her fears out. "I'm sorry. You're going to be okay."

"We're all going to be okay," the police officer said. "Hey, look at me." Nicole met mahogany eyes that soothed her hysteria. Despite the horrific scene around them, this officer's face reflected calm and control. "We're not going to get him out. I don't know what you think police officers do, but extrication is definitely a firefighter's job. We're just going to keep him alive until they get here to save the day."

Nicole couldn't believe the easy humor in the officer's voice pulled a small smile from her. But suddenly she felt responsible for this kid, and if she was going to trust this woman with his life, she couldn't keep referring to her as "the officer." She glanced at the silver nameplate on the officer's chest. T. SAM.

"Against my nature, Officer Sam, I'm going to let you take charge."

"Call me Traci. And keep that pressure on. I'm coming in." Traci worked her way into the cage formed by the broken tent poles. She rested her hands on Nicole's shoulders and slid in behind her, then somehow tucked herself into the space on the far side of Nicole, closest to the kid's injured leg. She flicked her wrist, and the blade of a pocketknife popped out. "Okay. Let's take a look at this wound."

Together, they managed to cut open the leg of his jeans to his mid-thigh, revealing a jagged laceration.

"Hey," Nicole called out to a man who was escorting several people with minor injuries past them. "Give me your shirt."

He glanced down at the bright-orange T-shirt that identified him as a festival volunteer.

"Hurry up. Take it off." As he yanked it over his head, she spotted something else she wanted. "And your belt." She glanced at Traci. "Do you know how to apply a tourniquet?"

Traci nodded. "We were trained on them. I carry one in the first-aid kit in my patrol car. Good thinking."

Nicole folded the T-shirt and pressed it against the wound, closing her eyes briefly to shut out their patient's whimper of pain. "If this doesn't control the bleeding, you need to use the belt."

After a few seconds, when it became clear that direct pressure alone wouldn't work, Nicole handed over the belt. Traci wrapped it around the boy's upper thigh, pulled tight, and had just finished securing it when two firefighters arrived. The two couldn't have been more different. The woman moved confidently, a reciprocating saw swinging easily from one hand, eyes constantly assessing the scene around her. The man's eyes darted as well, but with fear. He carried a backboard and kept looking at the woman, clearly drawing strength from her confidence.

"Oh, thank God, Everett. I thought you'd never get here." Traci put her hands on Nicole's waist. "Let's get out of here so these guys can work."

Nicole nodded and carefully climbed out of the wreckage, pausing when her sleeve snagged on the sharp edge of a broken pole. When she reached back, Traci caught her hand, carefully freed the fabric, then nodded for her to continue. As she moved, she felt Traci's warmth closer behind her now. They got out of the way almost as one, and the firefighters rushed in and went to work. They cut out a large section of metal, enough to get the backboard in close to the patient. As they were positioning the board, a paramedic came over, carrying a navy backpack with a reflective star shape Nicole recognized as a medical symbol. While Everett put a cervical collar on the patient, the paramedic shucked the pack and started pulling out IV tubing and other supplies.

"We've got him now, Sam. We'll put him on the next ambulance out."

Traci nodded and turned to Nicole. "You should stay here and get in that ambulance with him. Go to the hospital and have yourself checked out."

"What? No. I'm not injured."

"That shiner says otherwise." Traci pointed at her eye.

"It barely hurts now. Adrenaline, I guess."

"The police have a staging area on the other side of the park and are conducting witness interviews before releasing people. Of course, in the aftermath, I'm sure some people left on their own. But you should check in over there before you go," Everett said, before turning away and moving toward another patient.

"Let's go. I'll take you over."

When Traci started in that direction, Nicole grabbed her arm and gestured at the people around them still lying or sitting on the ground, injured and/or dazed. How long had she been sitting with the boy? It felt like an hour, but could it have been only a matter of minutes?

"They probably have a ton of witnesses to interview. I'll just be sitting there waiting my turn. Let me help some more. Then, I promise, I'll go."

Traci narrowed her eyes, her bicep flexing under Nicole's fingers. "How much did you see?"

"I saw the car as it came through the fence and everything after. But I think I'm still processing it all."

"Okay. For now. But then you go give a statement."

"Deal."

"Let's start sweeping in this direction and triage as we go."

They escorted a handful of victims to a staging area the fire department had set up for medical triage. Once there, a paramedic evaluated everyone and placed them in a queue for an ambulance, based on the severity of their injuries. Some were just patched up and signed a form saying they refused transport to the hospital. Traci was enlisted to clean and bandage minor injuries. And Nicole helped those who needed a ride home make contact with family members and friends. She tried to inquire after the boy with the leg injury, but he'd already gone to the hospital, and none of the paramedics on scene knew his status.

When the festival grounds had been nearly cleared of patients, Traci commandeered a security UTV that had been used for the event, and they volunteered to deliver bottled water to the officers on the perimeter of the scene.

❖

Traci sat behind the wheel of the UTV, waiting while Nicole hopped out and handed a bottle to the officer securing the intersection. When she'd come upon a scared-looking Nicole sitting with that boy earlier, she wouldn't have guessed that she'd still be working this hard. Nicole looked so much more put together than the rest of the festival attendees. Most of the crowd wore shorts and T-shirts or tank tops, and several of the men weren't wearing shirts at all. Nicole had on shorts, but they were khaki, and Traci surmised they'd been freshly pressed when she'd arrived at the event earlier that day. Her sleeveless denim button-down shirt now had blood on the front, but Traci could imagine her putting it on with her strappy sandals earlier that day and checking her reflection in the mirror. Nicole kept shoving the sides of her windblown, shoulder-length red hair behind her ears, but still it shone in the sun.

Based solely on appearance, she would have expected Nicole to be high-maintenance and, thrown into a stampeding-crowd situation, all about self-preservation. But she'd watched her overcome her fear—or at least shove it aside in order to do some good. And she was still doing it. She chatted briefly with the officer, long enough to bring a fleeting smile to his face, before rushing back to the UTV.

"You okay?" Nicole slid in beside Traci.

Traci nodded and steered onto the street to the next post. She parked between two intersections, and she and Nicole each grabbed a bottled water and headed in opposite directions to hand them out. When she reached the officer blocking traffic at Eighth and Spruce, his face looked pinched, and he rocked from one foot to the other.

"What's wrong with you?"

"I gotta pee."

"Why didn't you call in for relief?"

"We're already stretched thin keeping the perimeter secure, and I've been hearing on the radio how busy the scene is."

Traci glanced over at Nicole, who was making her way back to the UTV, then said, "Hold on." She jogged back to the vehicle. "I'm going to relieve some of these guys for bathroom breaks. Do you mind waiting for a minute?"

"I can keep going with the water."

"Technically that thing is city equipment, and I can't let you drive it."

"I'll grab four or five bottles and walk to the next posts."

"If you wait—"

"I don't want to sit here and do nothing." Nicole's voice had a desperate edge that hadn't been there before. Maybe she just needed to keep moving in order to avoid dwelling on this surreal situation. Traci could relate—she'd been running all over this scene to avoid writing up her supplement regarding the driver's statements in the car. She focused on finding places to help rather than process the fact that someone had caused this damage on purpose.

"Okay. Go ahead. I'll catch up when I'm done here." She returned to the officer needing relief and waved him in the direction of a line of Porta Potties set out for the event.

When, after a few minutes, he returned, she worked her way through several more officers on posts. She caught up with Nicole as they both arrived back at incident command. Traci returned the UTV and walked over to Nicole just as a detective told her she needed to give a statement before she could leave.

Nicole glanced over her shoulder, her gaze catching Traci's, and the plea in her eyes had Traci wanting to rush to her side. She gave in to that urge, closing the space between them and subtly touching Nicole's elbow. Oddly, the bubbling tension in her own stomach calmed as soon as she made contact.

"Are you okay?"

"Can you go with me?"

Traci met the detective's curious gaze over Nicole's shoulder, but she didn't care what judgments he might be making about her. Every officer had a story about a victim that was too needy or required too much handholding in order to be an effective witness. But that's not what this was. She slid her hand down Nicole's forearm and grasped her hand, feeling the almost desperate curl of Nicole's fingers against hers. She wanted to hold on, but she couldn't—not right now.

"I need to write up my own report about what I saw when I got to the car. I can wait if you're not finished by the time I get done."

Nicole's small nod accompanied an uncertain expression. She clearly didn't like asking—but what was she asking for?

"Ma'am, if you'll come with me." The detective swept a hand toward the command vehicle, a converted RV used for large-scale incidents.

Traci gave Nicole one more encouraging nod, then circled the RV to a table that had been set up as a workstation for the officers on the scene. She logged in to the laptop there and opened the report program. As she typed, the scene replayed itself. Reliving the moment when she'd realized that man had intentionally run his car into a crowd of people made her only slightly less ill this time. The scale of the incident was only now hitting her. She'd seen the local news vans arriving, thinking they were chasing the story because of popularity of this festival. But if word of the suspect's intent hadn't gotten out yet, it would, and probably soon. Then they'd attract national media attention. These things didn't happen in Bellbrook. But every town probably felt that way, until it did.

❖

"It all happened so fast. I heard the crash, and by the time I looked—God, this is horrible to say—people were being thrown through the air." The sounds and sights from the scene flashed in Nicole's head like an action movie she'd been forced to watch against her will. As her focus locked on one particular image, she snapped her eyes to the detective in front of her. "Was someone underneath the car?"

He nodded solemnly, his eyes gentle under graying eyebrows. With his thick hair waving back from his forehead and his old-fashioned striped tie and out-of-style suit, he reminded her of the detectives she'd seen on the ID channel. Some younger, more attractive actor typically played him in the reenactment. Then they'd cut to an interview with the real-life detective, and he looked like this guy.

"A woman. Did she make it?"

He glanced away, but given his expression, he didn't have to answer.

"What about the boy?"

"What boy?" He asked.

"We helped a boy over by the car until the firefighters arrived."

"Ma'am, even if I had specific patient information, I shouldn't be sharing it with you."

The paramedic—Candace's partner—what was her name? Nicole cycled through a series of images—of people she hadn't even realized she'd seen as they clamored to get away from the destruction. She recalled their faces, every detail down to the bright-red glasses one woman wore and the thick mustache a man sported. She even remembered seeing that elbow coming toward her head, almost in slow motion, though at the time it had happened so quickly she hadn't had time to react. Her cheek throbbed as if she were feeling the impact again, and hot tears welled up.

She closed her eyes, focusing on the present, in an attempt to regain control of emotions that threatened to spill over. When she felt a warm hand on her wrist, she imagined it was Traci's, but when she opened her eyes, the detective leaned toward her, his arm outstretched. She glanced down and he withdrew.

"I know this is difficult to go through."

She wanted to ask how he knew. Surely, he'd seen some tough things in his career, but she never remembered an incident of this scale happening in Bellbrook before. Maybe she was naive about what went on in her college town, but she'd always considered Bellbrook fairly safe. Certainly, they probably had their share of burglaries, petty crimes, and mischief. And anyone who thought their town or city, no matter how big or small, was free from drugs had to be deluding themselves. But she watched the news, and violent crimes were rare.

"It'll take time to stop those memories from creeping up on you." He cleared his throat. "Do you have family or friends you can talk to?"

She nodded. But she didn't have anyone close enough to talk with about this day. Certainly, she wouldn't easily leave this behind, but she'd have to figure out how to deal with it herself.

"That's all the questions I have for now. If you need anything—" As she stood, he handed her a business card.

"What happens next? I've never been a witness of anything at all, let alone something like this."

"Someone from the prosecutor's office will contact you if they intend for you to testify at trial. But I would expect that to be months or maybe even a year or more down the road."

She stepped out of the RV, pausing to let her eyes adjust to the change from the brightly lit interior of the vehicle to the darkening sky. Dusk had descended while she'd been inside, and the nighttime humidity draping her skin felt like one more oppressive layer added to an already heavy day.

"Hey, all set?" Finding Traci so close lightened the weight incrementally. Traci's confidence wrapped around her, and Nicole marveled at how she carried so much of it in her small frame. She seemed so sure, but not arrogantly so. The firm set of her angular jaw complemented the compassion in her deep-brown eyes, rather than contradicting it.

"Yes." She tucked the detective's card into her pocket, then left her hand inside. When Traci moved immediately to her side, she wanted to reach out, to find a physical connection to echo the emotional one she'd been experiencing, but she felt the detective's eyes still on her.

They walked together toward the area where an officer was allowing people to exit the scene; all other areas were still secure.

The scene around them still looked postapocalyptic, maybe even more so with the lack of victims in it. All of the vendors had abandoned their booths, yet their wares were still laid out on tables—those that hadn't been knocked over in the stampede. The ground was scattered with detritus from hasty medical treatments and trash from dumped-over waste bins. On the far side of the park, a crime-scene tech was photographing the car and several items on the ground nearby.

"Can I give you a ride somewhere?" Traci asked.

"I have my car. I parked near my office and walked over." She paused, mulling over why she felt such an urge to be nakedly honest with Traci. "I—don't know where to go. What am I supposed to do after something like this? Just go home, read a book, and go to bed?"

"Well, I'm probably going to take a shower first."

"That sounds amazing." Now she was imagining watching Traci step into her shower. And from the way Traci averted her eyes, her mind had gone to the same place. "A shower—getting clean, I mean. In my own shower—by myself." She was making it worse.

Traci glanced at her watch. "My shift is over. But you're right. It's not going to be that easy to unwind. Do you want to grab some coffee?"

Coffee sounded too normal for what she'd just been through. But the idea of spending more time with Traci was very appealing. "Okay."

"Great. But I wasn't lying about that shower. I feel like I need to wash off some of this grime before I can relax. My place isn't far. What do you say we run by there, grab *separate* showers, then go someplace and get some food? You can follow me, or if you're not feeling up to driving right now, we can go in my car, and I'll bring you back by yours after."

"Oh, so it's a meal now."

"You don't have to eat—just coffee is fine. But I didn't eat dinner, so by the time we get there I'll be starving." Traci gave her a quick once-over, and Nicole was disappointed that she didn't seem to linger anywhere. "I'm sure I have some clean clothes that will fit you."

"If you don't mind, I'll accept your offer of a ride. Maybe if the exhaustion hits, we can keep each other awake in the car." She didn't want Traci to have to bring her back here later, but she could always call a rideshare.

CHAPTER THREE

Traci unlocked the front door to her condo and led Nicole inside. She was glad she'd done some straightening up last night. Since she didn't enjoy cleaning, sometimes she let things go until her days off. But she had plans to go to a movie with Everett tomorrow, so she'd cleaned a bit. Now, knowing they'd both been at the scene for most of the afternoon and evening, she wouldn't be surprised to get a text cancelling. Plus, Everett had been seeing someone new and they seemed pretty serious, so she could imagine that after an incident like that one, she might want to be with her girlfriend tomorrow.

"Make yourself comfortable," she said as she glanced around, trying to see the small space like Nicole might. She'd accented her pale-gray furniture with yellow and orange geometric-patterned pillows. Pops of yellow ran throughout the art on the wall as well. The bright colors welcomed her home no matter what kind of day she'd had.

Nicole was looking around as well, and Traci hoped she wasn't being judgmental. Then she turned toward Nicole. "I don't want to sit on your nice furniture feeling this grimy." She glanced down at her shorts, where smears of black and gray slashed across her leg and hip. "Plus, I have blood on my shirt."

"Wait here." Traci ran into her bedroom and pulled open a couple of drawers. When she had an armful of clothes, she rushed back to the living room, taking a short detour to the hall bathroom.

"So, listen, this wasn't some creepy ploy to get you to my house and try to keep you here. I'm just now realizing that I have clothes for you, but offering you my undergarments is probably inappropriate. And I don't know about you, but I'm not necessarily interested in going back out in public. What would you think about staying here and ordering some food?"

"Do you have anything stronger than coffee?"

"Absolutely."

"Okay. Yes. I'd rather not go out."

"Good. Try these." She handed Nicole a pair of olive-green sweatpants and a soft, black scoop-necked T-shirt. "I laid out a towel and washcloth in the bathroom for you. First door on the right." She pointed in the right direction. "Everything else you need should be in there."

"Thank you." Nicole clutched the clothes to her chest and headed in that direction.

Traci waited until she heard the shower come on, and, assured that Nicole had everything she needed, she headed to her own bedroom and the ensuite inside. She removed her gun from the holster and locked it in a biometric safe on the nightstand. After hanging her duty belt on a large hook she'd installed in the walk-in closet, she unclipped her badge and nameplate and emptied her pockets.

As she stripped off her uniform, she dropped each article into a hamper. She kept two, side by side, in her large bathroom, because she didn't want her grimy uniforms mixing with her civilian clothes. After this day, she wanted the longest, hottest shower ever. But instead, she jumped in, scrubbed hard, then got out, so she wouldn't leave Nicole wondering where she'd gone. She put on a pair of zebra-print pajama pants and bright-red T-shirt and headed for the living room.

The guest bathroom door opened as soon as Traci exited her bedroom, and Nicole stepped out in front of her. Her hair was a shade darker when wet, and the tropical scent of shampoo wafted on the steam from the bathroom.

"Hey." When Traci spoke, Nicole turned her head. Her eye appeared more swollen than before, and the bruising was already deepening. But the skin hadn't been broken, so she wouldn't have to worry about a scar. "Do you want some ice for your eye?"

"Yes, please." Nicole followed her to the kitchen. "I'd also love a couple of ibuprofen."

"There's a basket of over-the-counter stuff in the cabinet next to the fridge. Glasses are the next cabinet over. Take whatever you need." While Nicole got her pain meds, Traci opened the lower freezer door and grabbed a bag of frozen peas. She held it up.

"These might be better than ice—more flexible. But I wouldn't eat them, since I have no idea how old they are. I don't like peas, so they may have come with the condo."

"We're still ordering food, right? Because now I don't want to eat anything in this house."

Traci laughed and handed over the bag of peas wrapped in a towel. She opened a delivery app on her phone and scrolled through the few restaurants that delivered to her complex. Being on the outskirts of town, she had fewer options than those who lived closer to the city center. They flipped through a couple of menus and settled on Chinese food, then ordered a sampling of dishes.

With dinner sorted, Traci turned her attention to beverages. "I have wine, white or blush. I don't drink red. Or there's some rum that I can mix with juice or soda."

"Wine is perfect—any kind. I don't think I should do anything harder than that after today."

"That's probably smart." She pulled down two wineglasses, then opened a bottle of Riesling.

As they returned to the living room, Traci turned off the overhead light and switched on a lamp in the corner. They settled on the sofa to wait for their food to arrive. Nicole held the bundle of frozen peas against the side of her face, resting her elbow on the arm of the sofa. She still looked stressed, the unobscured side of her face appearing tense and her gaze darting around the room as if searching for more danger.

"How are you doing?"

"This isn't how I expected to get my first black eye."

"Your first?"

"You seem surprised. Do you hang out with a lot of women who get in fights?"

"Well, yes. Bellbrook PD doesn't see a ton of action, but we've all been in a tussle with a suspect at one time or another. I actually got my first black eye in high school, though."

"I need to hear this story."

It wasn't a story she wanted to tell, but she had brought it up, and Nicole's interest relaxed the planes of her face. "The boys in my class started a fight club, and I wanted to participate. They obviously didn't want me involved."

"It's admirable that they didn't want to hit a girl."

"Not likely. They didn't want one to kick their asses."

"How'd you get them to let you in? I assume you did and that's where the black eye came from."

Traci looked embarrassed. "I'm not proud of it. The ringleader—his sister had been pursuing me and I'd been resisting. So—I let her kiss me, at school, where I knew it would get back to him."

"You goaded him into a fight? And, let me guess, you beat him."

"Hell, no. But that would have been a better ending to my story." She rubbed her cheek, below her right eye. "Getting hit in the face really hurts."

Nicole pulled the peas away from her cheek and gave her a look that said she didn't have to be told that.

"He knocked me out. Come to think of it, that was my first time being unconscious, too. When the principal found out, she shut the whole thing down, and they all got detention—all except me."

Nicole laughed, toying with a lock of hair. "You're right. You really aren't the hero of that story. You used the girl to incite a fight, then lost, and then got out of punishment. I'm guessing the principal didn't want to get sued by your parents?"

"That sounds about right. But I didn't use the girl—I mean, maybe initially, but I ended up dating her for a year afterward. To this day, I've never had a more awkward relationship with a girlfriend's family."

"You wouldn't have to worry about that with me."

Traci raised her brows. "Are you offering to be my girlfriend?"

Nicole flushed. "No. Well, I just meant that *I* don't have a relationship with my family, so my partner certainly doesn't have to."

"Oh. I'm sorry."

She waved a hand dismissively, but a shadow of hurt passed over her expression. "I was raised in a super-conservative household. Being gay wasn't even on my radar as an option until I went away to college. When I was a kid, my father joked that I was the son he never had because I was just like him. I had a golf club in my hand at four, and by the time I was fifteen, I was golfing with him and his buddies at the country club. I even followed in his footsteps professionally—getting a degree in finance and my MBA at his alma mater."

"Sounds like you guys were close."

"We were. Until he found out that we both liked women. We don't have the same taste, though. He likes them with low enough self-esteem that they won't threaten to tell my mother he cheats on her."

"Wow."

"I was twenty-two when I caught him kissing another woman—ironically, at the country club. I may have been trying to get back at him by telling him I was gay. I mean—I absolutely was, and I'd been working up the nerve to come out to them, but the timing of my confession was totally vindictive. Though it did make it easier for me to accept the job offer here and move away from them. I knew they believed it was a sin, but I thought they might get over that prejudice for their own daughter."

"And they haven't?"

She shook her head. "My father told me not to come back until I was ready to repent. I could see in his eyes as he said it that he knew he was a hypocrite and was terrified I was going to tell my mother about the other woman."

"Why didn't you?"

"I think she already knew. She never let on to him, but I got that idea. I'd just made her face the fact that her daughter was gay and didn't feel up to ripping away her illusions about my father as well."

Traci covered Nicole's hand with hers. "I'm so sorry that happened."

"What about you? Are you close to your family?"

"Yeah, I am. Though it's just my mom and her family. She raised me by herself."

"From what little I know about you, she did an admirable job."

"I'll tell her you said so. She would agree. And believe me, I wasn't easy. But I will say, having my mom find out I was gay and had been knocked unconscious at the same time was the way to go. She was so glad I didn't have any permanent damage she couldn't be mad that I was a lesbian."

"Maybe I should have tried that."

"It's not too late. Maybe knowing what you've been through tonight will soften their feelings a bit."

She seemed to consider that suggestion for a moment, then shook her head. "No. I don't think it will. And if that's the only reason they would consider a relationship, I'm not sure I care to."

The doorbell signaling their food delivery ended that conversation. They returned to the kitchen to fill plates with noodles and chicken dishes, and Traci refilled their wineglasses. Then they perched side by side on stools at the island separating the kitchen and living room.

"That detective said I might have to go to court." Nicole twisted a long strand of noodles around her fork, seeming content to twirl it rather than actually eat it.

Traci shrugged. "If this thing even makes it to trial, there'll be tons of witness statements to go through before the prosecutor decides who they'll put on the stand."

"Why wouldn't it go to trial?"

"He was sitting in the car when he was arrested. His attorney will have one hell of an uphill battle if they don't work out a plea." If there was a trial, Traci would definitely take the stand, unless his attorney got the driver's damning statements to her excluded from evidence.

"Do you know why he did it?"

She shook her head. "He didn't say." She'd known better than to question him once he made it clear he'd driven into the festival on purpose. From that point, everything they did had to hold up in court. In-depth questioning about his motive and the events leading up to the crash would come only after he'd been read and understood his rights. Her concern had shifted to the welfare of the nearby victims, and that's when she'd happened upon Nicole tending to the injured teen. "His reason, if he has one, might come out eventually. Or we may never know. Could be his attorney will say he was mentally ill."

"Do you believe that?"

She shrugged. "I didn't spend enough time with him to know. There'll probably be a court-ordered psych eval, so I'll leave that to the professionals."

"I don't even want to watch the news coverage. I'll probably leave my television off for the next week."

"Not a bad idea."

"Thank you. For keeping me sane this afternoon. And for this." She raised her glass and took a sip. "I should be getting home so I can figure out how to get some sleep."

"I'll drive you."

"I can—"

"Please. I'd like to see you safely to your car." She didn't like the desperation in her voice—mostly because it was genuine. She needed to know that Nicole was okay. And despite the connection they seemed to have, Nicole might walk away from this day and never look back. When she'd had time to process her emotions, she could avoid any reminders of this experience, Traci included.

The fifteen-minute drive back to the center of town passed with casual conversation—Traci pointed out the street she'd grown up on and where she'd gone to high school. And they compared the sizes of their schools based on how many people were in their graduating class.

Traci parked next to Nicole's car in the otherwise empty lot of her firm. What should she say now? After this day, "nice to meet you" or "see you later" didn't seem like enough.

"Can I get your number?" Nicole asked boldly, like now she might be able to appreciate living life in a way she hadn't before. Then Traci saw doubt creep into her expression. "So I can return your clothes after I launder them?" Now she spoke evenly, as if she were offering Traci investment advice instead of saying good-bye after a harrowing journey together.

She could tell Nicole to keep the clothes. After all, they weren't even her favorite sweatpants. But leaving open the possibility that they might meet again—well, she needed that more than she was ready to admit. So she took the phone Nicole held out and typed in her number.

"Thanks again." Nicole opened the door and climbed out. After Nicole closed the door, Traci rolled down the passenger window.

"Just doing my job, ma'am." Why did she say that? And why was she suddenly quoting Joe Friday?

Nicole must have thought she was making a joke, because she gave her one last smile before sliding behind the wheel of her own car.

❖

Nicole arrived at the office just before nine a.m. Monday morning. While an acceptable hour for many professionals, it was the latest she'd arrived in months, maybe longer. Luckily, by her firm's standards, she was starting her workday late, and everyone would already be ensconced in wading through the weekend's emails. If she could slip past the receptionist, she could be inside her own office without having to interact with anyone. She hadn't been able to completely cover up her black eye with makeup and didn't want to answer any questions about it.

As she reached the front door, she took out her cell phone and switched it to vibrate so it couldn't ring and give her away. Then she held it to her ear as she walked in, pretending to be on a call. She walked by the receptionist with a wave, but pointed at her phone when the woman tried to talk to her and breezed down the hallway and through her office door, closing it behind her.

She leaned against the wall beside the door and stared out the window behind her desk. She'd been so proud when she'd graduated from a cubicle in the big room down the hall to this office. She'd traded her cloth-covered pseudo walls for this view, and the change had made her feel important. She strode across the room and glanced at the parking lot below and the side of the brick building next door—some view. She couldn't see the downtown park where the music festival had been held from here, but she knew where it was, four blocks east.

An alert pinged a new email notification on her cell phone, pulling her back from the edge of melancholy. Work had always kept her busy when she just wasn't quite satisfied with some area of her life. And it would do the same now. She circled her desk, dropped into her chair, and logged on to her computer.

Normally, her Monday email wasn't overwhelming because she'd kept up with it on the weekend. But after Saturday, she hadn't felt like looking at her phone on Sunday. She'd slept late, as if her body had shut down to take care of her exhausted mind. So this morning, she had more than the usual backlog of messages.

She spent the next two hours working her way through the email, replying to as many as she could and carefully flagging those messages she needed to follow up on later. Then she moved on to a proposal for a new client she'd been wooing. Just last Thursday she'd locked him in for a meeting next week, and now she had to impress him. For the rest of the morning, she immersed herself in the details that would show him that she understood his financial needs. By lunchtime she had everything roughed out, and after she'd polished her proposal this afternoon, she'd be ready.

Her stomach rumbled, reminding her she'd skipped breakfast and her third cup of coffee could no longer suppress her appetite. She'd left a low-calorie dinner in the freezer last week, and if no one had snagged it, that would suffice for lunch. She grabbed her phone on the way out of her office in case she had to employ the fake-call trick again. Glancing out and finding the hallway clear, she beelined to the office kitchen.

She had forty-five seconds left on the microwave timer when one of her colleagues entered the kitchen. She'd almost made a clear escape.

"Hi, Nic." He grabbed his lunch out of the fridge and came to the microwave next to hers.

"Gary." She gave him a tight smile in response. She didn't like the nickname and had corrected him politely many times, yet he continued.

"Crazy what happened at the music festival, huh? Didn't you have tickets to that?" While he waited for his food to reheat, he stood almost shoulder-to-shoulder with her, leaving awkwardly little space between them.

"I did." She didn't correct his use of the plural. He assumed she'd have a friend or someone to invite along.

"Were you there?"

"I was." She took a step away.

"Wow. Did you see anything?"

She'd hoped her short answers would have discouraged further conversation, but she understood the fascination people had with catastrophic events. Or, at least, she'd had before being involved in one herself. Now she felt there should be more privacy around the incident.

"It was chaotic." She glanced up to find his gaze on her face and knew he was looking at her injured eye.

"The news said three people died and a bunch of others were hurt. Did you—"

She held up her hand. "I'm sorry. I really don't want to talk about it."

"But—"

"Gary, seriously. I'm not interested in giving up the gory details to satisfy your grotesque curiosity."

His expression immediately changed, and he had the nerve to look offended. She'd tried to be nice. She'd practically apologized for not wishing to discuss the horrific ordeal she'd witnessed. And now he was angry with her?

"I was just trying to be social."

She wanted to launch into all the reasons why that was not only wrong, but seriously rude. Instead, she grabbed her lunch from the microwave.

"I'm pretty busy right now, anyway, and don't have time for chitchat."

He huffed as she turned away, and she didn't stop to find out what he muttered under his breath because she suspected she knew and might lose her cool and her job if she actually heard him call her a bitch.

Chapter Four

Fifteen-Adam, you're responding to a report of vandalism at the Westside Baptist Church, at 745 Allen Avenue."

Traci had just finished gassing up her patrol SUV, a Ford Explorer. She got inside and glanced at the screen on the laptop mounted to the center console, reading the description of the suspect at the same time as the dispatcher verbalized it over the radio. Witnesses reported two males—one white and one black. The dispatch center had received two calls from people who had seen these guys in the area breaking the windows and spray-painting the side of a church van.

She didn't need to check the map to locate the church, which had been in the neighborhood for decades. Westside was one of the largest and most established churches in town, and everyone knew where it was. While she'd been assigned to this patrol sector for only a couple of years, she'd worked some in bordering sectors as well.

She acknowledged the dispatcher's transmission and pulled out onto the street. While making the five-minute drive to the church, she coordinated with another officer who was also responding. He approached from the front, while she came in through the alley, hoping to catch them trying to flee when they saw his car.

As she turned into the lot on the east side of the building, she saw two subjects running around the corner of the building, followed closely by the other officer. She angled her car to funnel them close to the building, where they had less room to escape. Throwing open the door, she took a line to cut off the guy in the front, leaving the second man for her fellow officer.

Her suspect, a white guy wearing a dark-colored hoodie and carrying a backpack, saw her coming and tried to juke away from her. But she anticipated his move, and as he spun away, she grabbed his backpack in both hands and yanked him toward her. As he stumbled, she adjusted her stride to keep her balance. Changing their momentum, she steered him against the brick wall of the church. The other suspect flew by with the officer still on his heels. But Traci stayed focused on the man in front of her. He struggled for only a few seconds before giving in and spreading his arms on the wall in front of him.

"I guess you know the drill." She tapped the inside of one of his feet with her own, and he spread them farther apart. She pulled off his backpack and dropped it behind her, out of his reach.

"I didn't do anything."

When she tugged down his hood and he glanced over his shoulder, she got a look at his face for the first time. She put him in his mid-teens, his face retaining some of the roundness of adolescence. Free of the hood, long hair flopped into his eyes, and he tossed his head.

"I don't think I believe you." She pointed at the red paint residue around his fingertips. "We'll get to that, though. First, do you have anything on you that's going to stick me or hurt me?"

"No."

"Shouldn't you be in school?"

He shrugged.

She searched him carefully but efficiently, then snapped a pair of handcuffs on his wrists, holding them securely behind his back. She walked him over to her SUV and had him stand nearby while she set his bag on the hood and unzipped it.

"You can't do that."

"Come on, kid. I'm betting this isn't your first time, so surely you've heard of search incident to arrest." She set each item out carefully on the hood—a notebook with doodles all over the front, a wallet, and a flashlight. She gave him a look as she pulled out a can of spray paint.

"You're going to arrest me for that? I bought it to paint my bicycle."

"I'll make you a deal." She held up the can. "We'll walk around to the van, and if the graffiti on it doesn't match this cap, you're free to go."

"Damn, lady." He hung his head.

She swallowed instructions for him to find a more respectful title for her. She'd been a smart-ass with him first. "Are we taking that walk?"

He shook his head.

As she was opening the back door to her SUV, the other officer came back alone.

"I lost him."

She looked at her detainee, already knowing the answer to the question she was about to ask. "Are you going to tell us his name?"

He lifted his chin, defiance shining in his eyes. She nodded, accepting that he wasn't ratting out his friend. Some guys did. Of course, the smart ones made sure to secure a lighter charge for themselves first.

She turned to her colleague. "If you'll grab some pictures of the van, I'll find a contact number for the pastor and start working on the report."

Bellbrook didn't have CSI guys to come out on every scene, like some of those shows on television. But last year, they'd invested some serious money in a new records-management system. She could complete her report on the computer in her car, then upload the photos of the damage to the church van and attach them to the same file. The RMS program had been a joint venture with the district attorney's office, and prosecutors also had access to the files.

She opened the back door of her Explorer and guided the kid inside. After she finished her report, she'd take him down to the Bellbrook Juvenile Justice Center to be booked. His parents would be contacted, and with their cooperation he'd be home by dinnertime. Eventually, he'd appear in court on charges of vandalism and truancy. His buddy would be free and clear unless he decided to give him up or the church had security cameras. But she doubted he'd have learned his lesson, so they would probably encounter him again some day. Scared straight only worked if they actually caught him and he got to spend some time in a cell.

After dropping off her prisoner, she took a quick break to grab lunch, then got back on the street. Her patrol district encompassed one of the most affluent neighborhoods and one of the least, and they were less than a mile apart. She started her afternoon with a drive through the lower-income complex. The city-subsidized apartments had been renovated by the housing authority a few years back and looked a lot nicer than when she'd first starting working over there. The brick had been painted light gray, and dark shutters were added to the sides of the windows. But the lack of central air meant many of the apartments had an air-conditioning unit sticking out of at least one window.

She drove through all the parking lots, keeping an eye out between buildings for any suspicious activity. When she neared the playground, she backed into a parking spot where she could watch the kids playing. Several mothers and fathers sitting on benches watching their children glanced her way, and a couple even waved. She made it a point to come through here at least once a day. Even when nothing was going on, her presence—or rather letting the marked patrol vehicle be seen in the area—made it safer for these families.

As she left the apartment complex, she turned right and passed a public elementary school. Then, a few minutes later, she drove by a larger school, this one private and more of a campus really, with several buildings on the grounds. Students there began in kindergarten and attended for the duration of their education. The subdivision just past the school was comprised of some of the more expensive houses in town.

The main street into the neighborhood was divided by a grass median lined with flowering trees. At the first intersection a wrought-iron fence surrounded the community pool. Large estate lawns cut by meandering driveways led to ornate brick and stone homes, which, at night, would be illuminated by tasteful landscape lighting. As she passed one woman weeding a flowerbed surrounding her mailbox, she waved. In another yard, two kids with gloves tossed a baseball back and forth.

By the time she finished a pass through the subdivision, she caught a call on a domestic disturbance at a familiar address a couple of miles away, on the outskirts of town. She'd been there before, and she knew some of the guys on the other shifts had as well. The residents— husband and wife—engaged in regular shouting matches. Usually, the call came from a neighbor who'd heard the noise. The last time Traci had responded, things had turned physical, and the woman had an angry, red handprint on her face. She hadn't wanted to press charges, but they'd taken him in anyway. That had been just last month. But without the victim's cooperation, too many of these cases got dropped or pled out by the prosecutor for little or no punishment. She didn't expect this time to be any different.

❖

By Friday evening, Nicole was exhausted. Putting in a full day took enough energy, but remaining polite while deflecting questions about the festival sapped her even more. When she'd bought the ticket, she'd told only one or two other people that she'd planned to go. She didn't socialize much outside of work with her colleagues, or at all unless she was meeting an existing client or trying to woo a new one. But somehow, word had gotten around that she was there. She could easily deflect her coworkers by saying she was too busy, but having a client corner her could be more difficult to wiggle away from without seeming rude.

She'd turned down an invitation to happy hour with one of her best clients, unwilling to spend her Friday night sidestepping questions about that day. She'd really wanted to go home and sink into a nice, hot bath, so she did just that. But she wasn't one of those people who could just soak idly in the bathtub for an hour. Her mind didn't shut off, and she'd end up staring at the ceiling and thinking about work, or how she really needed to paint her ceiling. So she took her phone into the tub with her, distracting herself with her favorite app, a puzzle game that involved connecting a series of dots in order to complete the required tasks.

Four levels later, one very difficult one that took several attempts, and her bath water had gone tepid. She opened the drain and grabbed a towel off a nearby hook as she got out. Maybe she would find a good book and go to bed early. She picked up her phone as she left the bathroom.

She'd been thinking all day, for several days if she was honest, about calling Traci. But what would she say? *Hey. Why doesn't my life seem normal when I'm not talking to you, even though we knew each other for one day?* That didn't sound crazy at all. But it was true. Six days had passed since she'd asked for Traci's number, so why hadn't she used it?

She didn't have an answer, but, knowing what little she did about Traci, she wouldn't ask it anyway. She would just engage Nicole in conversation and let her come around to it in her own time. And maybe that was why. She hadn't wanted to need Traci's quiet confidence. No. She would prove that she could get through this week on her own—dealing with both the questions and the memories they stirred. And she had, so didn't she deserve a reward? Like hearing Traci's voice. That would be a suitable reward for a week of hard work and avoidance.

❖

Traci's cell-phone screen lit up on the side table next to her chair. She glanced at it, aware that two other pairs of eyes tracked to it as well.

"Who's Nicole?" Her friend Candace nearly strained her neck trying to get a look at the screen.

"Just a woman I met recently." She shifted in the uncomfortable hospital chair where she'd been sitting for the past two hours. But she couldn't complain about her discomfort, not when the friend she was currently visiting was laid up in bed after shoulder surgery the day before.

Traci hadn't found out that the car had hit Jenna until late on the evening of the incident. She hadn't checked her messages while she and Nicole were together and didn't see Candace's text until she got home from dropping Nicole off at her car. Still, she found it hard to believe Candace and Jenna had been only feet from her while she looked in on the driver of the vehicle, and she hadn't even seen them in the chaos of those moments. She, Candace, Jenna, and Everett, all women first responders, got together at least once a month to swap stories and commiserate over work and their personal lives. Traci and Everett were the founding members of the group, Everett had then introduced Jenna, and Candace came along when she and Jenna were partnered together.

"I'm going to take this." She snatched up the phone and headed for the door to answer the call in the hallway.

"I hope it's okay that I phoned," Nicole said after Traci's greeting.

"I did give you my number." She continued down the hall until she found an empty waiting room. Inside, she crossed to the far floor-to-ceiling window, overlooking the large parking lot and the ambulance entrance to the emergency department.

"I haven't washed your clothes yet."

"That's not the only reason I gave you my number."

"Oh."

The silence on the line had Traci wondering if she should have been a little less honest. "If you aren't ready to return my clothes, why the call?"

"All week, all anyone wanted to talk about was what happened at the festival. Some of them knew I was there, and some didn't, but every conversation came back to that."

"It's natural they want to hear about it. We've never had an incident of that magnitude in Bellbrook, and everyone's trying to make sense of it."

"But it didn't happen to them."

"No. But it could have. And that's a shocking realization for some people. It's okay for you to tell them you don't want to discuss it. Or just remove yourself from the conversation. You don't owe them an explanation."

"I guess." She sighed, and then Traci could almost feel a shift in her mood. "Tell me how your day was."

"Same old stuff. You know," she gave an exaggerated sniff, "just a little crime-fighting."

"Oh, gosh, my hero. You can't see, but I'm swooning over here."

Traci chuckled. "I'm glad you're impressed."

"I am." Nicole's voice grew serious. "You are an impressive woman."

"You haven't known me long enough to see my faults."

"Then tell me what they are."

She hesitated as the conversation moved from friendly to flirtatious. She liked Nicole—what was not to like, really? She was smart and beautiful, and when it came time to step up, she'd run toward danger, and Traci had to respect that trait. But they'd been through an ordeal together. It was one thing to hang out and commiserate about their experience, but she got the impression Nicole was floundering a bit. Would moving beyond friendship be taking advantage of the situation?

"I leave my dishes in the sink. Sometimes for a couple of days. Can't even be bothered to put them in the dishwasher." She couldn't stop herself from wanting to get to know Nicole better. Maybe they'd find that they only worked as friends or acquaintances anyway. It was arrogant of her to assume Nicole would fall at her feet after a little flirting.

Nicole's soft laughter vibrated through the phone. "Oh, so that's why you don't have a girlfriend."

"Yep. Can't keep a woman because of my dirty dishes." A small group of people came into the waiting room, worry etched on their faces. Traci gave them a moment to get settled, then made her way out of the room. She didn't want to disturb them while they waited for their friend or family member.

"What else? I know you can go deeper."

"I'll trade you one for one." She strolled down the hallway, reaching an area of the hospital that had been heavily renovated several years ago. An elevated glass bridge spanned one section of the second floor to the other. She paused in the middle and leaned against the railing, looking down over the first floor inside the main entryway.

"I dye my hair." Humor lifted Nicole's voice at the end of her statement. "Actually, my hairdresser dyes it. And I'm not ashamed of it."

"Why should you be? It's a flattering shade."

"I'm going to fight aging every step of the way—to a point. Nothing surgical, but hair dye and skin creams, absolutely. Your turn."

"I don't trust easily. I have a handful of friends, all first responders, but I don't have a lot of relationships outside of that."

"I kind of get that with your job. Besides, it's not like I'm a social butterfly. My career is my life. I come home to a frozen dinner and a glass of wine—when I don't end up sleeping on the sofa in my office." Nicole made a small sound of frustration. "One minute, I'm reminding myself not to be reactionary. Then the next second, I'm thinking maybe I should quit my job."

"I don't think that's a good idea."

"That's easy for you to say. What you do makes a difference."

"Give yourself a break. That day—it shook all of us. And I'm used to seeing the worst of people. It's going to take time to come to terms with what happened."

"What if I don't want to? I can't forget. But I don't want to have to change. I was happy with my life. Or so I thought."

"Then don't."

"What?"

"I understand you're examining your priorities. I've seen a lot of people do that in the wake of life-changing events. But this may not be the best time to blow up your life."

"Every day that I don't do something better—"

"What we went through brings home the fact that our days here are numbered. But why is this an all-or-nothing situation?"

"What do you mean?"

"You could start with small changes." She chuckled. "How about no more sleeping in your office? Or don't take work home with you in the evening."

"How can I do that? My accounts need—"

"You're talking about leaving your profession altogether. Is that any more feasible for you?"

"It feels like the only way."

"Why don't you try my way first? What do you have to lose? For a week, you come home at a set time every night. See how it feels."

"I—I could try. One week."

She laughed. "You could start with saying it like it's not torture."

"One week."

"Better." She glanced at her watch. Visiting hours were over in thirty minutes. She should head back and say good-bye to Candace and Jenna. "I hate to cut this short—I really do. But I'm actually at the hospital right now—"

"Are you okay?"

"I'm fine. I'm visiting a friend." She didn't mention how Jenna got hurt, not wanting to steer the conversation back to that day. "I'm going to check in with you sometime next week, and you'll tell me how great it's been focusing more on yourself and less on your career."

"Home at a decent time."

"And leave your work at the office."

"Got it."

"I look forward to hearing all about it."

After they disconnected, Traci made her way back toward Jenna's room, replaying parts of the conversation in her head. She definitely liked Nicole—a lot. But she'd been telling the truth when she admitted she didn't trust easily. So when she began feeling like that wouldn't be an issue with Nicole, she then told herself she only felt that way because of the emotional, traumatic way they met. Now she couldn't even trust herself to know what she was feeling.

Candace and Jenna both looked up as she walked back into the room. She flushed under their scrutiny.

"You were gone an awful long time for some woman you met recently. What's the deal?" She could always count on Jenna to get right to the point.

She considered downplaying the situation, but she could use a second—and third—opinion on the situation. So she spilled the details of their meeting and their interactions up to this point.

"Wait. Did you say she helped a teenager right near the car—a boy, right?" Candace asked.

She nodded.

"Redhead. Well-dressed?"

"Yeah."

"I met her." Both Traci and Jenna gave Candace a skeptical look. "Really. Before anyone got to us—to you—" She looked at Jenna, the care she placed in their friendship evident in the shadow of worry still on her face. "She was there helping us. And I sent her to help that boy while I waited with you."

Traci narrowed her eyes, trying to remember the sequence of events Nicole had relayed to her. "She told me she helped a couple of people, but she was with the boy when I found her."

"She's pretty, and from the way she helped out that day, she seems to have some real substance to her—not like your last girlfriend. You should ask her out."

Jenna laughed. "If she was well dressed, you may not have to worry about this one stealing your money."

Traci rolled her eyes.

"Oh, I know. You should ask her to go bowling next weekend with Everett and her new chick. Jenna's not going to be up for it—"

"I can bowl left-handed." She nodded toward her right arm, which was in a sling.

"As I said, Jenna's not lifting anything heavier than a pound, per doctor's orders. And I'll be out of town. But you and Nicole should definitely go."

"The new chick's name is Claire," Jenna said. "Having Nicole along might help Claire feel less like an outsider. You know how when we get together we all start talking about stuff only our little group knows about."

"I'll think about it." She was already imagining how it might be to have Nicole there. She'd been thinking about backing out, knowing Candace was out of town and Jenna wouldn't be up for it. She didn't want to be the third wheel with Everett and Claire. But she couldn't tell Everett, or she might feel she couldn't invite Claire, since the bowling outing had started with their group. For now, she decided to stay busy this week until her planned call with Nicole, and staying busy would almost certainly involve finding reasons not to call Nicole earlier. She needed to give her some space right now to explore some changes in her life.

CHAPTER FIVE

Jared Ackerman, the man accused of intentionally driving his car into a crowd at the Bellbrook Jams music festival, appeared in court today."

Nicole glanced up at the television hanging over the console table on the wall opposite her desk. The reporter cut to video from the courtroom, and Nicole couldn't pull her eyes from the man in the center of the screen. His hands were cuffed in front of him and secured to a chain around his waist, but if not for that and the orange jumpsuit, Nicole might not have given him a second look. He was clean-shaven, and though he could use a trim, his hair had apparently once been cut neatly over his ears and off his neck. When the camera zoomed in on his face, she noticed some acne scarring on his cheeks and that his pale-blue eyes stayed downcast. In street clothes, he wouldn't stand out in a crowd.

Between the reporter's voice, too perky for the situation, and the crawl of text along the bottom of the screen, she gathered that this was a preliminary hearing, during which he was denied bond. He'd stay in jail until the criminal trial. The reporter speculated on his motive, throwing out all the usual reasons—mental illness, some type of protest, or extremist activity. But from what Nicole gathered, no reason had been confirmed from a reputable source, so everyone was just guessing right now.

She picked up the remote from the edge of her desk and muted the sound, but continued to stare at the picture. At last count, five people had been killed—three at the scene and two more who had died at the hospital days later—and twenty-four people were injured, ranging from serious and requiring hospitalization to those with minor injuries who weren't transported from the scene. She hadn't seen any solid stats on how many of those afflictions were a direct result of the car's impact into the festival and how many people were hurt in the ensuing panic, but she'd seen a couple of people knocked down by the crowd.

As the five o'clock news drew to a close, Nicole saved her progress on the file she'd been working on and began to pack her bag. Instead of the check-in call Traci had promised, she'd sent a text asking Nicole to meet her for dinner Thursday night. They'd settled on a restaurant downtown, not far from her office.

She turned off the television on her way out the door, pleased to see other offices with the lights still on as she passed through the hall. She never thought she'd take satisfaction in not being the last person out of the office.

As she stepped outside, she considered walking to the restaurant, but something pushed her toward her car. Though Bellbrook was relatively safe, as a woman, she always tried to be more aware of her surroundings when she was alone downtown. Today, Jared Ackerman's energy felt like a cloud over an otherwise sunny day. So she drove the five blocks, finding a parking spot on the street near the front of the restaurant.

Inside, she gave Traci's name to the hostess, who led her to the back of the dining room. Traci stood as the waiter pulled out Nicole's chair, and then they settled across from each other. Nicole ordered a white wine, Traci asked for water, and the waiter left to give them time to check out the menu.

Nicole opened hers, but she couldn't focus on reading. Traci's light-blue paisley-patterned button-down was open at the neck, and a silver medallion on a chain rested in the hollow between her collarbones. She glanced up to find Traci looking back at her as well.

"How's the first week going?" Traci asked.

"Torturous." Nicole referenced their earlier conversation with an easy smile. "I've been home every night by seven like a good girl."

"Seven? I'm guessing you were in the office before eight. That's more than a regular workday."

"Don't you ever work longer than eight hours?"

"Sure. But I typically pull only five shifts a week. And I bet you usually hit six days more often than you'll admit right now."

She glanced down at her menu, more to avoid eye contact than to actually peruse the selections.

"Okay. Can you at least admit that five days would be a short work week for you?"

She nodded. "It would."

"So, home by seven? What do you do with yourself every evening?"

"I don't bring work home, if that's what you're thinking?" She glanced up, intending to convey her sincerity.

Traci quirked her lips and lifted her brows skeptically.

"I don't." She sighed, preparing for what she'd been hoping to avoid admitting. "I binge-watch *Friends*."

"What?"

"The TV show from the nineties."

"I'm familiar with it. But why do you sound so guilty?"

"It's a total waste of time."

"I'm not sure it is."

"Name one redeeming quality."

Traci paused when the waiter delivered their drinks. After he'd walked away, she said, "Jennifer Aniston."

Nicole gave a nod of acceptance. "I'll give you that."

Traci grinned.

"But endless hours of television won't give my life any more meaning than filling that time with work. This isn't the answer to my search for deeper meaning."

"I'm not advocating for continued bingeing as a way of life, but—"

"I know. You think I should give myself a break and time to figure it out."

Traci lifted her glass in salute. "You said it."

Their waiter returned and took their orders—steak frites for both of them—then slipped away quietly. Nicole liked that he wasn't chatty. Friendly servers annoyed her—she felt bad about it, but they just did. She understood the various motivations: better tips, a more enjoyable way to pass the day, or possibly just because they liked to talk. Maybe because she had business dinners so often, she thought of them as meetings, with goals and objectives that inane banter could derail. She should keep that possibility in mind for the next time she and Traci discussed their faults. She was a rude diner.

"I don't know if you remember my friend Everett—she was the firefighter that came to help the boy."

"Tall, dark, hero type? How could I forget?" She winked, then enjoyed watching Traci's expression change to something that resembled jealousy.

"Yeah, well, she's got a girlfriend. So don't get too excited."

She mimed snapping her fingers in disappointment. "Are they serious?"

"Hey. I'm not offering to hook you up. I'm trying to ask if you'd want to double-date with them. And yes, they're serious."

"A double date, huh?"

"Everett and I bowl every now and then with some friends. This time it's just us, and she wants to bring Claire along. So I thought it might be nice to invite you as well."

"So you don't have to be the third wheel. I get it."

"And because I like spending time with you." The sincerity in Traci's gaze hit her squarely in the chest and left her a little breathless.

She took a sip of her wine, fortification for the journey she was about to take. "So this is a *date*-date, then?"

"Only if you want it to be. Otherwise, I'd be embarrassed and wishing I hadn't said anything."

"No. I want. I do. I just wasn't sure if you did."

"I don't want to be a distraction in the middle of everything you've got going on right now." Traci set down her glass and left her hand resting next to it on the table.

She appreciated Traci's concern, and out of respect, she took a moment to consider again if that's what she was doing. But it wasn't. She'd dealt with major life stuff in the past without needing to turn to a woman, or a friend, or anyone really, to get through it. When her grandmother passed away, she'd taken a couple of days to go to the funeral but never told anyone at work why. She'd sat in the back of the church and said her private good-bye, never speaking to either of her parents. She'd handled her emotions entirely on her own.

But this time, she didn't want to. Whenever the events of that day floated into her mind, she also saw Traci's face, bending near to ask if she was okay, then crawling inside the mangled tent poles with her. They'd experienced something intense in those moments, and maybe that had been the genesis of their connection, but she didn't want it to be the only thing they ever shared.

She covered Traci's hand, then slid her fingers up to trace the single, royal-blue line tattooed around Traci's wrist.

"What is this?"

"The thin blue line."

"Something to do with police solidarity? I've seen it on license plates."

Traci nodded. "There's been some contention around what it really stands for. And like any other symbol, it can be distorted to suit one purpose or another. But to me, it means that we stand as the line between chaos and order. I can trust that the men and women who serve next to me have my back, because we have a common goal."

"Some would say that's an idealistic way of looking at things." Nicole imagined that the surety behind Traci's words had been tested a time or two, and most definitely at the festival incident. She hadn't sensed a line between chaos and order that day. Nothing that happened had seemed logical, and the police officers she'd seen, Traci included, appeared to just be hanging on as tightly as they could to their training and the tools they had. But even that response couldn't be enough to combat a lunatic willing to use a car as a weapon.

"And they're not totally wrong. We're all still human, after all. Fallible." She captured Nicole's hand and intertwined their fingers. Her eyebrows drew together, and Nicole felt the question in her eyes as clearly as if she said it aloud.

"Yes. I want to double-date with you and your hot firefighter friend." She smiled when Traci rolled her eyes.

"You couldn't find another way to say it?"

"I thought that was pretty perfect." When Traci looked away, she squeezed her hand to draw her attention back. "But let me try again. You're even more hot."

"Better."

"I really like you. And I'm looking forward to spending more time with you and getting to know your friends."

Traci's slow smile and the smoky change in her eyes were worth the cost of a little bit of vulnerability.

❖

Nicole entered the darkened bowling alley and glanced around, spotting Traci with her friends about halfway down the row of lanes. As she walked over, the concrete floor felt slightly sticky under her shoes. The building was old and smelled like a combination of French-fry grease, floor wax, and a musty odor she didn't want to identify.

The bowling alley was in a complex that also boasted a movie theater and an indoor go-cart track. The theater had been completely renovated last year. The rows of folding seats with torn and dingy fabric had been removed and power recliners added in their place. The snack bar got an upgrade, now with several "cooked-to-order" offerings.

The owners of the complex promised that the bowling alley would get a face-lift next year. Nicole wasn't sure what they had planned, but anything would be an improvement over the old booths, arched around the scoring table and cracked Formica tabletops. The only upgrade since the 80s was the installation of computerized scorekeeping.

As Nicole approached, Traci spotted her and waved. Traci's plaid button-down shirt over khaki shorts gave her a sexy, preppy look. As Nicole stepped down into the area around the start of their lane, Traci came over and gave her a hug.

"Hi." Traci's quiet greeting felt like stealing a moment just for them before joining her friends. As she eased back, she turned Nicole toward the other two women in the lane. "Nicole, you remember Everett." Traci's introduction was polite, but the quick way she met Nicole's eyes when she said it carried a plea for her not to say anything about how attractive Everett was. She gestured to a pretty blonde standing next to Everett. "And this is her way better half, Claire. Guys, this is Nicole Klein."

"Hi. It's good to see you again—under better circumstances."

She liked the direct way Everett addressed the last time they saw each other. "You, too. And really nice to meet you, Claire."

Claire was a couple of inches shorter than Everett, and she was light, fragile beauty in contrast to Everett's dark, earthy good looks. They looked great together.

Everett lifted her chin in the direction of the alley in front of them. "Are you any good?"

"Not really. I'm wildly inconsistent." She thought that might sum her up in many areas of her life—all but her work.

Traci threw up her arms in frustration. "So, we're screwed then. Everett's a pro. It usually takes me three games to warm up enough to be passable. I was hoping you'd help me have a shot against her."

"You should've asked when you invited me. I'd have told you to find another date."

"Would you?"

She shook her head.

"Whoa, so you two are on a date here?" Everett waved her finger between them, giving Traci a saucy look. "Is this the first date? Are we all on a first date?"

"Everett." Traci's warning tone was laced with humor and embarrassment.

"Behave, Britt," Claire said. "Why don't you and Traci go get us some shoes."

"Sure thing." Everett slid her hand across the small of Claire's back as she headed toward the shoe-rental counter.

"What size?" Traci asked close to Nicole's ear.

She fought the urge to slip her own hand around Traci's waist and move into a more intimate embrace.

"Later," Traci said, as if she could see the struggle in Nicole's gaze. "What size shoe?"

"Eight, please."

"Back in a sec."

She watched Traci leave, but, no, she wasn't looking at the way her jeans fit. Claire shifted beside her, and she glanced over, afraid she'd been caught checking Traci out. But Claire's eyes were on Everett as well.

"How long have you two been seeing each other?"

Claire's face colored when she realized she'd been caught, but Nicole gave her a sympathetic look. "Not long. A month and a half."

"You seem good together."

"Oh. Thanks. I think we are." Claire smiled shyly, obviously at ease with her feelings about Everett.

"Are you a firefighter, too?" She tried to remember what, if anything, Traci had told her about Claire.

"God, no." Claire smiled. "I work at Release the Hounds. It's an animal rescue."

"Sure. I've heard of it. One of my coworkers has adopted about a half dozen cats from you guys."

"What do you do?"

"I'm a financial advisor—nothing exciting or noble like the rest of you."

"Don't nominate me for sainthood just yet. I started out in a corporate job—sales, actually."

"Really?"

Claire nodded. "It's a long story. But the rescue thing—it's as much for my own health and sanity as anything—or at least it was in the beginning. Now when I spend six days a week at work, it's because I love it, not because I feel I have to."

"Here we go, size eight." Traci handed over a pair of maroon, white, and blue shoes with Velcro closures.

They changed their shoes, and Everett entered their names into the scorekeeping computer.

"You're up, Sam."

Traci stood and strolled forward to pick up her ball. "You know I like to lead off."

"That's why I put you in first. I'm doing what I can to make you look good in front of your date." She gave Traci a wink and a finger-gun gesture.

Traci chuckled, then quickly transitioned her expression to a deadly serious one. "You're going down, Everett."

Claire and Everett beat them easily in the first two games, though Nicole and Traci came back to win the third. They turned in their shoes and moved to the bar area for a couple more drinks, wings, and French fries. They all walked out together, but after Claire and Everett got in Claire's Subaru and left, Traci and Nicole lingered in the parking lot.

"Did you have a good time?" Traci rested her butt against the passenger side of her car.

"I did. Everett and Claire are great." Nicole stepped into her, reaching out and dipping her fingertips inside the edge of her front jeans pocket.

"Claire's really good for Everett. She can sometimes take herself too seriously. But Claire reminds her there's more to life than firefighting." Traci nudged her hips forward, into Nicole's hand.

"Speaking of which—did you set me up?" Nicole glanced around, and seeing they were alone, she moved even closer, pressing her lips to the side of Traci's neck.

"What do you mean?" Traci gripped the back of Nicole's shirt.

"You don't know anything about the conversation I had with Claire—her talking about how she left her sales job?" She eased back to study Traci's face as she asked.

Traci shook her head and held up her hands, palms out. "I didn't even know about all that. It was just a happy accident." She grinned. "Or someone up there putting you right where you needed to be."

"Maybe." For all her talk about the possibility of leaving her job, meeting someone who had been brave enough to do just that made her realize that she wasn't ready for such a drastic measure. Seeing the joy in Claire's eyes did drive her desire for change, though.

"Your friends call you Sam."

Traci nodded.

"You told me to call you Traci," she said, justifying why she did so.

"Yeah, the last names—it's a first-responders thing. Now that I think about it, some of us do and some don't. Our paramedic friends prefer their first names. I guess it goes along with the whole pseudo-military structure of police and fire services."

"I can call you Sam, if you'd prefer."

"No."

Nicole narrowed her eyes. "Okay." She drew the word out, almost turning it into a question.

Under the circular glow of the streetlamp, Traci's cheeks colored, and she averted her eyes.

"What am I missing?"

"I like the way you say my first name." Traci still didn't look at her. "Besides, outside of work, I often go by Traci, so it's really not that unusual—"

She grabbed Traci's hand, stopping what was sure to be an epic rambling backpedal. "You could have stopped with your first statement. That was the perfect answer."

Traci slipped her hand into Nicole's hair, at the base of her neck, and drew her close. Nicole's heart rate kicked up as she realized what was about to happen, and she had only a moment to appreciate the desire in Traci's gaze before their lips met and she let her own eyes drop closed.

Traci's mouth moved against hers, both commanding and gentle. The flame that had been ignited with their teasing touches roared to life, and she pressed against Traci, uninhibited in her need to be closer.

Traci's hands circled her waist, her thumbs pressing into her hips. Nicole traced her tongue along Traci's lower lip and sucked gently, and Traci moaned in response. Suddenly, Traci squeezed her hips and pushed, restoring some space between them.

"You're going to make me lose my mind right here in this parking lot."

"Would that be so bad?"

Traci stroked a finger along her cheekbone. "It's been a perfect first date."

"Yeah. Who would have thought I'd ever say that about a night at this bowling alley."

"Hey. I'm a regular here. What are you saying?"

"God, are you really?"

"We like to bowl, and it's not worth the drive to Indianapolis just for a nicer place. The balls still roll down the lanes here, and the beer is cheaper."

"Hm. I'm going to pretend you didn't say all that."

"When can I see you again?" Traci asked.

"A second date?" Nicole raised her eyebrows. "How about in ten minutes at my place?" She slipped her hands around Traci's waist and kissed her jaw.

CHAPTER SIX

Traci stared at Nicole's taillights as she followed her into her gated apartment community. The complex of buildings, faced with brick and stained wood, had been built only a year ago. The exteriors were modern, and the areas between buildings were immaculately landscaped; Traci had no doubt the interiors were well styled, too.

Nicole parked in a numbered spot, and Traci chose one of those marked for visitors. She took an extra second to get out of the car. She hadn't hesitated when Nicole asked her to come home with her. Another moment of making out in the parking lot, and she might have suggested they climb in the back seat of her car. She took an extra breath, attempting to slow her racing heart. She didn't want to embarrass herself by pushing Nicole against her front door as soon as it closed behind them.

As it turned out, Nicole was the one who did the shoving, but Traci didn't mind that the back of her head hit the door. Nicole laughed and rubbed her hand over Traci's hair.

"I'm sorry. Are you okay?"

Nicole's breasts against her, her hips sandwiching her to the door, helped ease any pain. "I'm good."

Nicole swallowed the end of her words with a kiss that Traci returned just as ferociously. She clutched Nicole's hips, then slid her hands down to cup her ass.

"Bedroom?" Nicole rasped between kisses.

"Yes, please."

As Nicole grabbed her hand and pulled her through the apartment, Traci registered sleek, tasteful decor in a compact space but didn't bother noticing the details. Through a doorway just off the living room, Nicole paused beside a bed piled high with pillows and a fluffy comforter and unbuttoned Traci's shirt. When it fell open, Traci shrugged it off and reached for Nicole's flowy blouse. When she started to tug it upward, Nicole stopped her.

"There's a button in the back." She spun around, and Traci found the tiny pearlescent button and fumbled it through a tight loop.

With the neck more open, Traci grabbed the back of the hem and pushed it up and over Nicole's head, leaving Nicole to shrug her arms out of it while Traci trailed a row of kisses down her back. Traci lowered herself to her knees, just as she placed the last kiss in the hollow at the base of her spine.

"You're beautiful," she whispered as she curled her fingers into the waistband of Nicole's jeans. "Undo these."

Nicole quickly worked open the fly, and Traci dragged them down her shapely legs. Nicole turned as she stepped out of them, and Traci pressed her lips to her belly, inhaling her scent.

"Get undressed." The urgency in Nicole's voice matched the pressure that grew in Traci.

They needed to feel each other's skin—had wanted to since the first day they met, if she was being honest. Only the fear that the adrenaline of surviving had fueled their desire had held her back. But the pounding in her chest and the tightening in her thighs had nothing to do with that day and everything to do with the amazing woman standing before her.

"You good?" Nicole must have sensed her moment's hesitation.

"So good. Come here."

Nicole moved into her arms, then pushed her onto the bed. But when Nicole would have moved over her, Traci flipped her onto her back. Nicole's warmth against her, smooth and strong, and—she discovered—wet and slick, inspired patience she didn't know she had. She took her time, exploring and measuring Nicole's reaction to every touch and kiss.

And when Nicole tensed beneath her, Traci closed her eyes and reveled in the abandon with which she released, crying out and tightening around her.

❖

"What type of women do you usually date?" Traci asked the next morning over coffee and peanut-butter toast. They'd lingered in bed, making love before getting up and showering together. As a nod to their first evening, Traci now wore a pair of Nicole's sweats and one of her Notre Dame T-shirts. Her feet were bare and her hair stuck up in a faux-hawk that both their active evening and Traci's sleep habits had formed. Nicole had never slept next to someone who moved around so much during the night.

Nicole gave her a curious look. "I don't usually date. Why do you ask?"

"I can picture you with professional, white-collar types—women who wear skirts with their suit jackets to show off their amazing legs, which are most likely toned from hours of yoga or spin classes or something."

Nicole forced a laugh, but Traci's assessment of her social life somehow felt like a dig. She had acquaintances and colleagues who fit the description and didn't like hearing the judgment in Traci's tone. "You have an active and very specific imagination."

"That may be. But women like you don't date women like me." She took a big bite of her toast as if punctuating her point.

"Women like me? What part of my behavior since we met has led you to believe that I think I'm somehow better than you?"

"No, I just—"

"I don't date. Once in a while, when I'm out of town, if I get lonely enough, I might hook up with someone, but it's never been anything long-term. Is that what you want to hear? Or did you want the details, too?"

"Nicole, I didn't mean—"

"Don't be an ass and lose all the points you gained last night." She picked up her coffee mug and headed back to her bedroom, where she went straight to the bathroom and began brushing her hair.

"I'm sorry." Traci propped a shoulder against the doorjamb, her arms folded against her chest. "But look at this place. It's gorgeous. And you—you're amazing, successful, beautiful, driven, and fun to be with."

"If you say 'what do I have to offer?' I'm going to throw you out of my house."

Traci pressed her lips together, indicating she'd been about to toss out some version of that statement. She'd been so confident from the day they met that it never occurred to Nicole she might have a self-esteem issue when it came to them. Or maybe *she* had put that on Traci. She'd assumed a woman in uniform, who carried a gun and arrested the bad guys on the daily, wouldn't have insecurities about anything.

She sighed and set down her hairbrush, then met Traci's eyes.

"I have a nice apartment because it's where I spend what little downtime I have. But what I own doesn't reflect who I am, any more than what you have does for you. Got it?" Traci nodded. Nicole caressed a hand down Traci's arm to grasp her hand. "You are who I want to spend my time with, or you were until you started with this shit. And I don't think I have to stand here and extol your virtues for you to understand why. But if that's what you need, I will."

"No. I'm good."

"Great. Because I can think of some things I'd rather be doing with my mouth right now." She planted a hand in the center of Traci's chest and guided her back into the bedroom.

❖

Traci parked her car in front of Rock Solid Insurance, taking a moment before she got out to change her status on her laptop so the dispatcher would know she'd arrived. She was barely out of the car before an older man charged out the front door of the business. His wispy hair floated around his head in the afternoon breeze, and when he waved his arms to get her attention, the edges of his cardigan flapped.

"Officer, I'm the one who called."

"Yes, sir. What can I do for you?"

"This homeless guy has been sleeping behind my building." The man planted his hands on his hips.

"Has he been causing a disturbance or bothering your customers?" Bellbrook didn't have a large homeless community, but there were some, many of them familiar to the police. They tried to get them into the shelter, but it didn't always have room, and some people preferred the street to the shelter environments. Some had addictions or mental illness that contributed to their circumstances.

"No. But he can't stay back there."

"I'll talk to him." If she came in contact with someone who wanted help, she tried to assist them in any way she could. But she didn't like to bother people who were just trying to get by and had no place else to go.

"Let me show you where he is." When he stepped in front of her and headed for the alley, she stopped him.

"Just in the back there? I can probably find him. If I have any trouble, I'll come talk to you." Until she could assess the situation, she didn't want him to stir things up more than necessary.

He huffed in obvious displeasure but didn't argue.

"I don't want to keep you from your work. Go back inside, and I'll speak with you before I leave."

Her assurance that he'd get the last word was enough, and he went inside. She walked down the narrow alley between the insurance agency and the neighboring building. In the shadows, the humidity magnified a mix of unpleasant odors that Traci had no desire to dissect.

The confines of the alley spilled out into a more open space behind the building, and she paused there to look around before she proceeded. A dumpster with a stack of trash bags and empty boxes beside it took up most of the space in one corner. Several empty pallets leaned against the exterior of the building, near a door marked *Shipping/Receiving*, though Traci didn't know exactly what an insurance company was shipping or receiving that mandated a separate entrance.

She didn't immediately see any occupants in the alley and thought maybe the person had moved on and would save her the trouble of rousting him. Her boots echoed against the stone walkway as she continued, but then movement rustled the boxes near the dumpster.

"Come on out." She rested her hand on the case containing her pepper-spray canister, thinking she wouldn't need it but wanting to be ready for a panicked attempt to ambush her and escape.

The boxes moved again, and a figure emerged from under them. When the business owner said "homeless guy," she hadn't pictured this skinny wisp of a kid. He was taller than she was, but only by a couple of inches, and she probably still had thirty pounds on him. His denim jacket was dirty but in otherwise good condition, as were his pants and shoes. He hadn't been out here too long. As he stood, he swept a hand across his forehead, shoving his shaggy white-blond hair to the side.

"What's your name?"

"Caleb."

"Got a last name, Caleb?" She watched his eyes for signs of intoxication and/or drug use, but didn't see evidence of either.

He glanced quickly at her badge, then away, and she knew she wasn't going to get a last name from him. He'd been on the street long enough to learn that knowledge was power, and if he wanted to stay alive, he shouldn't give his away.

"How old are you?"

He lifted his chin, now initiating eye contact in order to show her he wasn't intimidated. "Over eighteen." Just barely over eighteen, if she had to guess.

"Okay." She purposely kept her voice soft and her gaze gentle, not needing a show of strength. "You can't stay back here. The business owner called in a complaint."

He nodded and retrieved a backpack from next to the dumpster, then shrugged one of the straps over his shoulder.

"Can I give you a ride somewhere? I know a guy over at the shelter, where I can get you a bed for a couple of nights."

He shook his head. "I'll move on."

Something in the defeated slump of his shoulders touched her, and she reached out a hand to grasp his arm and stop him when he started to pass her. Even as he tensed up, the sparse muscles in his thin arm didn't provide much resistance.

"When was the last time you ate?"

"Are you going to arrest me?"

She stared at him for a moment, letting the silence defuse his contention. "No." She pulled out her wallet, opened it, and grabbed a couple of twenties. "Get a hot meal."

"Lady, this is more than one meal."

"You don't want it?" She held out her hand for him to return the money, but he clutched it in a fist against his chest.

"I didn't say that." He shoved it into his pants pocket. "What will it cost me?"

She clenched her jaw against the idea that someone had already taught this kid that an act of kindness had to have a price. But was it a lesson he'd learned on the street? Or something in his past that had helped drive him there?

"Nothing."

"You don't want anything?"

"I'd like to get you some food at that place next door and maybe talk a little." She pointed at the pocket the money had disappeared into. "But what I gave you isn't contingent on that. You can walk away right now. And as long as you don't come back around so this business owner calls me again, you and I don't have to have any further dealings."

He seemed to be considering her offer, or maybe he was just sizing up whether he could trust her.

"You buy the food over there," he hitched his head toward the building next door, "and I get to keep your money for later."

"Deal. Let's go." She headed back through the alley toward the front, confident he would follow. As they reached the sidewalk, she turned to him. "You go start looking at the menu. I'll be right in there."

She turned toward the insurance agency, catching movement behind the glass pane of the door, and caught the owner still trying to scurry around a desk as she entered. He glanced up and froze, then grabbed a stapler off the desk, but she suspected it just happened to be the closest thing to him rather than something he actually needed.

"You shouldn't have any more problems with Caleb." He gave her a blank look, and she realized that he didn't even consider that she might have learned his name. She shook her head and said, "The kid was just trying to get some rest. But he knows not to come back here again."

"Good. It's nothing personal, you know. But letting vagrants hang around only encourages more of them."

Traci didn't respond, because suddenly this situation felt very personal to her. She left the insurance agency and headed to the sandwich shop next door. Caleb stood outside staring in through the window.

"What are you doing out here?"

He shrugged.

She looked inside and saw the employee behind the counter staring back at them. "Did they tell you to leave?"

"I told them you were coming. Then I said I had my own money. But they said they didn't have to serve me."

Traci had been in the shop before and had never had a problem. In fact, the employee even looked familiar. She considered her options. If she took Caleb in, they likely wouldn't have a hassle, but the defeat in his eyes made her angry.

"Wait here." She jerked open the door and stopped just inside it, so she would have to speak loudly enough for the other patrons inside to hear. "Did you refuse to serve my friend out there?" She jerked a thumb over her shoulder. She saw a couple of customers trying to covertly angle their phones in her direction, so she knew she was being recorded.

"It's our right." The woman hadn't even spared Caleb a glance before she'd answered.

Traci nodded slowly. "If you don't want his business, then you don't need mine either. And I'll be sure to let any of my friends who eat here know how you treated that kid, too." She purposely didn't name her friends as fellow officers, so they couldn't construe her words somehow as a threat to withhold police service. She wouldn't do that. But she wouldn't dine there again, either.

She left without waiting for a response and didn't stop when she hit the sidewalk. To Caleb, she said, "You like pizza?" He nodded, and together they crossed the street to a pizza place instead.

Less than ten minutes later, she watched as Caleb cut his slice of pizza with a fork and knife. She paused in the middle of shaking Parmesan cheese over the top of her piece.

"That's how you eat pizza?"

A blush crawled up his neck and he nodded.

She shrugged, picked up her slice, and folded it in half before taking a bite off the end.

He smiled as he speared another piece with his fork.

"How long have you been out here?"

He rolled his bottled water between his hands, avoiding the question.

"You don't have to answer. We could sit here in silence." She took a bite of pizza and chewed slowly, letting him decide.

"A couple of months." He shrugged. "It's not that bad."

He hadn't even been through a winter yet. She didn't want to see his bravado deflated, but she knew it would happen. She slipped a business card out of her front shirt pocket, wrote her cell number on the back, and set it on the table between them. He picked it up and held it between his index and middle fingers.

"Get-out-of-jail-free card?"

"Not exactly. No promises, depending on the charge." She smiled, and he gave her an answering grin that lit up his eyes, a hint of the boy inside this young man. "But you get in trouble, I'll be there, no matter what the outcome is."

"Yeah. You up for sitting in court and playing the supportive friend while your coworkers try to put me away?"

"Planning a crime spree?" She liked his wit and hoped homelessness wouldn't beat that out of him.

"Nope. Just trying to survive this life."

"You could hope for more than survival if you want to accept a little help."

"I'll think about that." He lifted his napkin out of his lap and wiped his mouth. Something about the gesture sparked an idea in her, and suddenly she was reviewing their whole interaction.

"Don't you think your parents are missing you?" God, she hoped she was wrong. She hadn't been trusting her instincts lately, not since the day of the festival.

"Ha. They're probably glad I'm gone."

"I don't know. A lot of kids think their parents would feel that way, but when it really happens—I've seen them beside themselves with worry after I go take a runaway report."

"I bet that's what they'll call it, too. They'll tell all their friends that I ran away, and they'll all believe it because I'm so troubled." He pursed his lips, and she could see the effort it took for him not to cry. "They'll never tell their stupid Republican friends they kicked me out because I'm gay."

"Caleb—"

"What would your mom say if you came home one day and told her you were a dyke?"

She flinched, exactly as he'd apparently hoped she would at his choice of terminology. But this wasn't the time for a discussion on the different ways their generations interpreted that term. "She took it hard at first. But she came around eventually, and now we're pretty close."

He blinked and stared, clearly taken aback, though she wasn't sure if the answer or the calm, direct way she delivered it threw him off. He regained control, but he wasn't as steady as he was before.

"I don't need the it-gets-better speech."

"And I'm not delivering it." She leaned closer, lowering her voice. "I don't know if it will. I hope, for your sake, it does. But if it doesn't, you can use the number on that card any time."

He nodded, swallowing hard, and stood up. "I should go. Thanks for this."

She didn't know if he meant the meal or the talk, but it didn't matter. When he went to use the restroom before leaving, she bought him two more slices of pizza and a bottle of water. As the cashier was bagging his food, Traci asked her to add a couple of chocolate-chip cookies, because she didn't think a kid could ever get too old for cookies.

He returned from the restroom and met her at the front door, and she handed over the bag. "A little something for the road."

He took it with a grin and held it up. "Or the street, as the case may be."

"Caleb."

"Yeah?"

"Be careful." She didn't say anything else, despite all that she wanted to tell him. She couldn't force her help on him. But now he knew it was available if he was willing to ask.

"Good to know there are some stand-up cops out there." He extended a hand, and she shook it. "Who knows? You might hear from me someday."

"Any time."

He nodded and slipped out the door. She followed and watched until he reached the end of the block, then turned left and walked out of sight. She'd been distracted by his living situation and ignored her pinging gaydar until well into their interaction. On some level, she was shocked that some parents still disowned their kids over sexuality. She recalled Nicole's story of her family, but Caleb was eighteen years old. His parents were from her generation. She was lucky enough to have had so many supportive people in her life that she needed reminding the whole world wasn't like that.

CHAPTER SEVEN

Traci parked in a visitors' spot in front of Nicole's place, cut the ignition, and sat staring up at Nicole's living-room window. The faint glow meant she was already home, sticking to her plan to avoid working late. Nicole seemed to be adjusting to her new schedule and only occasionally complained that she had work she should be doing instead.

She'd considered going straight home after she got off. Her confusing emotions about Nicole were still warring in her head and her heart. Being with her this past weekend had been amazing. Every time she thought about it today, she would swear she could still feel Nicole's touch. But they'd had that moment when she'd let her doubt creep in and, stupidly, voiced it aloud. A part of her still wondered if Nicole's feelings were, at least in part, affected by what they had gone through at the festival. But, she'd decided, she would enjoy the time they had together, and if after getting to know her better, Nicole didn't feel the same way, she would deal with the heartache. She already knew she'd be devastated, but maybe it would be worth it to feel the way she did now.

In the window, she saw the blinds move, opening slightly, then snapping back into place. Knowing Nicole was waiting for her started a bloom of happiness in her chest. She wouldn't mind coming home to this feeling more often.

She was still enjoying that thought as she knocked on the door, her backpack slung over one shoulder. Nicole opened the door and moved aside slightly, welcoming her inside. As soon as she entered, she was enfolded in Nicole's arms.

"I missed you today."

"Yeah?" Traci gave her a kiss that lingered pleasantly, not hurrying into anything more.

As they parted, Nicole slipped the strap of her bag off her shoulder and dropped it onto a bench by the door, then took her hand and led her to the sofa.

"I'm not used to thinking about anything but work while I'm in the office, but today, I kept finding myself distracted by you."

"I thought about you today, too." She settled at one end of the sofa and pulled a pillow to lean against her thigh. She patted it, and Nicole lay down, her head resting half on Traci's leg. "I met this homeless kid today—well, he's grown, but barely."

"A homeless guy made you think of me?"

"Yes. Now shush, and I'll tell you why." She stroked her fingers against Nicole's temple, and then, as she sifted them through the soft strands of her hair, she talked about Caleb.

"He really made an impact on you." Nicole tilted her head to meet Traci's eyes and touched her knee. "I'm guessing you made one on him, too."

She huffed. "Or he tossed my card into the nearest trash can as he rounded the corner."

"I doubt that. I know a little something about feeling like your family refuses to see you—to accept you for who you are. And when someone finally does, it means a lot."

"I hope so."

"He's got someone to call if he gets into trouble or just wants to change his situation. He didn't have that before he met you." Nicole sat up and cuddled close, slipping her left arm around Traci's shoulders while she ghosted her other hand across Traci's thigh. "I know how much it's meant to me, having you to talk to."

Traci kissed her and Nicole shifted to straddle her lap. Traci caressed up the side of Nicole's thighs, thankful for the cut-off sweatpants she wore because they stretched to make room for her hands.

"So, you enjoy all the talking we do?" she asked with her lips against Nicole's throat.

"Hm. Yes. I've been in relationships with amazing sex but always lacked a great conversationalist."

"Oh yeah?"

Nicole laughed, and Traci shifted and dumped her onto the sofa. Just as she knelt between Nicole's legs, her phone's text notification pinged from across the room. She straightened and glanced that way.

"Oh, hell, no. You are not about to check your phone right now." Nicole grasped the front of her shirt and pulled her down over her. "If you know what's good for you."

She grimaced and gently took hold of Nicole's wrist. If that was the text she'd been waiting for, she needed to check it before it got too late in the evening to politely respond. She eased Nicole's fist open and sandwiched Nicole's hand between her two palms.

"I have to check it."

"Is it work?"

"No."

Nicole narrowed her eyes, and when she released Traci, she detected a warning in her gaze. She grabbed her phone off the kitchen island, where she'd dropped it along with her keys earlier. She unlocked it, though she'd seen the notification she was waiting for on the lock screen. She took a second to read it, then typed a quick reply. When she glanced up, Nicole was still staring at her. She set her phone back down and returned to the sofa.

"Where was I?" She dropped one knee between Nicole's and bent over her, intending to brace her arms near Nicole's shoulders. But in a surprisingly quick move, Nicole shoved her back and slid into a sitting position.

"Do you remember? Because you were pretty distracted there."

"I was checking that for you." She settled onto the sofa next to her and took her hand.

"For me?" Despite her sarcastic tone, humor touched her eyes, and she let her hand rest passively in Traci's.

"Yep. So now I can ask, are you busy tomorrow evening?"

"Hm. Tomorrow evening. I don't know." She braced a hand against Traci's shoulder and held her at arm's length. "I'm waiting for a very important letter to come in the mail, so I should probably be here—" She broke off, laughing when Traci growled and tugged her closer.

Nicole grabbed the sides of her head and pulled her down for a kiss, and Traci lost her entire train of thought. She closed her eyes and let Nicole dominate the kiss, while she followed blissfully. The heat of Nicole's mouth fused to hers, melted, and flowed, filling spaces she hadn't even known were empty. When they inched apart, she panted a couple of soft breaths and gave a small sound of satisfaction.

"I don't want to ever stop doing that," she said quietly before she realized the words were out.

"Ever?" Nicole didn't looked freaked out—just curious. Was she wondering how serious Traci was?

"Is it too soon?" She could have backed it up and made her comment into a joke, but she didn't want to play those games. No matter how much this situation scared her, or how uncertain she felt their future still was, she was already invested in finding out.

"No." Nicole touched Traci's chin with her index finger. "I'd like to kiss you for a very long time."

Traci narrowed her eyes. "But I said 'ever' to you. And I have to settle for 'a very long time'?"

"Let's just see how things go." Nicole's smile sparked all the way into her eyes.

She pretended to consider this possibility, then nodded and steered them back on track. "So, about tomorrow, there's someone I want you to meet."

"Who?"

"You'll see."

"That's all you're going to tell me? If you're introducing me to your family, you have to let me know. That's not something you surprise a girl with. I'd have to mentally prepare to impress your mom."

"It's not my family. Since we're just seeing how things go, we're not quite there yet, right?"

"I have to simply trust you and go along?"

"I wish you would. I promise you'll like it."

"Okay."

"Good. I'll pick you up."

"At home? Or at the office?"

"Doesn't matter. Either place, at six."

"Let's make it here. I want to freshen up first. But you realize I'll have to leave the office by five in order to be ready?"

Traci shrugged. "That's just a bonus."

❖

"When are you going to tell me where we're going?" Nicole rubbed her palms nervously against her thighs. Who was she supposed to be meeting? After Traci had said she wasn't introducing her to her family, she'd thought maybe more of her friends. But now she didn't think so. They were thirty minutes away from Bellbrook, about to enter a neighboring town.

Traci turned down a side street just at the edge of town and drove into a subdivision of modest houses. The lots were small but well kept, and children played in several of the yards and on the sidewalks.

Traci pulled to the curb, glanced at her phone screen, then checked the number on the mailbox. "This is it." She opened her car door. "Come on."

"Did you buy a house? You talk about me making rash decisions," she joked.

"It's not my house." Traci was halfway up the walk, but Nicole still stood next to the car.

"Then who lives here?" She hurried to catch up.

"You'll see." Traci knocked on the door, and a woman about Nicole's age answered.

"Officer Sam, come in, please." She stepped back to make room for them.

"I told you to call me Traci. This is Nicole Klein. Nicole, this is Stephanie Ward." She turned toward the living room as they entered, then looked back at Nicole with a huge smile. "And this is Brandon."

A teenage boy half reclined on the sofa, his legs stretched out in front of him. His athletic shorts revealed a line of sutures along his thigh. Nicole immediately recognized his face, though now his expression was alert and smiling. His round face had a ruddy complexion, instead of the pale hue she remembered. The day of the festival, she hadn't noticed the beginnings of a sparse mustache shadowing his upper lip.

She took a couple of tentative steps forward, and Traci rested a hand against her lower back supportively. She was embarrassed to find her eyes filling, and she blinked several times to combat her tears. She would not cry in front of this kid.

"Hi," Brandon said.

"Please, have a seat. Can I get you two anything to drink?" Stephanie asked.

They both declined as they sat together on the love seat and turned toward Brandon. Stephanie sat at the end of the sofa, near Brandon's feet.

"How are you doing?" Nicole asked.

"Fifteen stitches." He spoke like they were a badge of honor. And maybe they were to a kid his age. "And I get out of gym class until the stitches come out."

"You don't like gym?"

"I'm not an athlete."

"What do you like to do?" She felt strange chatting idly with him, but she didn't know if he wanted to talk about the incident.

"I like video games. And some guys and I just started a band."

"Drummer?" she guessed.

He shook his head. "Bass guitar."

"Cool."

They fell silent for a moment, and Nicole glanced out the window behind him. They had a decent-sized yard, and the grass needed to be cut. Was that Brandon's job?

"He started asking to meet you almost as soon as he left the hospital." Stephanie touched one of Brandon's feet and looked at him, motherly love evident in her gaze. Nicole couldn't fathom Stephanie's panic when she learned about what was going on at the festival, knowing her son had been there. "We didn't even know who you were. So I reached out to the paramedics who transported him in the ambulance, and they remembered hearing that a police officer had been with him."

"My sergeant called me a couple of days ago and put me in touch with Stephanie. As soon as we started talking, I knew I wanted to surprise you with this visit."

"I was at the festival with my bandmates, and when everything started to go down, we got separated. I don't remember much, except your voice and a lot of pain."

"The doctor said if you hadn't controlled his bleeding, he might not have made it to the hospital." Stephanie's voice broke, and she took a deep breath before speaking again. "I can't thank you enough for being there. Both of you."

Nicole swallowed past the emotion rising in her throat. "I'm glad I was able to help." She glanced at Traci, not sure what else to say. She didn't want to go into any details that might make this harder for Stephanie.

"Traci said when she found you, you'd already started helping him. Do you have medical training?"

She shook her head. "I was there to see a band I liked later in the day. The first person I found was a paramedic who was injured." She'd been blown away when Traci had shared that her friend Jenna had been the injured paramedic and that Candace remembered her. She couldn't wait to meet them both. "Her partner was with her. And she told me to help Brandon." She chuckled. "At first I thought she'd sent me over to him just to keep me out of her way while she took care of her friend. But when I got to him and saw he was hurt badly, too—everything happened so fast."

"You didn't run away from the area?"

"A lot of people did," Traci said. "I met so many people trying to get out when I was going in."

Nicole glanced again at Brandon, recalling his distant gaze and the shock of dark, sweaty hair falling across his forehead. "I don't remember thinking about it one way or the other. I just wanted to help."

They chatted for another twenty minutes, but when Brandon began to look tired, she and Traci excused themselves, promising to keep in touch. Stephanie squeezed Nicole extra hard when they hugged by the front door. And her whispered "thank you" tied a fresh knot of emotion in Nicole's throat. She couldn't speak her reply, so she simply patted Stephanie's back and gave her a watery smile as they separated.

She and Traci walked silently to the car and climbed inside. Traci tapped her thigh, and when she looked at her, Traci seemed to be searching her expression for something. Then she gave her a small nod, started the car, and steered out onto the street.

The drive home was quiet, and Nicole appreciated the time to reflect on the experience. She'd been reevaluating her life before the festival and finding it lacking. But she hadn't realized that not a single day before that one mattered because, as she'd said, she'd chosen to stay when it counted, and that was the core of who she was. She just needed to find more opportunities to uncover that part of herself.

Traci parked in front of her apartment building. Without a word, she got out of the car, circled, and opened Nicole's door. After Nicole got out, Traci enfolded her in a short hug, kissing her temple, then released her and stepped back.

"You'll call me if you need anything?"

"Are you leaving?"

"Unless you don't want me to. If you need space to process, my feelings won't be hurt."

"I'd like for you to stay." She laced her fingers into Traci's, but when she would have pulled her toward the building, Traci tugged back. She opened the trunk of her car and lifted out a backpack.

"I was hoping you'd ask."

After they got inside, Nicole turned on the first movie in her favorite action series to distract herself from what she was feeling. She'd need to unpack some more of this day, but she'd do that later. For now she just wanted to sit here, cuddled into this amazing woman who had come into her life, and enjoy a movie.

"Thank you for today." She touched Traci's arm, then pressed a kiss to her cheek. "That was an amazing thing to do for me."

"I'm glad. His mom wasn't being dramatic. That kid is alive because of you. That's something you did. So whatever else you're feeling about your contributions to the world, no one can ever take that away from you."

She nodded, tears filling her eyes. "This. In case, you haven't figured it out, yet, *this* is what you have to offer me. Understanding exactly what I needed."

❖

By the time they started the second movie in the series, Traci could tell that Nicole was no longer paying attention. Before they'd settled in, they'd both changed into more comfortable clothes for an evening of vegging. Since Traci was pretty certain Nicole had seen this one before, she didn't say anything. She wrapped her arm around her and quietly let her mind work.

She hadn't realized she'd been drifting from the plot as well, until she opened her eyes to find the credits rolling up an otherwise black screen. She glanced over to see if Nicole had noticed and found her amused gaze. Sitting up from her slouched position, she closed one eye and rubbed the other one with the heel of her hand.

"Was I snoring?"

"No more than usual."

"Great."

Nicole picked up the remote and muted the pounding action-movie theme music accompanying the credits. The sudden silence felt louder than the sound had been. Traci suppressed her need to fill it, though, waiting to follow Nicole's lead. She'd expected today to bring up some things for her. In truth, the visit had affected Traci more than she'd thought it would as well. Over the years, she'd had a few follow-ups with victims and been thanked by family members. But none had touched her as much as Nicole's interaction with Stephanie—simple yet poignant. It reminded her of why she'd wanted to be a police officer to begin with—before the profession became so completely laden with politics and social tension. She'd wanted to feel good about herself and to do something worthwhile for her community, she'd wanted the ideal of serve and protect, and she'd wanted to wear a uniform—to be honest about that point. It made her feel good to get back in touch with those motivations.

"I've been thinking about what you said—you know, small changes. And I have an idea." Nicole shifted, turning toward her and reclining against her chest.

"Yeah?"

"Could you put me in touch with Claire? I'd like to talk to her about volunteering with her rescue."

"That's a great idea. Why there?"

Nicole shrugged. "I like animals, but I've never had a pet because I spend so many hours at the office. And Claire seems great. I enjoyed meeting her."

She glanced at her watch. "Do you want to call her now? It's not too late. I actually wouldn't mind a shower, which would give you time to chat with her."

"Sure. I guess."

Traci pulled up Claire's contact in her phone and texted it to Nicole so she'd have it for future use. Then she handed over her phone with the contact still on the screen, ready for Nicole to press the call button. "Use mine. Unlike most people, she probably answers numbers she doesn't recognize, but just in case."

She kissed the top of Nicole's head as she passed by on her way to the master bedroom. Her long, hot shower filled the bathroom with a steamy cloud, scented with Nicole's shampoo. She dried off and wrapped herself in one of Nicole's fluffy robes. As she walked through the living room, Nicole was still on the phone, so she continued to the kitchen to forage for snacks in case they decided to watch the third movie in the series.

By the time she'd popped some popcorn, poured it into a bowl, and grabbed two diet sodas, Nicole had finished her call.

"I guess you got her." Traci handed over the bowl, then dropped down onto the sofa next to her.

"I did. We had an awesome talk. We even started brainstorming some ways for me to help out."

"Like what?" She threw a piece of popcorn in her mouth.

"Well, first and foremost, I can go play with the puppies and kittens."

"Of course. I might even join you."

"And I could offer free financial planning for the rescue, too. Maybe help them figure out how to maximize their donation funds to really get the most out of them."

"That's a good idea. But I'm probably not helping with that."

Nicole laughed. "I'm sure Claire can find something else for you to do."

CHAPTER EIGHT

Nicole leaned back in the grass, locking her arms and bracing her weight on her hands behind her. Five eight-week-old puppies crawled across her lap, and when the smallest of the litter got his back legs hung up climbing over one of her thighs, she gave him a little boost. She'd been volunteering at Release the Hounds for a month now and loved it.

She hadn't been able to stick to her shortened workdays all the time, because sometimes forcing herself to leave a project unfinished caused more stress than staying and finishing it. But she'd found a nice balance between spending her downtime with Traci or here at the rescue. And that made the time at work even more productive.

When she glanced up and saw Claire walking across the lawn with a small cooler, she waved. Claire detoured in her direction.

"How are these little guys doing?" Claire squatted beside her and caught one of them as it waddled by. She picked him up and hugged him close. "Oh my God, puppy breath."

"They're great. I think I might have to adopt the runt." She pointed at the speckled little body trying to wiggle into the pile of his siblings currently dousing themselves in the large water bowl she'd put out for them.

"That's the danger of volunteering here. I don't have a single volunteer who hasn't taken one home with them at some point or another, sometimes more than one at a time."

"I'm not home enough. Maybe if I lived with someone and our schedules overlapped enough to provide for a dog." She looked across the lawn to where Traci and Candace worked with two of Claire's employees repairing one of the storage sheds.

"You two are getting serious, then? Talking about moving in?"

"Not yet. But I can see us getting there eventually."

"You're good for her. I'm glad she found you."

"She's pretty good for me, too. How's Caleb working out?" She nodded in the direction of the lanky guy currently horsing around with Traci.

"He's a good kid. From what I can get out of him, he's had a rough time. But he seems to open up only to Traci. I'm glad he's got her looking out for him."

"Me, too." He'd called Traci a couple of weeks ago in the middle of the night after some other homeless guys had assaulted him. They'd taken everything he had and left him with a broken nose and some cracked ribs. Traci had gone out and picked him up, and he'd been staying with her these past couple of weeks.

Traci had gotten him the part-time gig working for Claire, saying she wanted him someplace she knew was safe until he got on his feet. Nicole had talked to her boss about hiring him to do some courier work for them as well. She hoped that someday, when she asked Traci to move in with her, he might be ready to sublet Traci's place for whatever very reasonable rent she came up with.

Claire stood and cupped her hand around her mouth. "Guys, come take a water break." She opened the cooler.

Nicole scooped up her little speckled pup, laying claim before the others could come play with the dogs. As she stood, he burrowed in under her chin, nuzzling her neck.

"Seriously, little dude. I can't take you home."

"I bet you will." Claire gave her a knowing smile.

While Claire passed out bottled water, Traci came to stand close to Nicole.

"Who's your friend?" She rubbed one finger over his tiny head.

"I don't think he has a name yet. I've been calling him Runt."

Traci laughed. "That's a horrible name."

"I don't know," Candace said. "It seems to suit him. It's not like you're any good at nicknames. You usually call everyone by their last names, except Jenna and me."

"And Claire and me."

"Yeah. I don't know why. But girlfriends have first names," Candace said.

"Yep." Traci clapped Candace on the shoulder. "And you're next in line to get one. Make sure she doesn't have a weird first name, okay?"

Candace nodded, but she didn't meet Traci's eyes. Nicole didn't know too much about Candace's dating history. This was only the second time they'd hung out. The first time, they'd talked extensively about the day of the incident and the coincidence of Candace and Traci being good friends, while Nicole connected with them both that day. She'd met Jenna the same day, but they hadn't got on that well. Jenna seemed more reserved and not into talking about the festival, which was understandable.

She turned to Claire. "I forgot to tell you, but Brandon and his mom are coming to the adoption event next weekend. We need your help convincing his mom he should get a dog."

She'd left her number the day that they visited, and Brandon had started texting her a couple of days later. At first, he seemed awkward about it, saying he thought she might not have time to talk to some kid. But she'd assured him she wanted to and that she understood how he was feeling. Despite how many people had been there that day, only they knew exactly what they'd gone through. She and Traci had been group texting with Stephanie, too, making sure she knew they were in contact with Brandon. She'd given Stephanie a heads-up on the puppy thing, not wanting her to be blindsided, and she seemed like she might be on board.

"Maybe he could take Runt," Traci said.

At first Nicole clutched him to her more tightly, resistant to the idea. But then, she couldn't really take him right now anyway. And if Brandon had him, she could always visit. Claire had said when the family that had found the litter brought them in, they'd been cold, and hungry, and separated too early from their mother, who they believed had been hit by a car and killed. Runt had been in the most dire condition, and Claire was actually surprised he'd pulled through. Nicole remembered Stephanie saying the doctors stated that if they hadn't controlled Brandon's bleeding, he might not have survived.

"If he wants him, I think they'd be a perfect match," she said.

"Then it's settled. Claire, can we hide him from all the other guests until Brandon gets a chance to see him?"

"Why don't we just tell Stephanie to bring him a little early?" Nicole rubbed her chin on the top of Runt's head, and he pressed back against her.

Traci turned to stand in front of her, bending her head to talk to Runt, whispering something only he could hear. Then she straightened and stared into Nicole's eyes.

"I know you love him. But I think Brandon might need him."

Nicole's eyes welled, and she bit her lip to keep from crying as she nodded.

"Someday, we'll find another special little guy or girl for us. Okay?" The tenderness in Traci's gaze enveloped her heart, healing and expanding it. And suddenly she couldn't hold back.

"I love you."

Traci's eyes widened.

"Whoa, was that the first 'I love you'?" Everett exclaimed loudly enough for the rest of the group to hear. Nicole had been so caught in their bubble she hadn't noticed Everett join them. "Claire, we got to be on their first date, and now we just witnessed the first 'I love you.'"

Nicole's face flamed hot, and she started to turn away from the others. But Traci caught her and pulled her into her arms. She kissed her gently, then with her mouth close to Nicole's ear, she said, "I love you, too."

Runt wiggled and whimpered at being pressed between their chests. Traci smiled and kissed his head. "We love you, too, little Runt."

HEALED

CHAPTER ONE

Jenna Teele opened her eyes to the peal of her alarm clock, though she suspected she'd been on the verge of wakefulness already. She tapped the button to silence the squeal and flopped over as if she had a prayer of going back to sleep. A twinge in her shoulder as she rolled onto it reminded her of why she had to get up today. It would be her first day back since being injured on the job—she needed to return to work strong.

She had to shove aside potentially debilitating memories of the moment when a man had intentionally driven his car into a crowded music festival. She'd been lucky enough to escape with a badly broken humerus, an injured shoulder, and a lot of bumps and scrapes. That's what she needed to focus on. After twelve laborious weeks of recovering from having her upper arm surgically put back together with plates and screws, she'd been cleared to return to work.

She forced herself out of bed, stretching and raising her arms just to prove she could. The right one didn't go all the way up, and the shoulder still felt stiff and swollen, but the doctor had said she could get back on the rig, and that's all she cared about.

A hot shower and a couple of Aleve should get her going. She'd weaned herself off the good drugs weeks ago, and not coincidentally, that was the last time she'd had a good night's sleep. She passed her roommate's closed door on her way to the hall bathroom. Daide had won the coin toss and got the bigger room with the ensuite, so technically her bath was for guests, too.

By the time she got out of the shower, Daide was in the kitchen.

She entered just as he slid two eggs onto a plate already loaded with bacon and two slices of toast.

"Disgustingly over-easy, just how you like them." He set the plate on the bar-height table that occupied the eat-in area near the French doors leading to the deck off the back of their house.

"You can't sop your toast in hard yolks, my friend," she said as she sat down.

"Thank God for that." Two more eggs, well-done, went onto his plate, and he took the chair across from her.

People often mistook them for siblings, especially since she'd been wearing her natural hair shorter, in a faux-hawk style. He kept his a little tighter on the sides and top than she did. They had similar skin tone and bone structure. But mostly their familiarity gave people who saw them interact the impression that they were close. From the first day they'd met, on the scene of a fatal motor-vehicle crash, they'd gotten along as if they'd known each other forever.

In those early days, they'd shared an apartment because they were both broke. But now they could each afford to live on their own. Yet Jenna just didn't want to. She liked having someone around sometimes when she came home. When she wasn't in the mood for company, Daide knew how to stay out of her way, and vice versa. Since they weren't broke anymore, they'd upgraded to a small house near the university several years ago. They talked about renting but ultimately wanted something they could work on together, so they purchased a bungalow, agreeing that when one of them wanted a change, they'd settle on a fair price to transfer ownership.

"What's the occasion?" She waved her hand over the plate, then picked up a slice of bacon and took a bite. "Not that I'm complaining."

"I figured since you were luxuriating in the shower, I might as well help you get a jump on the day—first one back and all."

"I couldn't force myself from under that hot water." She'd practically felt her muscles loosening as she let the stinging spray beat down on her shoulder, neck, and back.

"Forget it. I know what you do in your long showers, and it ain't that much different than what I do in there."

"Ew." She'd regretted her drunken confession about how much she enjoyed the massage setting on the handheld showerhead. And she didn't need a visual of what he might do either.

"Yeah. Eat your runny eggs and try not to think about that."

She grabbed her fork and powered through a bite, just to prove his attempt to gross her out had failed. Making a point of swallowing hard, she pointed her fork at him. "You just lost all your good karma for making this breakfast."

He chuckled, then sobered. "Seriously, I know today's going to be tough."

"Just another day, man." Even she didn't believe that.

"I've never been injured on the job, but—"

"I'm fine." She didn't want to wade through her feelings right now. She just wanted to get to the station and rediscover her work routine. Logging some miles in an ambulance next to her partner would be a step in the right direction. "Are you working today?"

"Yep. In fact, I need to jump in the shower and get ready." He picked up his plate and carried it with him toward his bedroom. "I'll have to finish this in there."

"You home tonight? I'll bring dinner." She heard his affirmative response as he closed the door behind him.

He worked eight-hour shifts as a police officer and was usually home before her twelve-hour-day had finished. So, often, he had dinner ready by the time she got there, but since he'd handled breakfast, she made the gesture. She didn't think she'd be up to cooking, but she'd grab his favorite takeout on the way home. His boyfriend had just been promoted to sergeant and pulled the second shift, so he and Daide could spend their evenings together only when their days off lined up.

Jenna rinsed her plate and put it in the dishwasher. She eyed the pot of coffee Daide had brewed earlier, then headed for her bedroom before she could give in to temptation. Before, she'd needed at least one cup in the morning to get going, but she'd given up caffeine while on medical leave. She'd like to go back to work without picking it up again, but the next couple of days would determine whether she could.

Getting dressed for work felt both familiar and foreign. She hadn't put on her uniform in three months, not since waking up in the hospital to find that doctors had cut her logoed polo shirt off her. After a quick check from a neurologist and a consult with an orthopedic surgeon, she'd been wheeled back for surgery to repair her arm and shoulder.

After three days in the hospital, she'd traded the cotton gown that opened in the back for T-shirts and sweats. That had been her uniform for the next three months, though even getting into a T-shirt was a challenge, and some days, she had to grab a button-down shirt for easier access.

She'd supplemented her required several days a week of physical therapy with stretching and exercises at home. Two weeks in, she'd suffered a setback her therapist blamed on her overdoing it in her haste to get back. After her doctor had threatened her with extra weeks off work if she didn't cooperate, she complied with his instructions and was happy to be getting back in uniform.

She tucked a pair of angled scissors into a pocket on the side of her navy BDU-style pants and pulled her gray polo over her head, then adjusted her collar. Socks, shoes, belt threaded through the loops— every piece of the uniform returned a layer of the old Jenna to the stripped-down version she'd become during these last several months.

The rain had just started when Candace Cooper parked her car behind Bellbrook Fire Station 2. She grabbed her backpack and darted inside the back door. After she stowed her bag in the locker room, she checked her reflection in a cheap, plastic-framed, full-length mirror fastened to the wall, re-tucking the hem of her polo shirt. She slipped a hair tie from her wrist and smoothed her strawberry-blond hair into a ponytail. She grabbed a lint roller from her locker and obsessively rolled it over her pants—even she had to admit the particles she sought to eradicate were probably invisible.

But her nerves had her searching for ways to occupy herself. She'd barely slept last night, and this morning she found herself awake well before her alarm. Rather than lie there, she'd gotten ready and arrived at work early. She still had thirty minutes until her shift started, and every one until Jenna entered would be excruciating.

Rather than sit around inside, she went to the vehicle bay and began a pre-shift inspection of the ambulance. The overnight crew had just returned from a call, and with luck, they wouldn't get another before swapping out with Candace and Jenna. Candace circled the outside of the ambulance, checking for any new dents or dings since her last shift. She didn't want the blame for damage that no one discovered until after her twelve-hour turn in the rig.

She opened the back doors and climbed inside, running a quick inventory of supplies and drugs.

"I bet you'll be happy to have your partner back today." EMS Chief Barb Warnke stood in the open doorway of the patient compartment. Warnke had been their chief since before Candace was hired. She was smart, fair, and intimidating as hell. At six foot two, she towered over Candace by more than six inches.

"You don't even know. I've been saddled with a dud for weeks." By her third shift with the floater, she'd been ready to break her own arm—or maybe his—to avoid working with him. He talked too much, thought he knew it all, and acted like politics kept him from realizing his full potential. He'd been thrilled to spend more than one shift in a row in one station and acted like he thought he could keep Jenna's spot even when she came back. Had he actually tried, he would have had to fight both Candace and Jenna for it.

"He wasn't that bad."

"He cut his fingernails in the rig—while I was driving—and one hit me in the cheek." If they hadn't been on the way to a call, she would have pulled over and left him on the side of the road.

"Teele's back, and since she never calls in sick, you don't have to worry about him ever again."

"Thank God."

"How she's doing? I visited her in the hospital, but after that she ducked most of my phone calls."

"Don't feel bad. She ignored a lot of mine, too. I could get her to reply to text, but if I wanted more than a one-word response, I had to drop by. Luckily, Daide conspired to let me in when she would've ignored the doorbell." She hopped down out of the rig just as a crowd of firefighters rounded the front of the engine. When Jenna had missed one of their regular gatherings with their friends, the five of them had shown up at her door with food and drinks. Jenna hadn't seemed thrilled at first, but she'd settled in and seemed to have a good time.

"Teele just pulled in. We thought we should all welcome her back," the captain on the engine said as he hit the button to roll up one of the big overhead doors.

"Great. She'll love that," Candace said sarcastically.

"Should we hide?" One of the rookies seemed way too excited by the idea.

They all turned toward the open bay door, searching expectantly for Jenna.

"Yes. Go get in the big tool compartment in the truck," Jenna said as she strolled into the vehicle bay from the other direction, coming up behind them. "I'll try to control the urge to lock you in."

Candace hung back as, with a chorus of welcomes and cheers, they descended on Jenna, some hugging and some just bumping fists or offering a high five. After the crowd had dispersed, Candace held out a hand to Jenna, offering a handshake.

"Welcome back, partner. You have no idea how happy I am to say that." She hoped her voice sounded more even than the tremors she felt inside. She'd complained to Jenna about her substitute a couple of times but had tried to limit her bitch sessions, to avoid throwing a guilt trip on Jenna.

"Happy to be here. I've been bored as hell the last couple of weeks."

"How's the arm?"

"Ready to go." Just as Jenna spoke, the alert tones sounded over their radios, and the dispatcher announced a report of someone having chest pains.

"Ask and you shall receive."

Candace climbed behind the wheel of the ambulance, and as the bay door rolled up, she took a second to appreciate Jenna sitting in the seat next to her. She flipped on the lights and siren as she eased onto the street, waiting for a couple of slow-to-react drivers.

"Get the hell out of the way." Candace tapped her fingers against the wheel.

"Idiot drivers."

When Candace glanced over at her, Jenna winked. The flutter in Candace's stomach shouldn't have taken her by surprise. They'd been partnered together for three years, and she'd been feeling that weightlessness when Jenna looked at her since six months in. She'd almost told her several times during the ensuing year, but she'd chickened out. She liked working with Jenna and had been through four previous nightmare pairings on the rig. Jeopardizing their partnership wasn't a risk she wanted to take, so she'd learned to absorb her feelings and turn them into the most amazing friendship she'd ever had.

CHAPTER TWO

Butterflies fluttered in Jenna's stomach as they rolled into the apartment complex where their patient lived. Of course, she hadn't forgotten her training in twelve weeks, so she shouldn't be nervous. She fought the urge to roll her right shoulder, a habit she'd developed when it was injured as the small stretches helped it stay loose. But now she didn't want to draw questions from Candace.

Candace had been an amazing friend during Jenna's convalescence, when she hadn't been completely annoying. The first couple of days home from the hospital, Candace had helped her get in and out of the shower, once Jenna had conquered her discomfort. It wasn't like they hadn't seen each other practically naked in the locker room at work. But somehow the act of having someone help you undress in your own private bathroom felt much more intimate. Candace seemed as— embarrassed wasn't the right word—maybe thrown off by the whole experience as she was. She'd drawn the line at asking Candace to get in and help her wash her hair, and had done the best she could one-handed. Then after she got out, she let Candace help her moisturize it. It wasn't as if she were going out in public trying to impress anyone anyway.

Jenna had wanted to focus on her physical recovery and ignore all the emotional shit. But after the first couple of days, Candace kept trying to get her to talk about it. That's why she'd started ignoring her calls. When Candace had called her on it, she'd just say her pain pills made her sleep a lot.

Those pills had been a godsend for the first several weeks. In fact, she wouldn't have been able to get through those days after the surgery without them. As a paramedic, she'd always known how dependency worked, but experiencing the relief from that level of pain brought a new understanding. After about three weeks, she'd weaned herself down to taking the pills only before bed. She needed to be clear about how much pain she was feeling if she wanted to return within the minimum time set by her doctors.

"Jenna."

She blinked and found Candace standing outside the rig with the jump bag over her shoulder and the cardiac monitor in her other hand.

"Where were you?"

"Sorry." She shoved open her door and hopped down.

As they headed for the building, she grabbed the monitor in her good hand and followed her up the walk.

"You okay?"

"Yeah. What apartment was it again?"

"Three-oh-six."

"Ugh. Third floor." They entered the breezeway and started up the metal stairs. "We're going to need the stair chair."

"Let's see what we've got. Then one of us can run back for it."

Jenna grunted her approval, growing winded as they approached the third-floor landing. Depending on how large the patient was, they might have to call for some firefighters to come help get him down the stairs.

Candace raised her fist to knock on the door to 306, but it swung open before she hit it. A short, plump woman holding a cell phone up to her ear filled the doorway. She ran her free hand through the front of her hair, pulling at it until it stuck up.

"Yes, they're finally here," she said into the phone before disconnecting. "9-1-1 said they'd stay on the phone with me. But I bet they didn't know how long it would be."

Jenna tensed, and Candace rested a hand on her back, saying, "Ma'am, can you show us to the patient?"

Candace was far more even-tempered than she was. Jenna got her short fuse from her mother, whose explosive temper had intimidated both Jenna and her younger sister when they were growing up.

"He's back here in the bedroom."

They followed her down the short hallway and found a red-faced man half reclined in bed. He was conscious, but diaphoretic and breathing hard. Candace dropped to one knee next to the bed, on the side closest to where he was, and began taking his vitals while Jenna set up the cardiac monitor.

While Candace ran the cardiac strip, Jenna returned to the rig for the stair chair. The guy was in his seventies and had a wiry frame that had gone frail from various health issues. His wife said that he'd had cardiac issues since his fifties, when he'd been thirty pounds heavier. She and Candace shouldn't have any problem getting him down the stairs themselves.

She grabbed the chair and hurried back up. When she reached the top again, she paused, disguising her need to catch her breath by taking the time to unfold the chair, which was basically like a hand truck with a seat on it for transporting patients.

By the time she returned, Candace had him ready to go. They got him into the chair and secured for the ride down the stairs. Jenna grabbed for the handles on the back of the chair, but Candace stopped her with a hand on her arm.

"I got this."

"I can do it."

Candace simply shook her head. "That's three stories. No need to put your shoulder through that so soon."

The person on the back of the chair controlled the descent as the chair rolled carefully over each stair tread, while the person in front steadied and took some of the weight as needed. Despite their patient's stature, by the time they reached the bottom, Candace's face was flushed, and Jenna knew Candace had made the right call. Her shoulder would have been burning had she been in Candace's place.

When they reached the rig and got the patient loaded, Candace jumped into the back, leaving Jenna to drive. That was fine. They usually took turns in the back anyway, but she'd kind of been looking forward to losing herself in patient care on her first day back.

❖

"You don't have to baby me, you know. I got clearance to come back. I'm fine."

"I wasn't—"

"Don't even. I'm not talking about the stair chair."

"Then what?"

"Jumping in with the patient and letting me drive. You're the one who exerted yourself coming down the stairs. I could have handled patient care."

Candace shrugged. "We usually split anyway."

"Okay. So, I get the next one?"

"Sure."

They got their second run of the shift just as they were leaving the hospital. A passing pedestrian called in about a person who appeared under the influence of some type of controlled substance. The patient had been yelling at others on the street, tried to start a physical altercation, and pulled a pocketknife on a business owner who attempted to intervene. Police were called, and when they got on scene, the guy said he needed to go to the hospital because he was having trouble breathing.

As they rolled up, one of the police officers approached the ambulance. Jenna hopped out of the driver's seat.

"Hey, it's Officer Sam." Jenna grinned as Traci Sam lifted her chin in greeting.

Sam was part of her circle of friends, and Jenna had missed seeing her when they all got together. She'd been making excuses not to hang out because she didn't want to talk about her injury or the day of the festival. She'd heard after she woke up in the hospital that Sam had been there as well. In fact, she'd met her current girlfriend at the scene when they'd helped an injured boy only feet from where Jenna lay unconscious.

"How are you feeling?"

"Perfect. Glad to be back." She glanced at the patient, who was sitting on the curb and seemed to be breathing just fine on his own. "You got me a welcome-back gift?" Candace had already grabbed the jump bag and was on her way over to the patient.

"He's got that disorder where hearing the word 'jail' makes him short of breath."

"It's common and contagious, my friend. I think the beds in the hospital are softer than the ones at the jail."

"That's probably it." Sam touched Jenna's good shoulder as she passed on her way to help Candace with their assessment. "Now that you're back, are you planning to stop ducking our monthly bowling nights?"

"Not sure the shoulder is up to bowling yet." Jenna rolled it gently, as if that somehow demonstrated the strain swinging a bowling ball would put on it.

"You don't have to. Just come hang out. We miss you." Sam followed her over to the patient.

"I'll think about it."

"Do that. Plus, I want you to get to know Nicole better."

Jenna nodded, but her attention was already shifting to the guy on the curb, handcuffed behind his back. His long hair fell across his face and he twitched his head, but it swept aside and landed right back. His eyes jerked from side to side, and he flinched as if some figment of his imagination had darted at him.

"They started it." His voice was hoarse, no doubt from the yelling he'd been doing when they rolled up. Jenna didn't ask who "they" were.

"He's stable," Candace said, unnecessarily, as she glanced over her shoulder at Jenna.

"Good." Jenna looked at Sam. "Are you riding along?"

Sam nodded. "He's in custody."

"Okay. Get him up. Let's go."

Sam grabbed the guy's upper arm and helped him to his feet. His shoes were missing the laces altogether. And Jenna didn't know if the sheen of sweat on his face was due to whatever drugs he was on or to the wool trench coat he wore.

Sam led him to the ambulance and guided him up to sit on the stretcher. When Candace put one foot up on the back step, Jenna touched her elbow.

"My turn."

"I don't mind. I know you hate dealing with the high ones."

She did. But she shook her head and repeated, "My turn."

As Jenna climbed in, Candace shut the door behind her. The box that was the patient-care area of the ambulance quickly filled with the sour scent of body odor, and she wrinkled her nose. Damn her need to prove herself. She should have let Candace take this one.

"I don't want to go." Her patient rolled his head against the back of the stretcher.

"Yeah?" Sam said from her spot on the bench next to him. "We can get you back out and take you to booking instead."

Candace had just climbed into the driver's seat. She glanced over her shoulder through the opening between the cab and patient compartment, waiting for the go-ahead to start driving. They didn't take people to the hospital against their will.

"No." He drew out the *o*'s.

"All right. Keep quiet then until we get to the hospital." Sam gave Candace a circular signal with her index finger, indicating she could take off.

Candace pulled into downtown traffic, then headed for the loop around the main campus that led to University Hospital. Their patient wasn't in distress, so the lights and sirens remained silent during transport. Jenna checked his vitals again, breathing shallowly through her mouth when she had to bend too close to him.

When they rolled up to the emergency-department doors, he tried to stand up, but Jenna put a hand on his shoulder and held him in place.

"Nope. You get to ride in on this end of the trip." By the time she stepped out of the ambulance, Candace had come around from the front and moved in to grab the stretcher release.

"Sam, help me out with this."

Before Jenna could protest, Sam and Candace had the stretcher out and the wheels dropped and were rolling him into the ED. Jenna grabbed the tablet and followed them, already planning Candace's lecture for when they were alone in the rig again. She'd sent the pre-hospital report through via the tablet just before they rolled up. About a year ago, University had wanted FD to make the switch to electronic run sheets, because their shiny new patient-care system had a module that would interface with them. FD claimed the city budget wouldn't cover it, and after some back-and-forth the university came up with some grant money, no doubt from a generous alumni donor, which made the project more affordable. Jenna hadn't minded the old paper-and-pen method, but she had to admit, this system was faster, both for relaying information to the hospital and for billing. It also had improved the continuity of patient records exponentially.

She trailed along behind the stretcher until a nurse and a PA met them and directed them to an exam area, and then she consulted the tablet and recited the last set of vitals. Despite sending the run sheet ahead, they still did a verbal hand-off so that no new, last-minute information could be missed.

Jenna grabbed for a corner of the sheet to assist in transferring the patient to the ED stretcher, but Sam had already gathered it up in her hand. She and Candace helped the medical staff move him, then maneuvered the stretcher out of the room. Candace headed for the paramedic workroom, little more than a supply closet, with enough space for the stretcher and two people. Sam had stayed with the patient, so Jenna followed Candace inside.

She dropped down into a chair at a computer workstation, unlocked the tablet she still carried, and clicked through several options to complete their portion of the patient care on the case. As she did, Candace stripped the stretcher and tossed the old linens into a laundry bin. She sprayed the vinyl mattress with disinfectant, then wiped it dry. Jenna finished, letting her passivity convey her mood as she watched Candace unfurl a new sheet and fold it smoothly over the corners.

"What lengths are you willing to go to, to make sure I don't have to do any actual work?"

"What?" Candace continued working and didn't meet Jenna's eyes, a sure sign she knew exactly what she was referring to. Candace was big on eye contact while having a conversation, except when one of them was driving. Then she got mad if Jenna took her eyes off the road too often.

"Are you going to work my overtime shifts with me, too?" She regretted her question as soon as she'd spoken. She'd talked Candace into working in the first-aid tent with her the day of the festival. Candace didn't need the money; she lived frugally. But Jenna had convinced her because she wanted the company, asking her how often she could get a free soundtrack for her life. Candace had checked out the festival lineup and decided to sign up, too.

"You don't need to work overtime yet."

"You know I'm helping Mom pay for Aliyah's living expenses." Jenna's sister was smart—smarter than Jenna. So when she'd expressed an interest in medicine, Jenna had promised to help her pay for her expenses while she got her undergrad degree so she could concentrate on getting into a great medical school and not have to work.

"I'm aware." Candace never liked that Jenna worked as hard as she did to spare her sister from having to struggle. But Jenna's mother had taken on two jobs to send them to private school growing up. And now she wanted to give her mother that break and help Aliyah along. "I thought they could figure out how to cover it themselves while you're injured. You were unconscious, for Christ's sake." Candace's language was always a good barometer for how irritated or angry she was. When she started throwing out F-bombs—look out.

"How many different ways do I need to say that the doctor cleared me?"

"I'm just worried about you."

"Well, don't be." She hadn't meant to sound so snappish. Candace had been right next to Jenna when that car hit her and was lucky she hadn't been hurt as well. And Jenna had to remind herself that she might also carry some emotional and mental effects from that day. She sighed. "I know that was a tough day for you, too. But I'm really okay. And I just want to move past it."

Candace nodded and turned away, pushing the stretcher out of the room. Jenna wished she'd been able to read her expression. She grabbed her tablet and headed for the ambulance. Hell, that was only run number two. They still had more than half their shift left, and the afternoon portion was sometimes the busiest.

CHAPTER THREE

Medic Two, you're responding with PD to an assault at the Bell Bar and Grill. The complainant advises that four to five people are involved, and several parties are ETOH."

"Corporate lunch?" Jenna guessed.

Candace shook her head. "Baby shower."

Jenna laughed, and Candace's heart lifted with the sound. Jenna wasn't one of those women who laughed all the time—like everything was funny even though it wasn't. So when she did, something was humorous enough or witty enough to tickle her.

But when they walked into the restaurant, gear in hand, she wondered if she hadn't been right. Six women crowded around a table, all raising their voices to be heard over one another. One woman already had a trickle of blood running down her chin and a rapidly swelling lip. She was obviously the patient, but if the officer didn't get here soon, there would be more.

"Hey, let's break this up," Jenna said.

"Or we could wait for the police."

Candace barely got the words out before one of the women reared back and punched the other one in the face. The victim spun around, hit the wall, and slid to the ground. She might not have felt that last impact though, because Candace thought she was unconscious before she landed.

The assailant pulled her foot back for a kick while the other woman was down. Jenna leapt into the space between them and grasped the woman by the shoulders, but the woman resisted. Her hands shot out, and she locked her elbows with the force of a shove that sent Jenna flying back against the same wall that had injured her last victim. The impact obviously caught Jenna off guard. Candace imagined she could hear Jenna's breath leave her body on a whoosh, but of course she couldn't have really heard it over the noise of the other women shouting.

"Shit." Jenna pushed off the wall, which only put her face-to-face with the woman again.

"You want some more?" The woman stood up straighter and pumped her fists in Jenna's direction.

If the woman hadn't looked so angry, Candace might have laughed. Instead, she held up her hands in surrender as she moved between the woman and Jenna. "I just want to check on this lady." She pointed at the victim at her feet, who was starting to come around.

"She's fine." The slurred response didn't instill confidence.

Just when Candace was deciding whether to take this woman on, too, two police officers showed up. Candace glanced at them and almost laughed. It was as if dispatch had sent the tallest, burliest men they had, because even the woman ready to fight a moment ago looked like she knew better than to mess with these guys.

While one guy put the suspect in cuffs, Candace dropped into a squat to check on her patient. They'd need the backboard for this woman, but the one with the fat lip could ride along, so they wouldn't have to call for another unit. She glanced over her shoulder, seeking Jenna's gaze. But Jenna had closed her eyes and slumped back against the wall, holding her bad shoulder in her opposite hand. Her face had gone pale, and she looked like she was in a lot of pain.

Remembering how Jenna had reacted at the last two scenes, Candace didn't say a word, even though everything in her screamed to check on her. Instead she said, "You got the jump bag?"

Jenna straightened and handed it over; then, after a moment, she crouched next to Candace. Together, they assessed their patient and loaded everyone into the ambulance. Candace went directly to the driver's seat, letting Jenna have the back.

But once more at the hospital, after they'd handed off both women to medical staff, she couldn't stay silent any longer.

"Do you want to get that shoulder checked out before we leave?" she asked as they both spread a sheet over the stretcher in the workroom.

"Nope."

Candace shook her head and turned away. She hated how much she cared about Jenna. The incident at the festival had driven home to her just how fragile time is. And she yearned to tell Jenna how she felt, now more than ever. But Jenna's inability to let her in told her everything she needed to know about how well a confession about her feelings would be received. Jenna didn't even do relationships; she only got involved with women casually. To admit her crush—because she refused to call unreciprocated feelings love—could irreparably damage their friendship.

"Come on, Candy."

"Don't fucking call me that." She hated that name, and Jenna knew it. No one but her mother called her Candy. Jenna used it only when she wanted to get a rise out of her, but Candace was usually better at letting it slide by.

Jenna didn't respond, knowing when to let her be. In fact, neither of them spoke on the way back to the station, and once they got there, they separated. Candace went to hang out with the guys from the engine, and Jenna went to the weight room, daring Candace to say she shouldn't be lifting weights. And though she managed to control the urge, she did hope Jenna was smart enough not to injure herself out of spite.

Jenna shoved open her front door with her good shoulder, balancing her duffel bag in the crook of her elbow and a paper bag of takeout Thai food in her hand. She went to the kitchen first and placed the food on the counter. Then she grabbed a beer out of the fridge and headed for her bedroom to drop her gear bag.

When she returned to the kitchen, Daide was already there peeking into the bag of food. Seeing how comfortable he looked in his sweatpants and T-shirt, she couldn't wait to get out of her uniform.

"Rough first shift back?"

She nodded. "How'd you know?"

He glanced at the beer bottle in her hand. "Because you work tomorrow. And you never drink on a school night. Do you want to tell me about it over dinner?"

"I really need a shower first."

"Go. This will stay warm, and if not, Thai reheats."

"Don't wait for me."

He grabbed two plates out of the cabinet. "Okay. I'll meet you out back."

She left him opening cartons and filling his own plate while she ran back to the bathroom for a quick shower. She never felt like she could settle in until she'd washed away the grime of being on the streets and in and out of the hospital. When she was on shift, her multi-shower days could really dry out her skin, so she took the time to moisturize after she toweled off.

By the time she fixed herself a plate and wandered, barefoot, out to the back deck, Daide had finished half his dinner. He was the youngest of five kids, so he'd learned early to eat fast if he wanted his fair share. He waited until she got settled at the patio table across from him to make a "go ahead" motion with his fork. She picked up her own fork and took a big bite of noodles, then gestured as if to say she couldn't say anything with her mouth full.

After he'd let her eat in peace for a few minutes, she started talking. "It was just a long day. Candace kept trying to do my job for me, or make Sam do it. And I just want to act like everything's normal again."

"Were you in pain?"

"Not really. Maybe when that woman shoved me against a wall, but just while I was working, no." She rotated her shoulder forward, tensing as she remembered the jolt of pain the impact of the heel of the woman's hand had caused.

"What woman? A patient?"

"The woman who assaulted my patient."

"Let me guess, you stepped between her and the patient."

She shrugged. "That's my job."

"No, ma'am. That's *my* job."

"You weren't there."

"Was that the fight outside the bar this evening? I heard that go out over the radio. Officers were on the way, and you could have waited for them. It was a little early for a drunken brawl, wasn't it?"

"Nobody told these ladies that. I think they had an early happy hour."

"Candace will be all right. She just needs some time to see that you're okay."

"It's not like she hasn't seen me during these three months. She knows how seriously I took my recovery."

Daide bit his lip and returned his attention to his plate.

"What?"

"You should have seen her at the hospital. She was a mess, and that was hours later, when I got there and you were in surgery." Candace had called Daide shortly after Jenna had gotten to the hospital, but he'd been out of town visiting his family that day, which was why he didn't get dispatched to the festival when it all went down. He immediately made the two-hour drive home, then came to the hospital right away.

"Okay. But, Daide. Three months ago."

"Have you put yourself in her place?"

"Hm. She got to get up the next day and keep going to work like nothing had happened. Is that what you mean?" She couldn't keep the sarcasm from her tone. Some days, especially in the hospital, she'd thought about how unfair it was that all her friends came out of that day feeling like they'd helped in the face of tragedy, but she wound up feeling helpless. Hell, even Sam's new girlfriend had apparently saved some boy's life.

"Is that really what you think? That she went on like nothing happened?"

"Yeah. While I had to sleep with that damn sling on every night." For weeks she'd been unable to get comfortable. If she didn't stuff the pillows under her sling just right she'd wake up in agonizing pain.

"Candace was lying on the ground next to you when Nicole found you both. Yeah, she wasn't hurt, and she came around quickly. And then she stayed with you, insisted on riding with you to the hospital. She wouldn't talk to any of us—just sat by your bed. And even when you came home, she called me every day to check on you. Of course, since you stopped answering her calls, she had to."

"What's your point? That was all weeks ago."

"My point is, this is an adjustment period for her, too—having you back at work and wanting to make sure you really are okay. So take it easy on her, because that day didn't happen to just you." He stood and picked up his plate. "Just think about it."

He took her empty plate and went inside. She slouched in her chair, her good arm against the armrest and her bad one bent and cradled against her stomach. She'd started sitting like that out of habit when her arm was in the sling, then later to take some of the weight off it rather than just have it hang. Funny how just the force of gravity could cause her pain.

She slapped a mosquito that landed on her arm. The night air had started to cool, and she wanted to stay out a bit longer. Grabbing a lighter off the table, she lit several glass citronella-oil torches around the railing of the deck. She and Daide had built this deck themselves, after tearing off the old, rotted one. This main fifteen-by-twelve foot platform stepped down to a concrete pad they'd had poured to hold the five-person hot tub Daide insisted on when they bought the house.

This day didn't happen to just you. She'd been focused on herself—she'd needed to be in order to reach this place. And she'd expected Candace to be there—to be the friend she needed—to support her when she struggled. But had she been the same for Candace in return? How long had it been since she'd asked Candace how she was doing—if she was okay?

She picked up her phone off the table, ready to send a text to Candace, then decided against it. She'd talk to her tomorrow. Instead, she grabbed her beer and sat on the deck steps looking out over their small yard, enclosed by a horizontal-slat privacy fence. You'd think after three months at home, she'd be tired of this view, but this was her happy place. Their house represented everything she'd accomplished. Being able to carve out this piece of the world and also help her sister move closer to her goal gave her the biggest feeling of accomplishment possible.

But tonight, she needed to think about focusing less on herself and more on her friends. So she sipped her beer, determined to limit herself to one. Daide didn't come back. After night fell, she went inside to get ready for bed.

CHAPTER FOUR

*T*he squeal of a siren pierced Jenna's already pounding head. She tried to open her eyes—but something was wrong. A haze covered her vision, and her eyes burned. She raised her arm to rub her face, and pain blasted through her right shoulder. She clamped her jaw against her scream, but a strangled grunt escaped.

"Hold still for a sec." The brusque voice didn't wait for agreement before she felt a pinch and then a sting near the inside of her elbow. She logged the sensation as an IV insertion.

She lay on her back on a stretcher. The IV. The chatter of a radio in the background. And a smell—or combination of smells—she couldn't exactly name but knew better than almost any. It all added up to the back of an ambulance. But why was she on the stretcher instead of leaning over it? The back door clicked open.

"I'm riding with her." The door swung shut before anyone inside could argue. The familiar voice washed over her, and she imagined she could hear the racing beeps of her heartbeat slow on the monitor somewhere nearby.

"Candace." In her mind her voice was louder, but she managed to get enough out to alert Candace to her consciousness.

"I'm here, Jenna." After a rustle of movement, Candace grabbed her hand.

"Let's go." The no-nonsense voice—a paramedic, maybe—was back. The ambulance started to move.

"I can't see." Through the blur of shapes and light, she made out the shape of a person leaning closer at her side. She made another

attempt to swipe at her face, this time with her uninjured arm, but Candace held fast to her hand.

"I know. You're kind of a mess right now. We're going to get you to a hospital. Can I at least have something to clean her face off?"

That last part wasn't meant for her. She'd just heard the mumbled response from the paramedic, when she felt something damp against her face. Gauze? Maybe.

"What?" She wanted to ask what was on her face, but she had to fight against the weight that tried to pull her brain away and couldn't get it all out. Shadows invaded the edges of her vision.

The paramedic spoke again, and a voice crackled through a radio speaker. She tried to hold on to the staccato rhythm of vitals being recited—her vitals being relayed to a nurse at a hospital. What were they? If she could make them out, she could figure out how serious this was. But she'd already missed them, and panic was edging into her muddled brain. The darkness was back, and it wouldn't stay in the periphery. As she faded, she felt Candace's hand tighten against hers.

Jenna jerked awake, sitting up quickly, then flinching as the movement tightened her shoulder. She rubbed a hand over her face. She hadn't had a dream like that in weeks. Her drunk assailant had aggravated her physical injury and no doubt dredged up a bit of the psychological trauma as well.

In her dream—more a memory, really—Candace had been a calming influence. Other than the pain, Candace's hand in hers was her most visceral memory from that day. Before this had happened she would have said that Candace was the only person she was okay with seeing her that vulnerable. But after yesterday, she wasn't so sure. Candace's memory seemed frozen on that image of her in the hospital bed. And Jenna needed her to be the one to see her strength.

She glanced at the clock. She hadn't missed getting up this early. She didn't want another day like yesterday. A small part of her contemplated calling in sick. Chief Warnke would probably chalk it up to her injury whether she said that was the reason or not. But she dragged herself out of bed, knowing she wouldn't be making that call.

Somehow she managed to pass up Daide's pot of fresh-brewed coffee again. In fact, she avoided the kitchen altogether. She'd grab a granola bar and an apple when she got to work.

❖

Candace pulled the handle on the coffee urn that dispensed only hot water, letting it stream into her oatmeal. As she walked to the long, industrial dining table, she stirred her breakfast, the scent of apples and cinnamon wafting up. She sat down and pulled the bowl close, sinking her spoon into the perfect texture of oats. Jenna would hate it. Oatmeal grossed her out. She said it tasted like paste. When Candace recited the flavors she loved, Jenna said that apple-flavored paste was still gross.

Three guys from Engine 2 slid into the chairs across from her, their plates loaded with the bacon and eggs one of them had cooked.

"Want some bacon, Cooper? There's plenty left."

"No thanks."

"You gotta get your protein to make it through the day."

She smiled. "Oatmeal has plenty of protein. And I need my carbs to keep up with Jenna."

"Speak of the devil." One of the guys raised his chin, gesturing behind Candace. She glanced over her shoulder. Jenna strode in from the direction of the front door.

"Hey, Teele. Bacon and eggs?"

"Nope." She sketched a wave in their direction as she passed through the living area and kept going. She headed for the ambulance bay, Candace assumed to do the supply inventory for their shift. Normally, Candace would join her, but she seemed to want some space from everyone.

"Man, what's her deal lately?"

Candace didn't respond, determined not to get involved in this conversation.

"Yo, Cooper. What's up with your partner?"

"Yeah. Why's she being antisocial?"

"She's fine." Candace unlocked her phone and opened a game, hoping they'd get the hint she didn't want to talk about Jenna.

She finished her breakfast, washed her bowl, and headed for the bunkroom. She hadn't slept very well. She wouldn't admit it to Jenna, but worry had kept her restless through the night—through most nights since the festival. She'd never experienced so many layers of anxiety in her life.

On a larger scale, she worried about a society where no one was really very surprised when someone targeted a crowd of people. She'd heard the guy's attorney was claiming he was mentally ill. And who wouldn't believe that? You'd have to be in order to drive your car into a music festival. But Candace wanted him in prison, and nothing less felt like justice.

The reality of that day brought home the truth that nothing was off the table. Police officers ran into danger, so she was used to being concerned about Sam and her colleagues. But firefighters and paramedics were everybody's heroes. Living in a world where that fact was no longer true made her uncomfortable.

For the past three months, she'd stressed about Jenna, on a personal level. Jenna filled her in on what the doctors said. She'd joked about how hot her physical therapist was and bragged about how she'd done more reps of her exercises than she had the previous day. But if Candace didn't know any better, she could have been recovering from a fall, or some random sports injury. She acted as if the psychological aspect of what they'd gone through didn't exist.

Alone in the bunkroom, Candace sat on one of the beds and allowed herself a rare return to that day. She didn't do it often because it amplified her stress too much.

She'd slumped in a chair in an otherwise empty hospital waiting room. After Jenna had been taken to surgery, a nurse had led Candace from the emergency-department waiting room to the med-surg floor. She'd been handed off to the woman who would be Jenna's nurse after she came out of recovery. Jenna would be admitted and spend at least one night in the hospital.

Candace's phone buzzed in her hand, and she glanced at it but didn't unlock the screen. She'd tried answering the texts from friends and coworkers at first, then abandoned her feeling of obligation to keep everyone posted about Jenna's condition. Several fellow paramedics and a few firefighters had stopped by after shift. But most of them had come from the mass-casualty scene and were as worn out as she was, so she'd sent them home. Only a couple had argued that she shouldn't have to wait alone. Then, when she assured them she'd be fine, they'd insisted she get some coffee before they left. She glanced at the Styrofoam cup sitting on the table near the window. Her stomach couldn't handle drinking it, and she'd let it go cold long ago.

For hours, she alternated between sitting in that chair and pacing to the window to stare aimlessly at the view of the roof of the adjoining building. She'd tortured herself trying to build a clear recall of the moments before the accident. After responding to countless tragic scenes in her career and hearing her patients say "it all happened so fast," she now understood what they meant.

She and Jenna had spent that morning working in the first-aid tent inside the music festival, one of the largest events every year in Bellbrook, treating victims of excessive heat, alcohol overindulgence, and the occasional cuts and bruises. Two medics had relieved them to go grab something to eat and walk around the grounds for a few minutes. She and Jenna had browsed a few artisan tents but hadn't made it to the food vendors.

In hindsight, she'd registered the rev of an engine as they walked through the open grassy area where music fans gathered in preparation for the next act. But she hadn't found the sound any more alarming than the occasional whine of a sport motorcycle or rumble of exhaust from a large pickup truck. Then the sounds of crashing and screaming had melded together and roared toward her like a freight train, but she couldn't see the tracks and had no idea from which direction the noise came. The next thing she remembered was being flung through the air and skidding, then tumbling across the grass.

The sensation of lying facedown and staring at a car crashed into one of the huge event tents was so vivid that her heart started to race again. As she'd rolled over and sat up, she'd braced for pain, thinking that the car must have hit her and flung her to the ground. But she'd felt only what would probably amount to a bruise on her hip and a twinge in her wrist.

That bruise had faded inside of a week, and her wrist hadn't even required a follow-up check from a doctor. She closed her eyes and tried to visualize something besides that moment, but her mind wouldn't clear of the fear and panic. She heard the screams of those around her and the exclamations as the crowd practically stampeded away from the area.

"Candy!"

Candace jerked back to the bunkroom, her arms stiff and hands pressed into the mattress at her side. She glared at Jenna for using the hated nickname.

"Well, I called you Candace and Cooper, and you didn't respond to either."

She forcibly relaxed her hands, uncurling them from the sheet she'd had a death grip on. "Did I miss a call?"

"No." When Jenna sat on the bed next to her, she wanted to scoot away or stand up, anything to put some space between them. She was too close to the moment she'd just relived to have Jenna this near. "I'm sorry if I was a bit of a bitch yesterday. I expected my first day back to go a little more smoothly."

"Give yourself a break."

"I can't." Jenna wrung her hands together. "We don't exactly work in a business that allows for distraction. I need to be as much on my game as the next guy—as you are—so no one else gets hurt."

Candace laughed bitterly.

"What?"

"If I learned anything after the festival, it's that we have zero control over whether people get hurt."

"You know what I mean. I can't be thinking about anything except our patient when we're on a call."

"That's nice to say. But can you do it?"

Jenna stood and took a few quick steps away. "Are you doubting me?"

"Maybe I'm doubting myself."

Jenna leaned against a cubicle-type wall that separated the beds. Her expression shifted to concern—her eyes softening and darkening. "I'm sorry. I haven't been a good friend lately."

"You basically took a car to the chest for me. I'm not sure how I'd find a better friend than that."

"No. I should have checked on you after—" Jenna stopped talking as Candace's words registered. "What?"

"You pushed me out of the way."

"I did?"

"You really don't remember?"

Jenna rubbed two fingers and a thumb against her forehead and squeezed her eyes shut as if this conversation was giving her a headache. Maybe she shouldn't push her.

"Bits and pieces, and I think it's still coming to me. But I may never completely recover those minutes before the accident."

"It wasn't an accident." Candace surged to her feet, suddenly finding a focal point for her anger.

"What?"

"Everyone keeps calling it an accident. But it wasn't, was it? Some maniac *purposely* drove his car into a crowd of people. There was nothing accidental about it. He wanted to hurt or kill as many people as he could. And you're such a goddamned hero you had to risk your life pushing me out of the way. I almost—" She coughed to cover the sob that surged up in her throat. She buried the words *I almost lost you* because they felt too personal—too vulnerable. "You could have died."

She shouldn't have looked at Jenna in the moment. Then she wouldn't have had to see her stricken expression. "Candace." Jenna crossed toward her, and she backed up until she hit the edge of the bed.

"I'm sorry. I shouldn't have said all of that. I—"

"Hey." Jenna grasped her shoulders, and Candace had to look away from the pain in Jenna's eyes. "I'm still here."

"I know that."

"Maybe you think what I did was foolish—"

"It was stupid, downright idiotic, even."

"A minute ago you thought I was heroic." Jenna smiled and, damn her, it was a cute smile.

Candace shook her head, both in disagreement and to dispel her growing forgiveness. "I said you were a goddamned hero. That's different. Don't you get sarcasm?"

"Regardless. It's done. It's over. He's locked up. And we're still here. We're going to be okay."

"You can't know that." The layers of uncertainty echoed back, covered in the scary reality that not just their lives but their relationship might be changed permanently.

Jenna stared at her, and she saw the moment Jenna understood her fear. "No, I can't. Not for sure. But I hope we are. And I'd like to think whatever happens, we'll get through it just like we did that day. Together." Jenna stroked her hands down Candace's arms and caught her hands.

Jenna's confidence was contagious, and Candace wanted to believe her. They could come out on the other side of all this even stronger. That's what friends did, right? And that's what Jenna was talking about when she said *together.* She was talking about their friendship, the veneer of which covered Candace's deeper feelings. Jenna wanted to reassure her that they were a team in whatever this was. But the reminder that they hadn't really been on the same page even before the festival had Candace falling back into self-preservation mode. She pulled her hands free and stepped away.

"You're right. We'll be fine."

"If you need to talk about what happened at the festival—"

"What, now you want to talk?"

"*Want to* is a strong way to say it." Jenna smiled. "I was going to say, I'm sure Claire would be up for talking. She's into being all touchy-feely." She was joking, of course. "I want to be here for you, Candace."

She closed her eyes against the soft way Jenna said her name. She'd always been able to melt Candace when she did that. And, damn it, she didn't even know it. If Jenna ever caught on to the effect she had on her, she wouldn't stand a chance.

Just then, alert tones sounded over the station speaker, and their unit number was called. Candace stopped herself from muttering, *saved by the bell*. But that's what she felt. Their conversation had been drifting dangerously close to the truth.

"We should go," Candace said.

Jenna looked at her for a moment longer as if trying to figure out a puzzle. "Yeah. We don't want any of the guys coming in and hearing us getting all mushy."

CHAPTER FIVE

H ey, Ito. How's it going?" Jenna called as she hopped out of the rig.
"My head hurts."

Ito had been part of the Bellbrook homeless community for longer than Jenna had been a paramedic. Over the years, and a number of trips to the hospital, Jenna had learned that he was a second-generation army veteran. His American father had met his Japanese mother when he was stationed in Okinawa during the Vietnam War.

He used to claim some other aches and pains, but Jenna suspected he'd learned the hospital would often keep him overnight for some priority symptoms. If he claimed severe headaches, or chest pain, even if the hospital suspected he made them up, they would sometimes monitor him overnight out of an abundance of caution. The last thing they wanted was a lawsuit for putting someone back on the street the one time his symptoms were real and having him die.

Chief Warnke's department SUV came to a stop behind the ambulance.

"What's she doing here?" Jenna asked.

Candace shrugged. "I heard she's been working on a proposal to cut down on repeat calls."

Jenna heard the words "frequent flyer," even if Candace didn't say them. These types of calls had been Warnke's pet peeve when she was on an ambulance, and she'd talked for a couple of years now about paring them down. Jenna thought she was taking on a losing cause.

"Okay, buddy." Jenna took his arm. "Let's get you into the ambulance."

"I really don't feel good, Miss Jenna." He bent at the waist and vomited all over both of their feet. She didn't even have a chance to think about her ruined shoes when he started to go limp against her. Reacting without thinking, she tried to catch him, but her weak side took most of his weight. Pain ripped through her shoulder as she stumbled, trying to hold him up.

Candace appeared on his other side, dipped to shove her shoulder underneath his, and lifted. Jenna grunted as the shift put even more pressure on her momentarily. Together, they managed to lower Ito to the ground and let him sit down.

"You stay with him. I'll grab the stretcher." Candace touched her good shoulder as she hurried back to the ambulance.

Trying to ignore her own discomfort as well as the watchful eyes of Chief Warnke, Jenna crouched to assess her patient. "How long have you been feeling badly this time, Ito?"

"An hour or so."

She grabbed his wrist and checked his pulse. "You scared me, buddy."

"Me, too." His voice wavered.

"Okay. We're going to get you to the hospital, and they'll fix you up." She and Candace moved quickly, recording his vitals and shifting him onto the stretcher.

But when they wheeled it over to the rig, Chief Warnke grabbed the end of it with Candace and lifted it. Candace engaged the button that raised the wheel assembly so they could push it inside and lock it in place. Jenna stood there helpless, trying not to look as pathetic as she felt, hurting and smelling of vomit.

Candace jumped inside with Ito, and Chief Warnke turned to Jenna. "Get the shoulder checked out when you reach the hospital."

"With respect, ma'am, I'm good."

"Great. Then the doc will have no problem writing me a note to that effect so I can let you stay on shift."

"Yes, Chief." She yanked open the driver's door with her good arm and climbed inside. When the smell of vomit filled the small space, she rolled down both front windows.

She had to focus first on getting her patient safely to the hospital. Then she'd have plenty of time to bask in her own irritation. She couldn't even be mad at Ito; clearly something was medically wrong with him that she would have dismissed because he called so often. She'd heard the warnings about becoming complacent regarding frequent callers. *It only takes one time.* That was the mantra of EMS trainers. This call wouldn't further the chief's cause.

At the hospital, she managed to help Candace unload the stretcher without putting too much stress on her shoulder. Ito was mumbling something about trouble, but she couldn't make sense of it. She and Candace exchanged worried looks as they wheeled him inside. As they handed him off in the ED, Candace rattled off his vitals, which had tanked considerably since they first found him.

As they left the exam room, Candace flagged down another doctor in the hallway. "Hey, Doc. Do you have time to look at my partner's shoulder?"

"Sure. Grab a seat over there." She pointed at a gurney nearby. "I'll be with you in a minute."

Jenna glared at Candace.

"What?"

"First, did you have to pick the hottest doctor in the place?"

Candace wrinkled her nose like she didn't find the doctor attractive, but Jenna knew better. The doc's thick, dark hair, pulled back in a low ponytail, and even darker, intelligent eyes made her both Jenna and Candace's type. Jenna had flirted a little before while dropping off patients but never gotten any return signals.

"Come on. *Dr. Maines?* We've caught each other checking her out before, and you know it." She wagged a finger at Candace, who didn't change her fake-innocent expression. "Second, I don't need to see a doctor."

"You heard what Warnke said. Are you just hoping she'll forget between now and when we get back to the station?"

"I don't want to go out on leave again—no, I *can't.*" She would probably go crazy if she had to sit at home any longer.

"If you need more time—"

"I don't." She cupped her left hand against her right shoulder. "It was just a twinge—nerve regeneration."

"Jenna."

"Are you a doctor?" Jenna snapped.

Candace didn't respond.

"Okay. Then just drop it."

"All right, ladies. What's going on with the shoulder?" Dr. Maines hurried back over.

Stubbornly, Jenna remained silent. Candace wanted her to see the doc, let Candace do the talking.

"She aggravated a previous injury."

"Aggravated how?" The doctor pulled a curtain around the gurney, then snapped on a pair of gloves. "Can you slip your arm out of your shirt? You don't have to take it all the way off. I just need to get under there." She tilted her head toward Candace. "She can stay or go. Your choice."

"I'm staying." Candace folded her arms across her chest as if daring someone to say something different, but Jenna knew better.

The doctor hovered her hands over Jenna's shoulder. "May I?"

Jenna nodded. The doctor guided her arm with one hand while gently probing her shoulder with the other.

"So what happened today?"

"The patient in exam two started to pass out on her, and this idiot tried to catch him," Candace said.

"Does your partner speak?"

"Sometimes." Candace smiled. "But I don't mind talking to you."

"I don't mind either." She gave Candace a wink that made Jenna narrow her eyes. "But it's customary to get the history from the patient."

"Unless she's incapacitated?"

"Is she?"

Candace shook her head. "Emotionally stunted, maybe."

"Okay, okay." Jenna started to wave her arms, but the doctor's hands still cupped her shoulder. "For your information, I am not an idiot. Or emotionally stunted. And I didn't just try to catch him. I *did* catch him. And—then he vomited on my favorite work shoes." She glanced at Dr. Maines. "Just in case you thought that smell was from me."

"That's a relief." Her eyes sparkled, but she directed her humor-filled gaze at Candace, not at Jenna.

"I'm really fine. Can I just get a note for my boss that everything's okay, and we'll get out of your way?"

"What about the previous injury?" Dr. Maines leaned closer as she palpated the muscles between Jenna's shoulder and neck. She smelled like vanilla, which Jenna would normally assert was an overused fragrance, but on her, it was nice.

"I—uh—I was hit by a car." That was the first time she'd said it aloud like that—not an accident, or the incident, or the festival—but the bare bones of what happened.

"Any other injuries?" If the doctor was fazed, she hid it well.

"A huge bruise on my hip. I guess I was reacting before the crash because the doctors said they thought it was a glancing blow. The shoulder is more likely from the impact with the ground when I was thrown."

"How long ago?"

"About three months."

"On the job?"

She nodded.

"That's funny. It's not a big town. Seems like I would have heard about a paramedic getting—oh."

"Yep." She pressed her lips together and nodded.

"Sorry."

"Why? You didn't run me over." Jenna felt a little bit of satisfaction at Candace's grunt of disapproval.

An awkward silence took over, which was usually the case when the subject came up. People never knew what to say. Sometimes it was "At least the guy is in jail," which was little comfort. Or they'd say "I'm glad you're okay," which she wasn't always sure she was.

Dr. Maines withdrew her hands and turned her back, pulling off the gloves, then throwing them away. Jenna shoved her hand through the arm of her polo and carefully smoothed it back down, noting only a slight pull of pain. She'd be sore later, but some anti-inflammatories and a heating pad would help.

"I don't feel anything new to be concerned about. You've put some stress on it and will likely be sore for a day or so."

Exactly as she'd thought. She stood and tucked in her shirt. "Can I get that note?"

"I'm not taking you out of work, but you should rest it as much as you can. I'll be right back with your note."

"Thanks." After Dr. Maines left, she said to Candace, "I'm going to use the restroom before we go."

She headed down the hall to the nearest one. And when she returned, she found Candace leaned against a counter talking to Dr. Maines. She hung back for a minute, telling herself she was giving her friend a minute to work her game. But, truthfully, Candace didn't have a lot of game. And, in Jenna's opinion, she didn't need it. She was gorgeous, with her strawberry-blond hair and lightly freckled skin, but in a girl-next-door way. When she did get involved with women, it was usually because they approached her. And she was so good with people, much better than Jenna, that everyone warmed up to her right from the beginning. It was part of what made her a better paramedic than Jenna.

Candace rested an elbow on the counter, bending slightly at the waist to do so, and Jenna noticed the way her uniform pants hugged her waist and flared at her hips. She said something that made Dr. Maines laugh. Candace's expression warmed, her smile lifting her cheeks and igniting something in Jenna's chest.

Jenna shook her head and forced herself to look at Dr. Maines. She was smoking hot, no doubt. So why then couldn't she stop staring at Candace? Maybe Candace was right: She was emotionally stunted, or at least a little fucked up in the head right now. Either way, she didn't enjoy the sick feeling in her stomach when Dr. Maines handed Candace a business card with what Jenna could only assume was her personal cell-phone number on it. What the hell was going on with her?

She approached just as Candace slipped the card into her pocket. Jenna curled her hands into fists at her sides when Dr. Maines followed the motion with her eyes, then lingered over Candace for a moment.

"Thanks again, Doc."

"Take it easy on that shoulder." When Dr. Maines held out her note for the chief, Jenna plucked it out of her hand with a forced smile.

"Will do." She walked off so she wouldn't have to witness whatever good-byes they exchanged.

By the time she reached the rig, Candace had caught up with her. Jenna keyed her radio and told the dispatcher they were back in service and available for calls. Candace didn't say anything during the ride back to the station.

Jenna wanted to ask if she was going to call Dr. Maines, if she thought they might go out. Normally she would talk to her best friend about such things. But she couldn't force the words out past the bitterness in her throat. What was that? Envy? Was she jealous that Candace had a shot with Dr. Maines? She and Candace had never competed for dates. In fact, it was almost an unspoken rule between them—if one of them was interested in a woman, the other didn't interfere. They'd both dated their fair share, maybe Jenna more than Candace. But Candace got past the first or second date more often than Jenna did.

That might be why this Dr. Maines thing was bothering her. Candace had a better chance of finding something meaningful with her than Jenna did. And that would leave Jenna as the last member of their group of friends still single—with no prospects on the horizon.

Candace flipped on the siren as she pulled out of the station behind the engine. Several other crews were already on the scene of a fire ravaging a well-known downtown business. The building had begun its life as a farm-and-feed store in the 1920s. Over the decades, it had been home to other businesses as well. Several years ago, it had finally found its next purpose as a farm-to-table restaurant.

As they rolled up, she parked far enough back not to be in the way of the firefighters swarming the scene. Flames licked out of the windows of the brick storefront. The bricks were keeping the exterior structure intact but also created a virtual oven while the consumable materials inside burned. A stream of water arced from a hose on the end of the aerial ladder that extended toward the building.

The fire chief was on scene. Candace had heard his voice on the radio directing crews. He'd been with the department a little over a year and was the best chief Candace had ever worked for. He employed the perfect balance of being hands-on and also stepping back and letting his chain of command do their jobs. On large-scale incidents like this one, he typically responded quickly and managed the flow of resources.

Candace slid out of the rig and circled to the front. The business hadn't been open yet, and the few employees inside, prepping for their day, had evacuated immediately. Their role at the moment was standby, in case a firefighter was injured. She leaned against the grill of the ambulance. Jenna kept walking, moving to stand next to a nearby engine and strike up a conversation with the pump operator.

Candace wasn't surprised. Jenna had been distant for the past two weeks. When they were alone in the rig together, they shared only awkward silences. At the station Jenna found ways to avoid her. On their off days she didn't even hear from her, and when she tried to ask Jenna what she'd done when they weren't working, she got the brush-off. But she wouldn't be able to ignore her tonight. They were supposed to get together with their friends for bowling, which was really just an excuse to drink and hang out. No one took the bowling seriously except Everett and Sam.

Tonight, Jenna would have to interact with her and, more importantly, with their friends. She might learn just as much from watching Jenna with them than trying to engage her directly. Maybe Jenna was mad because the chief made her get that note about her shoulder. The frosty attitude had started right around that time. But that didn't make sense, because the chief had seen her try to catch Ito. It wasn't like Candace had told her Jenna had been having trouble. Hell, she'd been covering for her, dismissing the concerns around the firehouse, saying Jenna was fine, or just tired, when really she was being kinda bitchy to everyone, especially her.

As the scene started to wind down, Jenna returned to the rig and got in the passenger side. Candace rolled her eyes. Nothing felt quite as lonely as being completely ignored by your best friend. It hurt, and that made her angry. One minute Jenna was talking about how they would get through everything together, and the next, Candace was invisible.

Jenna had always been this way. When she was angry or upset, her walls went up, and she shut everyone and everything out—almost everyone. Candace couldn't remember ever being on the outside of that wall.

When they got back to the station, the guys from the engine returned just behind them, and a couple of the guys talked about starting a card game. Candace grabbed a seat at the table, and Jenna sat down across from her.

"What's everybody doing after shift? Does anyone want to get a drink?" one of the guys asked as he started shuffling the cards.

A couple of others agreed, and they looked at Candace and Jenna.

"I can't. I already have plans."

"Hot date?"

"You bet." She winked at Jenna, who stared back at her.

"Jenna?"

"No thanks." She shoved the cards she'd just been dealt into the center of the table and stood. "I'm not really in the mood for cards."

They all watched her until she'd cleared the hallway, headed for the fitness room. Then they went back to playing cards. The first time Candace had played, she'd expected poker, and when they told her they liked rummy, she smothered a laugh. Three burly firefighters with big broad shoulders, two of them with shaved heads, sitting around playing a game she associated with old women struck her as hilarious. But then she joined in and was as addicted as they were.

Rummy with the guys and bowling with the girls later. No wonder her personal life was so nonexistent. The closest she'd come to an actual date lately was when she'd gotten Dr. Maines's business card. She'd given it to Candace and told her she could call her anytime. But Candace hadn't used it. She'd deluded herself into thinking that Jenna needed her right now. And then Jenna totally ignored her. So, she was the idiot in this situation. Maybe she should figure out where she'd put that card and make the call.

"What the fuck is Teele's problem lately?"

"She's too good to hang out with us these days."

"Come on, guys. She's been through a lot." Candace picked up her cards and fanned them in her hand to look at them.

"She's not the first person to be injured on the job. Half the guys in this room have been hurt at one time or another."

"But hey, man. We firefighters are tough. Maybe paramedics just aren't built to withstand what we can. Especially not *lady* paramedics."

Candace shook her head, deciding not to dignify that comment with a response. He was just trying to get a rise out of her, and she didn't think even he believed that.

"Well, whatever's wrong, she just needs to get her shit together, because we're starting to get tired of her sulking around here like we were driving that damn car."

Candace grimaced. That one was over the line, and she was about to tell him so, when she heard a noise behind her.

"You all don't have anything better to do than sit and talk about me when I'm out of the room like a bunch of gossiping old women?" Jenna stood in the doorway, hands planted on her hips. Her face shone with sweat, and a triangle dampened the front of her shirt from the neck down over her chest. Candace had to look away. She didn't work out with Jenna anymore for one main reason. Hot and sweaty, she was too much for Candace to handle.

"Relax, Teele," one of the guys said. He looked at Candace and grinned, and she knew what he was about to say was only going to make it worse. "Cooper, can't you keep this woman under control?"

"What?" Jenna strode several steps into the room. "What did you say?" she asked, louder this time.

Candace jumped up and crossed to her, sticking out her arm to bar Jenna from moving closer, though she could easily have pushed past her.

"Come on. Let's go talk." She grabbed Jenna's arm and steered her out of the room. Jenna let herself be led, but her stiff posture said she was still ready to fight.

"That's such bullshit. Would he tell one of the guys to keep the other one under control?" Jenna asked as they left the room.

Candace knew they could hear her, but thankfully, none of them responded.

"Yes, it is."

"And what were you doing? Just sitting there letting them talk?" Jenna strode into the bunkroom, then spun around and advanced back toward Candace.

"What? No." She tried to play back the conversation in her head. She'd defended Jenna, hadn't she? Not that she was obligated to. Their coworkers had a right to their opinions about her recent behavior. And Jenna hadn't done any explaining of her own. "I've been making excuses for you even when everyone says you need to get your head out of your ass."

"Who? Who said that?"

"It doesn't matter. They're all assuming this still has to do with your injury. And maybe it does, but that can't be all of it, because this pissy attitude of yours only started a couple of weeks ago."

Jenna rolled her eyes upward and shook her head.

"Just talk to me, Jenna. Regardless of what you think, I'm on your side."

"I didn't ask you to be."

"I'm your partner. You don't have to ask."

"Maybe we shouldn't be partners anymore."

Pain knifed through Candace, so severely that she grasped at her chest. Then, realizing what the motion gave away, she covered by opening her palm and smoothing her shirt as if straightening it.

"If that's what you want, I'm sure Warnke could get you a transfer. But you'll have to be the one to leave because I like it here." She wasn't so much attached to the rest of the guys, but this station was closest to her house. And if Jenna was going to initiate the split, then Candace figured that meant she had to be the one to leave.

She was honestly surprised she got anything out and wasn't doubled over right now. She forced her chin up, keeping her eyes straight ahead as she turned and left the room. What more could she say, after all? As much as she disliked every other person she'd been partnered with, and as much as she cherished the time she spent riding with Jenna, she was still above begging her to partner with her. She'd tried to be there, and now, more than ever, Jenna seemed determined to push her away. Maybe it was time to let her succeed.

CHAPTER SIX

Not really feeling a night out. I'll catch you guys later.

Candace stared at the message she'd just sent in a group text to her four other friends. She'd left Jenna off the text. She would find out when she got to the bowling alley that Candace had bowed out, but the petty side of her decided to let her wait until then. She actually did want to hang out with her friends and wasn't looking forward to spending a night alone at home.

She'd tried to psych herself up for the last hour to go face Jenna. She'd tried on at least a half dozen outfits, and every one of them lay discarded on her bed in a big pile of failure. She was standing in her bedroom in her bra and underwear when she decided to send the text.

Noooo. Jenna already canceled. If you do, too, then it's just the four of us AGAIN. No offense, Everett and Claire.

She smiled at Nicole's text, despite her sadness at knowing that while she'd been agonizing about whether to go, Jenna had already definitively made up her mind.

Now I don't want to go either. Britt's text had a sad-face emoji after it.

If Jenna wouldn't be there, then why shouldn't she go? She really did want some company tonight so she wouldn't dwell on the situation.

Okay. I'll be there.

She returned her attention to the clothes pile and fished out the last thing she'd tried on. She didn't need as much armor without Jenna there, so this embroidery-embellished top and a pair of jeans would be just fine.

When she walked into the bowling alley less than an hour later, she was so glad she'd come. She greeted each of her friends with a hug and already felt a little better. She resolved to enjoy this night and not think about what was going on with Jenna. They'd been through a lot together and would get through whatever this was, too.

Since they had an odd number, they bowled individually for their scores, not nearly as competitive as when they played teams. But for Candace it didn't matter because she wasn't very good in either circumstance. And Jenna, her usual teammate, wasn't a bowler either. They usually goofed around while Sam tried desperately to beat Everett, who almost always won.

She lasted through the first game until Everett asked her why Jenna had canceled.

"I don't know." She shrugged. "I guess she had other plans."

"She texted me that she wasn't feeling well." Sam narrowed her eyes. "Weren't you with her at work today? Was she sick? Or do you think it's the shoulder?"

"She was fine at work. Maybe she started feeling badly after she got home." She didn't want to blame the shoulder, though that might have been the easiest choice.

"She never gets sick and rarely skips bowling night. I know she missed some after her injury, but I thought she was doing better. Hell, she's the glue that holds this group together. We all come to see her smiling face." Sam raised her beer bottle slightly, almost as if toasting Jenna before taking a drink.

"Should we be worried about her?" Claire asked.

Candace stared at the Coke in front of her, wishing it were something stronger, though alcohol probably wouldn't make this night better. She really wished Jenna was here so she could tell her that whatever she'd done, she was sorry and wanted her friend back. She'd ignored her desire for Jenna for so long in order to hold on to her friendship, and she could do it again.

"Candace?"

"Huh?"

"Should we be worried about her?"

She shook her head helplessly. "I don't know."

"What's going on?" Everett, who'd been about to bowl her frame, set her ball back on the return and came over to sit beside her.

Candace couldn't hold it in any longer and started telling them how Jenna had basically ignored her for the past two weeks and she didn't really even understand why. She answered their pointed questions about the days leading up to the beginning of the freeze-out as well as she could, then ended with their blowup after Jenna heard the guys talking about her.

"Then she said maybe we shouldn't be partners." She shouldn't be sharing her drama with their mutual friends. But she needed to talk to someone. Everyone but Nicole seemed surprised by what she'd just said. She met Nicole's eyes. "What?"

"I'm new to the group. Maybe I shouldn't—"

"Just say it."

"Have you considered that it might be easier if you weren't partners?"

"No. I've never thought that." Why would Nicole even suggest the possibility?

"Really? I have to say, you're stronger than I am. If I had to work that closely every day with someone I was in love with—"

"Whoa. Who's in love?" Everett blurted, during what happened to be a lull in the noise from the business's other patrons. Several sets of eyes turned to their lane. Everett glared back, and Claire touched her shoulder.

"You're not denying it," Sam said more quietly from the chair behind the scoring screen.

She'd been hiding it for so long that denial had been her first instinct. But truthfully, she felt relieved that they knew. "No. I'm not."

"Wow."

"I'm sorry. I thought they must know. I haven't been around the two of you that much, but it's obvious in the way you look at her and the way you treat her." Nicole did look genuinely sorry.

"It is?"

Nicole glanced around the group as if searching for support.

"They're friends," Everett said.

"And partners," Sam added. "Of course they're close."

Candace looked at Claire, who just shrugged.

"I asked Britt once if you two had ever gone there. You do have this 'more than friends' vibe. But when she said no, I assumed I'd read things wrong."

"Thank you." Nicole threw up her hands in victory.

Sam touched her shoulder. "Honey, this moment isn't really about you being right."

"Yes, of course."

"Is this a new development? Like since the festival," Everett asked.

"Not really. That day, I guess it made me realize how fragile life really is and has made hiding my feelings more of a struggle. I mean, you hear people say we only get one time around, so do it right. But who really lives that way?"

"So then, how long have you had feelings for her?" Claire's question felt gentle, as if she already understood what the answer would be.

"Since not long after we were partnered together. So, about three years."

"The whole time we've known you, you've had this secret crush on Jenna?" Everett asked.

She nodded. Jenna had been friends with Everett and Sam first and had brought her into their group when they were paired together on the ambulance.

"Why didn't you ever say anything?" Sam asked.

"I never got the idea that she returned my feelings, and I didn't want to screw up the best friendship I'd ever had. Not to mention if we couldn't be partners anymore."

"You have to tell her now," Nicole said as if that were a foregone conclusion.

"What? Why does she have to do that?"

"She's already in danger of losing her as a partner. And the fact that Jenna canceled tonight says something about where your friendship is. Although I doubt it's irreparable, at the very least it's altered. All that's left to determine is, does she return your feelings? And you can find out by telling her how you feel."

Claire tilted her head while she considered Nicole's arguments. "She does have some points. It may not be a bad idea."

"Oh, my God. I should have been drinking tonight." Candace tilted her head back and closed her eyes. "Guys, I need to think about this before I decide to tell her. Let's just get back to bowling, okay?"

❖

"Then I said, maybe we shouldn't be partners."

"Wow. That's cold." Daide handed her a beer, her second of the night, and sat down across from her at the patio table. "I told you to try to see her side of things, not cut her off completely."

"Man, so much has happened since then." She took a long drink of her beer and stared out at the yard. "For starters, did you know that I pushed her out of the way of that car?"

He didn't have to answer, but when she glanced at him, his guilty expression said it all.

"And you didn't tell me?"

"I found out a few days after. I read the police reports. Candace told one of the officers she thought that's what happened, and a couple of witnesses confirmed it. The car was headed right for her, and at the last minute, you just shoved her out of the way, putting yourself in the path instead."

She rubbed a hand against her temple. "Why can't I remember any of that?"

"What's the last thing you remember?"

"We'd been given a break from the first-aid tent and were walking among some of the vendors. And then it's just a blank except for some bits and pieces of being loaded in the ambulance, then waking up in the hospital."

"Is that what your moodiness has been about lately? The festival?"

"Not just that."

"What else?" He stood to check the burgers he'd thrown on the grill when he found out she was bailing on bowling.

"Well, did you know that Dr. Maines is still hotter than sin, and yet, somehow, she doesn't hold a candle to Candace Cooper?"

"Wait—what?" He spun around, spatula in hand, and stared at her.

"Yeah." Had she really had only two beers? She felt buzzed and seemed to be losing control of her mind-to-mouth filter.

"You're saying that you—and Candace—"

"No. Nothing's happened. Not even close. I just—I don't know. I'm thinking of her differently these days. But she doesn't know about that."

"And what does Dr. Maines have to do with it?"

She quickly filled him in on their visit to the hospital with Ito and her subsequent checkup. "So, now, she'll be Mrs. Dr. Whatever-her-first-name-is Maines. And I'll be stuck here with you for the rest of my life."

"First, I am offended that you think I don't have my happily-ever-after. And second, did she go out with the hot doc and have a great time? Because for some reason, I suspect you don't have any of the details, and you're jumping to the biggest conclusions." She started to answer, but he held up a finger to stop her. "Ah. No need to respond. I already know. So the question then becomes, as Candace's best friend, why would you be freaking out about the possibility that she might find happiness?"

"I don't know."

"Oh, dear girl, that wasn't really the question."

She sat back and threw up her arms in defeat.

"The question is this. How long have you had an adorable little crush on your best friend?" He puffed out his chest, then folded his arms across it.

"Seriously, Daide."

"I am so serious."

"I don't—"

"How long?"

"A few weeks, maybe. I've always thought she was beautiful. But you know how it is when partners get together. And we got along so well and had so much fun, right from the beginning, that I would never risk that for a romance that might not work out. We've both had crappy partners before, and twelve hours with someone you don't like is miserable. So she's been my best buddy for the past three years."

"And how does she feel?"

"She probably feels like she wants to date a hot doctor, not some broken paramedic who's been treating her like shit."

"You're not broken, just a little bruised. I mean, they're kind of old bruises that aren't going away, and they're that ugly yellow-green color."

"Daide."

"But not broken."

She smiled. She wasn't convinced he was right, but she loved that he sounded certain.

"Your first move is to stop treating her like shit."

She nodded. That, of course, she'd known.

"And decide if you're going to ask for a transfer."

She shook her head right away. "I'm not. I was just frustrated. I could never leave her."

"Then tell her that, not me."

She pulled out her phone, intent on texting to ask if they could talk, but then paused. Candace was probably out with their friends having a good time. Maybe she should just chill with Daide tonight and discuss this with her at work tomorrow.

CHAPTER SEVEN

Jenna dashed from her car through the pouring rain, not bothering with an umbrella because it probably wouldn't survive the whipping wind anyway. The rain had started late last night, with two rounds of severe thunderstorms rolling through in the very early morning hours. Between the beer Jenna drank last night and lying awake listening to the storms, she hadn't gotten much quality sleep.

Inside the station, she headed straight for the locker room to drop her bag and brush away some of the moisture. She stripped off her department raincoat and hung it on a hook to drip dry before she had to head back out for their first call. On days like this they were sure to run a lot, just for the motor-vehicle crashes alone.

She went into the living area as the alert tones sounded throughout the hall. The dispatcher gave the location and details for a crash, directing the engine to respond. But a different medic unit went with them.

"Why aren't we going? Isn't Candace here yet?"

"She's in with the chief. And Warnke said to send you in when you got here, too." The engine crew headed out the door toward the vehicle bay.

Why was Candace in with Warnke? Had she changed her mind and decided to ask for the transfer herself? Damn. That would make this mess harder to fix. But she couldn't have had time to file any paperwork yet, so Jenna could still walk this back—though she might have to grovel a bit.

She knocked on the chief's door and heard her call out to enter. As she did, she said, "Why didn't we get that run?"

Warnke sat behind her desk, and Candace occupied one of the two chairs across from her with her back to Jenna. She didn't even look at her—that couldn't be a good sign.

"I put your unit out of service. Have a seat, Teele."

Jenna circled the chair next to Candace and sat down, chancing a glance at her. Candace looked just as confused about why they were here as she felt. Maybe this wasn't what she thought.

"I was just about to fill Cooper in, so I'm glad you're here." Warnke leaned forward, resting her forearms against the desk. "I don't know if you've seen the news, but the storms we got hit Henry County much worse than here. They had multiple confirmed touchdowns of tornados—the weather service is saying EF-3, maybe. I need the two of you to take your rig and go over there to assist them, ASAP."

"Henry County is a three-hour drive. Surely, there are crews that are closer," Candace said.

"Every place between here and there is dealing with storm damage as well, on a smaller scale. So rather than deplete one area, State Emergency Management is asking for one crew from any agency that can spare them. FEMA is probably on the ground by now and will likely take over coordinating some of this."

"Why us?" Normally, she'd jump at this opportunity to have a new adventure with Candace, but today it filled her stomach with a stone of worry.

"You two have search-and-rescue training."

They'd taken a state-level training course with some first responders from Bellbrook and neighboring departments as well. But that had been two years ago, and there wasn't much call for search-and-rescue in Bellbrook.

"Plus, you're two of my best. You're so in tune as a team, you could go out there and rock this job without even having to speak to each other."

And they just might, if the last couple of weeks was any indication.

Warnke met Jenna's eyes. "I know you're just coming off—something. And if you're not ready for this, let me know now. If you're going, I need you to get home, pack a bag, and be ready to leave within the hour. You'll probably be there for a couple of days."

"I'm good to go." Jenna's pride wouldn't let her admit she was even a little apprehensive about this. The shoulder had been pretty good this last week, with no new stresses since that day with Ito. But search-and-rescue could be labor intensive, and often no one was close by to help with lifting—of people or debris—so everyone had to carry their load.

"Good. Pack your bags and come back here. I'll start the paperwork. They'll find you a place to sleep when you get there. Keep track of any expenses as far as food and gas for the ambulance, and we'll get you reimbursed when you get back."

Jenna stood, already mentally running around her house and grabbing everything she'd need. Luckily she'd done laundry a couple of days ago and had plenty of clean uniforms. She let Candace leave before her, then followed her out and headed for her car.

Candace tossed her duffel bag and a backpack into the ambulance, then climbed the steps and stowed her bags in the space between the jump seat and the cabinet. She'd already loaded several cases of bottled water and a box of snacks and MREs, just in case they didn't have access to food and water. She'd also stopped at Walgreens and purchased a bunch of toiletries to donate when they arrived.

"Mind putting mine in there?" Jenna stood in the open door.

"Toss it in."

Jenna's bag hit the floor and slid toward Candace. She threw it in on top of hers, then exited the rig and closed the door behind her.

"Ready?" Jenna asked.

Candace gave her a skeptical look. "Are you sure you're good for this?"

"I said I was."

"Okay. I just don't want to get out there and find out your shoulder isn't strong enough. You could get me or someone else hurt." She could tell Jenna didn't like her implication. And she hated saying it. But lives could depend on what they were about do.

"I understand the risk." Jenna's jaw was tight and her voice cold.

"Okay. Let's go." Candace pulled the keys out of her pocket. She wanted to toss them to Jenna and make her drive, but she couldn't bring herself to do it. Jenna should be free to rest her shoulder, or move around and stretch it if need be during the drive.

She hated the tension between them, but it wasn't really her fault. Jenna had basically ignored her for the past two weeks, so why now, just because they would be spending the next several days together nonstop, was it on her to make the effort? She'd be cordial, so as not to be miserable for the next several days, but she wouldn't go out of her way to engage.

The drive was as uncomfortable as she'd thought it would be. They rode in silence, with Jenna playing on her phone while Candace navigated the boring three hours on the interstate. They spoke only to discuss which fast-food place to grab lunch from. She couldn't remember three hours she'd enjoyed less in an ambulance with Jenna. The rig was normally her happy place.

Last night, after talking to her friends, she'd been seriously considering confessing her feelings, until they'd gotten called into Warnke's office. Now she couldn't start that conversation, because what if it went badly? Jenna might not return her feelings. She'd eventually get over that, but in the short term, she'd be wrecked. How would they spend the next couple of days together after such an awkward situation?

She exited the interstate and started to see debris from the storms. The roads were littered with leaves and small branches.

"Turn left on the next street." Jenna had printed the directions to the community center that was being used as a command post, just in case they lost cell service and couldn't GPS their way there.

Many of the homes had shingles missing from their roofs and siding blown off into the yard. Several trees had large branches split off and lying in the grass. She saw one electric pole that had snapped, the top half dangling from the wire overhead. At the next intersection, they had to drive around a limb in the road, half onto the shoulder. Candace went slowly as the passenger-side tires rode the edge of a steep ditch.

"Easy," Jenna murmured while Candace gritted her teeth.

Back on the road, the rest of the drive to the community center was uneventful. The command post had been set up in the area with the least damage so they could coordinate the flow of large fire-and-rescue apparatus, as well as electric-service trucks and tow trucks.

She parked in a makeshift lot on a soccer field next to two other ambulances, left their gear in the rig, and went inside to check in and get their assignment. The community center was bustling with activity, and they were directed to the auditorium to check in with a staging officer.

The tall, very thin man wore a khaki uniform, his protruding hip bones no doubt holding up his duty belt. His hair stood up in the front, and when he raked a hand through it as he consulted some kind of list on his clipboard, she knew why.

"Emmanuel Sapp, chief deputy with the Henry County Sheriff's Department, currently the liaison between FEMA and the local crews working search-and-rescue. The FEMA guys are directing everything, securing aid, and coordinating rescue efforts. They're short-staffed, too. We got widespread damage across two counties, encompassing twelve small towns. So they're tapping us local guys to check people in and assign them to a sector."

He took down their names and jurisdiction information, as well as the chief's contact information. Since Bellbrook was paying their regular salary while they were here, as well as travel expenses, the city could apply for federal disaster-relief funds to offset some of the costs. Despite Emmanuel's frazzled appearance, Candace found him to be very organized. She supposed she'd be looking a little rough at this time tomorrow, too.

"The largest tornado cut a swath through the east side of town, which is our most densely populated area, and destroyed over two dozen homes. That's where we're focusing our search efforts right now. Luckily, it was late afternoon and school had already dismissed. The high school took a lot of damage, and the baseball team was practicing, but they were able to shelter in the cafeteria. No one was injured." He tapped the shoulder of a police officer standing close by. "Officer Deering was about to head over to that side of town. You can follow him in your rig. All the injured are going to Henry County Community Hospital for triage. They're keeping the most severe cases there and parceling out the rest to various locations."

Deering turned around. "One of our retired docs has been treating patients over at the veterinary clinic."

They followed Deering outside and headed to their rig. As Candace maneuvered through the parking lot to the entrance, she saw Deering's patrol car waiting for her. She followed him for fifteen minutes, picking their way through the increasingly damaged neighborhoods, once having to turn around and detour due to a huge tree down across the road.

"I'll never find my way back to that community center."

"We'll sleep in the rig if we have to. I'll even let you have the stretcher, and I'll take the bench." A hint of the old Jenna peeked through in her words.

"Right. So I can listen to you complain that your neck hurts all day tomorrow." She heard the smile in her own voice and both loved and hated it.

"That happened one time, and I slept on it wrong."

"Complaining. All. Day."

Jenna adjusted her helmet and put on her safety glasses. Candace, standing next to her, did the same, then picked up their medical bag and slung the strap across her chest. She'd insisted on carrying it. Jenna grabbed a pry bar off a rescue truck, leaving the heavier power saws to some of the guys.

They joined the rest of their search team—firefighters, police officers, and emergency-management specialists. They had a target one-block radius of homes to search for survivors. The homes in this area had all sustained heavy damage but weren't leveled like some of the neighborhoods they'd passed on the way in. The USAR markings in front of each dwelling indicated that those areas had already been searched.

"We need medical over here." The call came from a house across the street from where Jenna's team was about to search.

"Go ahead. We'll jump in here for you." Two firefighters who'd been floating among the teams when manpower was needed came over.

Jenna and Candace hurriedly picked their way around rescue apparatus and a downed tree in the yard in order to meet up with the team that had just come out of the house.

"We have a survivor trapped in the basement. She's got a probable head injury and is complaining of pain in her ribs and left arm." He led them into the house and to the kitchen. "We have access via the basement stairs, which are intact. But she's trapped under some debris right now. My guys are digging her out as we speak."

Jenna started down the open stairs to the basement, pausing to test each tread, though they felt solid under her feet. Candace waited until she'd reached the bottom to start down. Jenna found two team members pulling boards, large chunks of drywall, and other debris off a pile near the southeast corner of the basement. Jenna jumped in and began removing pieces of wood and setting them aside in a pile they'd started well away from the patient.

After they'd cleared enough debris for her to get a better look at the patient, Jenna squatted and shined a flashlight through the gap. The woman lay on her side, and Jenna couldn't see her face, but the limpness in her posture made her nervous.

"Hello? What's your name?" When she didn't get a response, she glanced over her shoulder at one of the guys standing behind her. "Was she conscious when you located her?"

"Yes. We heard her crying out. She responded to our calls, but it's been a few minutes since she said anything."

They increased their pace, pulling back debris until they reached the final large slab of drywall and found a bookcase under that, covering the patient, one of the shelves bisecting her back, which likely accounted for the rib pain she'd reported.

As two guys lifted the bookcase, Jenna started to scoot closer, ready to get in there with her patient. But at the moment she moved, something under the corner of the bookcase shifted. As one of the guys lost his grip on the heavy piece, Jenna shot forward into the gap before it closed, twisting and trying to get her hands on the bookcase to catch the weight somehow. She braced it with her bad arm, bent at an awkward angle, saved from the full brunt of the piece only by someone above her catching it. She felt her burden lighten as she turned to look up. Candace stood there with both hands bracketing the corner of the bookcase, staring back at her. Confident that her partner had her, she turned back to the patient.

"Let's get her out of here, guys. Give me a cervical collar and get the stokes in here. I need her out of this basement as soon as we get her stabilized. And for God's sake, somebody get that bookcase off us. I need my partner in here."

She heard a masculine chuckle but didn't know which guy it was. The bookcase moved away, and then Candace dropped down beside her.

Within minutes, they had the patient in a stokes basket being carried up the basement stairs. She and Candace hadn't exchanged more than a few words, but instead of the tense silence from earlier, this quiet was productive, comfortable, and efficient. It was everything that was good about her and Candace together.

Their patient was critical, but as they raced to the hospital, Jenna couldn't help but feel optimistic. Her vitals had stabilized in the ambulance, and she would make it there, hopefully in time for them to treat her head injury. But she'd have to be one hell of a fighter. Jenna rode the adrenaline of the rescue and of rediscovering the magic of her partnership with Candace. Together they probably boasted better stats than anyone else in the department, and though her theory wasn't scientific, Jenna sometimes felt they were able to transfer their synergistic energy to their patients.

They dropped her off at the hospital, stopping only long enough to grab a clean sheet for the stretcher and toss the old one. Jenna would prep it for the next patient while Candace drove them back to the search area.

For the next ten hours, they moved through the neighborhood, clearing houses and marking the front doors, garage doors, sheets of plywood—whatever they could find to indicate that residences had been checked off the list. They located and transported two more survivors.

Their whole group stopped for a quick meal break about halfway through, eating fast-food burgers someone had dropped off while sitting on benches in a park adjacent to the neighborhood they were about to search next. After fifteen minutes of swapping stories with the firefighters and police officers from other jurisdictions, they got back to work.

As dusk turned to night and lowered a curtain that made the shadows too deep to safely continue, they received orders to return to the community center. Once there, Deputy Sapp handed Jenna a hotel key—an actual one dangling from a square plastic key chain.

"We're putting the first responders up at the motel just up the road. It's not fancy, but it's a clean bed and a shower. We've got a lot of folks coming in to help out tonight and tomorrow, so I'm sorry we can spare only one room per crew. But hey, at least you're both ladies. It'll be a bit more uncomfortable for the coed crews."

Jenna nodded stiffly, prepping herself for an awkward night. But he made sense, and she couldn't ask for any further accommodations. She didn't even have a good reason. They were partners and, like he said, both women, so why should they have a problem sharing a room—a room they were lucky to have instead of a cot in the corner of the community-center gymnasium. She was sure that he wouldn't think the fact that they'd barely spoken in two weeks, because Jenna was having conflicting feelings about Candace, would be a good enough reason to come up with a valuable second room.

CHAPTER EIGHT

Candace and Jenna climbed out of the van, along with several other first responders. Because the motel had limited parking, Deputy Sapp had arranged the ride so they could leave their apparatus at the community center. They claimed their respective luggage as the van driver unpacked it from the back.

The motel had probably been built in the 1950s and undergone several renovations over the years, each leaving evidence of that decade someplace on the exterior. The sign out front appeared original and lent the motel a cool retro feel.

Candace opened the door to their room, saying a silent prayer that she would see two beds. The tension in her chest eased. The beds were covered in patterned bedspreads she felt sure would be polyester when she got a closer look. The room hadn't been updated in years, but as promised, it provided a clean bed and a shower. And right now, she wanted only to stand in that shower until the water went cold, then fall into bed.

She dropped her bag next to the bed closest to the window and immediately stripped off the bedspread. It was as scratchy as she'd thought, and she didn't want it touching her face while she slept. The sheet and blanket would be sufficient.

"You can have the shower first," Jenna said from where she stood near her bed.

"No. You go. I intend to use every ounce of the hot water you leave me."

Jenna laughed, and Candace almost cried. She waited until Jenna disappeared into the bathroom before she whispered, "God, I've missed you."

She grabbed her phone and checked her email while she waited for Jenna. When Jenna came out wearing a dark-gray silk pajama set— tank top and shorts—Candace almost whimpered aloud. She'd known about Jenna's penchant for cute pajamas, but she hadn't had time to worry about that while working today. And that was a good thing. She wouldn't have survived the day thinking about seeing Jenna like this. Jenna's shorts covered only the tops of her smooth thighs, and her tank top revealed her toned arms.

For the first time since right after her surgery, Candace saw the scar running down the front of Jenna's shoulder. The three-inch raised ridge, darker than her skin tone, reminded Candace of what she could have lost. Overwhelmed, she moved past Jenna toward the bathroom, carefully avoiding touching her.

Minutes later she stood in the shower while tears streamed down her face. She smothered her sobs so Jenna wouldn't hear her. Pride had kept her from reaching out. But seeing Jenna's scar, combined with spending the day amid devastation, put her stubbornness in perspective.

She dressed in her own pajamas, suddenly feeling dowdy in gray knit pants and an oversized T-shirt. When she came out of the bathroom, Jenna was already in bed, her back to Candace.

Candace got into her own bed and lay on her back, staring at the ceiling. As she'd been getting frozen out by Jenna these last couple of weeks, she'd been thinking she'd be damned if she'd be the one to apologize. But today, she just wanted her friend back. She wanted to celebrate that they were there together and healthy. And she didn't want to take another day for granted.

"How's your shoulder?" She was careful to keep her tone gentle, concerned, and not judgmental. This was an olive branch, not an accusation.

"It's okay."

She sighed. "Can I get more than just okay?"

Jenna was quiet for a long minute, and Candace wasn't sure she'd respond. "Will I be sore tomorrow? Yes, but let's face it, you might, too. I'll probably never fully trust the shoulder. But I'm feeling good right now. It's handled the stress of what we did today."

"That's good." Candace turned on her side, facing Jenna's bed.

"I'm sorry for whatever has been creating this tension between us. If I was too pushy making sure you were ready, or if you feel I didn't support you enough, I'm sorry. But I could have lost you. And I don't want to waste time being mad at each other."

Jenna didn't turn toward her. "It's not your fault. I've been a jerk these last couple of weeks. I've had a lot going on in my head."

"Since when can you not talk to me about something?"

Jenna sighed.

"Whatever it is, can it really make things worse than they've been between us?"

"Maybe. It could change everything."

Candace's heart raced as she felt like she was hurtling toward a dangerous confession. "Could be it's just time for us to evolve. That's what makes friendships last, after all."

Jenna sat up and looked over at her, conflict evident even in the shadows cast by the streetlight outside their window. She crossed her legs in front of her and rubbed a hand over her face. Candace waited, holding back the words she wanted so desperately to say. Jenna was working up to something.

"I was jealous." What Jenna finally blurted out didn't clear anything up for Candace.

"Of what?"

"Dr. Maines."

Candace rose and propped herself with her elbow and forearm against the bed. "Why?"

"That day in the hospital, I saw her give you her card."

"So you were jealous because you thought I got her and you didn't?"

Jenna didn't respond. Candace pursed her lips in frustration. Getting Jenna to talk when she didn't want to had always been an exercise in patience, but today felt especially difficult.

"We've never competed for women. If you were that into her, you could have just told me. Besides, I never even called her." The truth was pushing at her, demanding attention. But she hesitated. If Jenna was making it clear that she was attracted to Dr. Maines, Candace would only make a fool of herself by trying to compete with the gorgeous doctor.

"I wasn't—I didn't talk to you about it because I didn't want to hear about how great things are going with you and Dr. Maines. I'm happy for you if you're dating her, I really am. Or I want to be."

"I just told you, I didn't even call her. I don't understand—look, this isn't going to get us anywhere. I am not now, nor have I ever dated Dr. Maines."

"Why not?"

"I'm not interested—"

"Bullshit. She's obviously smart, and attractive. But you're right. She's probably not your type. Hell, Candy, she's everyone's type."

"You should ask her out, then."

"I'm not going to ask her out."

"Why not? You said you were jealous that she was going out with me. I told you, I'm not doing that. So you're free to." Candace could hear the tears in her voice and knew Jenna would, too. She'd convinced herself years ago that Jenna wouldn't return her feelings, and if she revealed them now, every moment that she'd hidden them since then would be justified when Jenna rejected her.

Jenna stared at her hands, poking at one thumbnail with the corner of her index fingernail.

Their friends had advised Candace to talk to Jenna, but they hadn't imagined this scenario when they suggested conversation. They were basically held hostage here. Whatever they said today, they couldn't escape tomorrow, when they would spend another entire day together. Suddenly, she felt like the past several months had been leading them to this place—Jenna's injury, Candace's worry and her desire to care for her during her recovery, and now their need to readjust to spending every day together in a rig. Whatever happened now, they weren't going to get back where they were. A man in a car whose motives she didn't even know had forever altered their worlds. Jenna had been through the worst of it, but Candace could no longer fool herself into thinking she'd escaped unscathed.

"I'm not going to ask Dr. Maines out." Jenna looked like she wanted to say something else, but Candace couldn't wait—couldn't draw this moment out any longer, or she might lose her nerve. She no longer had any doubt that she was supposed to be in this spot with this woman and that their friendship was strong enough to survive.

"Good. I don't want you to go out with Dr. Maines."

"You don't think I'm good enough for her, right?"

"It's not that at all. I've got someone else in mind for you." Candace pushed herself up and turned to sit on the edge of the bed.

"Have you been holding out on me? Where did you meet someone new?" Jenna moved to mirror her pose. Their knees almost touched in the space between the beds.

Candace sighed. "Could you just understand what I'm trying to say so I don't have to actually come out and say it?" Heat filled her cheeks, and her stomach flopped nervously. This would all be much more embarrassing if she passed out or threw up right now.

"What—I don't—"

If she weren't so nervous, Jenna's expression at the moment she put it together might have amused her. Her eyebrows shot up and her chin dropped slightly. Then her gaze darted down Candace's body and back up to Candace's face, but she avoided meeting her eyes.

"You—uh, you mean that—you and I—"

"See? It's not that easy to articulate, is it?"

"Shit, Candace. I don't know what to say."

They couldn't both be lost in this situation, and since this was new information for Jenna, maybe Candace needed to be the one to get herself together. She drew in a deep breath and tilted her head back to look at the ceiling for a second. Then she stood, putting a little space between them in hopes that might help. When she got to the wall by the television she whipped around, already throwing her next statement out between them.

"If it's totally out of the question, never happening, not something you'd consider, just tell me right now. Quick, like a Band-Aid, so I can work on getting over it."

Jenna shook her head slowly. "It's not. Out of the question."

"You need some time to process?" She read Jenna's still-confused expression. "Would this be a space-and-silence process? Or do you want to talk?"

"How long have you felt this way?" Jenna touched her eyebrow, a sign that she was feeling overwhelmed.

"Okay, so talking then. And we're starting with a tough question."

"Are there easy questions in this scenario?"

"Good point." Candace returned to the bed and sat down. She wanted to take Jenna's hand, but the only time she'd ever done that was the day of the festival. Over the years, they'd hugged each other, crammed way too close together in a car, and danced together—the drunk kind where there might be too much grinding. That last one hurt Candace, in a kind of good way.

But that day, she'd held Jenna's hand all the way to the hospital and every second she was in her room until she woke up. Then not again. What had Jenna asked her? How long?

"I've been attracted to you since the day we met. I've—" She hesitated, then decided she might as well be all in. "I've had deeper feelings since—eh, about six months after we met."

"Damn. You never said anything."

"And risk ruining our partnership? Maybe you've forgotten my stories about the loud gum-smacker, the one with too much perfume, and the guy who sang along with every song on the radio—but with the wrong words. I could not go through another one of those."

"Maybe not in the beginning, but after a while, you had to have figured out we could get through it."

She shrugged, as if this conversation weren't the biggest deal in the world. "I was scared."

"What changed?"

"The festival. I'd been telling myself *maybe someday* for so long. But that day started me thinking that we're not promised a someday. All we have for sure is today. Corny, I know. If I had lost you that day—" She cleared her throat to cover up the hitch of emotion in her voice. "So I've been trying to figure out how to tell you, and then you were suddenly mad for no reason. I was going to tell you yesterday, but when I got to work, Warnke called me into the office. I thought it would make the trip awkward."

"Because this hasn't already been awkward?"

"Who wants to share a room with someone who has just professed their feelings when the other person doesn't return them? Unless I really did want to sleep in the rig—"

"And you were sure I didn't return them?"

"Pretty sure. For years, I've watched you go after any woman you're interested in. I figured if I had a chance, I would've seen a sign."

"You're not just *any* woman."

"Before you say anything, I don't need you to try to spare my feelings. I can handle the truth."

"I guess the festival was a catalyst for me, too. Not right away. But recently, I've been seeing us in a new light. And when I thought you might go out with Dr. Maines, I felt this insane jealousy. I was jealous because I wanted *you*, not her."

They sat on their respective beds, mirroring each other but not touching. "What do we do now? I hadn't considered that you might also have feelings for me. I focused on prepping myself for rejection."

"It's been a long day. You look as exhausted as I feel. Let's table this subject for tonight and talk some more tomorrow."

CHAPTER NINE

Jenna rolled over as the alarm on her cell phone went off. Deputy Sapp was sending a car for them at eight. She'd set her alarm for six, leaving them both time to get ready and grab a quick breakfast at the diner attached to the motel. She didn't know how long it would be before they ate lunch.

Candace slept peacefully in the other bed. She lay on her side, her arms bent and her hands stacked under her cheek. Jenna traced her eyes over Candace's shoulder and down to her hip, then felt like a creep, even though Candace had a sheet over her.

"Are you going to sit over there staring? Or are you going to come closer and not make it so weird?" Candace didn't even open her eyes.

Jenna stood and approached Candace's bed. Candace's eyes followed her, dropping down her in a way that heated her from the inside. She sat on the edge of the bed, trying not to feel strange about the situation.

They'd shared a room before, so this shouldn't be weird. They'd even shared a bed once.

"What's going on in that head?"

"I was just thinking about that time we all went to Pensacola, and we rented that two-bedroom condo."

"Everett and Sam took the room with two doubles, and you and I shared—"

"A king bed." Jenna took her hand and stroked her thumb across her knuckles. "Was that—did you—I don't know how to ask this without sounding like a conceited ass."

Candace lifted her chin in a go-ahead gesture.

"Was that hard for you?"

"Because you're so irresistible, being in the same bed and not having sex is torture for any woman?"

Jenna laughed. "Okay."

"You're right. You sound like a conceited ass."

"I'm sorry. I didn't mean it exactly like that. But ever since I started noticing new things about you, I can't seem to stop. I can imagine that situation would be more difficult for me now."

"That was a crazy week. But for the most part it was about the four of us hanging out and long days at the beach. By the time we fell into bed, I was too exhausted to think about anything else. I remember one night, though, that was maybe harder than the rest."

"Yeah?"

"We all went out for drinks—you had a lot of tequila and—"

"And tequila makes me flirty," she grimaced, "and a little handsy. It always has."

"I woke up in the middle of the night, and you were palming my breast."

Jenna covered her face with her free hand. "Oh my God, I thought I dreamed that. No, I was sure that was a dream because your—" She stopped as a visceral memory hit her, and she could tell from the flush crawling up Candace's neck that none of it had been a dream.

"My nipple got hard. Yeah, one of the most humiliating moments of my life."

"What, no?"

"Oh, yes. I was saved from dying of embarrassment only because I could tell that you were back asleep in seconds. And when we never talked about it again, I wasn't even sure you remembered."

"I woke up with the worst hangover and the belief that I'd had a sexy dream about my best friend. I don't know if you noticed, but I never drank tequila again after that trip."

Candace pursed her lips as she considered Jenna's admission. "I didn't, but now that you mention it, I don't remember you drinking it again. Though it was never your go-to, anyway."

"Well, aside from my feeling you up, that was an awesome trip."

"Are you kidding? That was my favorite part." Candace smiled. "It was a great vacation. I knew you were drunk and asleep, so I didn't read too much into it. But you—ah, you squeezed my breast and made this sound—like a little growl in your throat—and snuggled against me, and it was the most erotic and most confusing moment."

"I'm so sorry, Candy."

Candace closed her eyes.

"You don't like it when I call you that. I guess I'm sorry for that, too."

"No. I—I usually don't, but you've never said it quite that way before."

"How did I say it?"

"Intimately and a little raspy."

"And you liked that?" Jenna raised her brows.

"Okay. Don't get full of yourself." Candace tugged on her hand. "I've been thinking about what we talked about last night, and I have an idea. But I need you to get in here with me before I can tell you about it."

Jenna stretched out beside Candace, and Candace rolled over and pulled Jenna's arm around her so that they were spooning. Jenna stared at the spot behind Candace's ear, wanting to kiss her there.

"What's your idea?"

"Before I get to that." Candace covered her hand and started to slide it up her stomach toward her breast. "Do you want to recreate that night in Pensacola? For old times' sake?"

Jenna snatched her hand back just as her fingers touched the swell of Candace's breast. "Cut it out."

Candace laughed. "About our dilemma, I'd like to propose an experiment."

"Okay."

"We already know we get along. You know my quirks and I know yours. As long as we both think we could live with those in the long term—now that I mention it, I'll be clear. I'm thinking about more than just a fling here."

"Me, too. I wouldn't risk what we have for anything less."

"Then there's only one thing we don't know."

"What?" Jenna asked.

"Do we have physical chemistry?"

"What's your plan?" She was certain they would, given the way her heart was racing just now with Candace in her arms, pressed against her.

"This hotel room is now Las Vegas. What happens in this room stays in this room."

"Seriously?"

Candace laughed. "Why not? At the end of this trip, we decide whether to give it a shot or not. But we both agree our friendship remains either way."

"How do we know we can do that? That one of us won't get our feelings hurt if the other one decides they don't want to pursue anything more?"

"I'm the one with the unrequited crush, so if I'm saying I can do it, then you can, too."

Jenna chuckled. "Unrequited crush? Feels dramatic."

"Maybe to you. But you know how you feel right now? Come talk to me in two and a half years or so."

"Okay. Las Vegas."

"Good." Candace turned in her arms until she faced her. "Now, let's see about that chemistry."

She took Jenna's face between her hands and looked into her eyes for longer than would have been comfortable for anyone else. Fear flashed and then melted away in Candace's gaze as she stroked her hands down to Jenna's neck. Jenna closed the space between them until her lips almost touched Candace's, then paused. She could feel Candace straining not to move the remaining inch. With tremendous effort, Jenna held herself back, enjoying the bloom of anticipation unfurling within her, tendrils of pleasure growing and reaching out to tingle along every nerve.

When she touched her lips to Candace's, those tingles turned to sparks, then bursts, bright and hot behind her eyes as she closed them. She slid her arm around Candace's waist and gathered her closer as the kiss ended.

"Well? Chemistry?" Candace's fingers still rested on Jenna's neck.

"You have to ask?"

"I could use a little reassurance that it wasn't just me."

Jenna replayed that kiss in her mind, capturing the feeling once more and bottling it in her mind. "Kissing you is like coming home to a surprise party."

Candace laughed. "I need you to explain that one, because I don't remember you having a surprise party, so I don't even know if you like them."

"Coming home is familiar and warm and comfortable, and surprise parties are exciting and unexpected."

"Kiss me again so I can feel the party, too." Candace slid her hands to the back of Jenna's neck and pulled her back down.

Jenna complied, pouring her feelings into the meeting of their lips—happiness, excitement, anticipation, and desire.

"Damn. I almost forgot about what you were wearing." Candace smoothed her hand over the silk covering Jenna's lower back. "You really sleep in this stuff."

"Just because you're sleeping doesn't mean you can't feel pretty," Jenna said with exaggerated flair.

She slipped her hand under the hem of Candace's T-shirt and trailed her fingers up her rib cage. Candace's skin was soft and warm, and Jenna wanted to map it under her hands.

Jenna kissed her again, and Candace rolled to her back, pulling Jenna on top of her. Candace's leg slipped between hers, and Jenna rocked her hips against it.

"Whoa." Jenna caught herself before she could embarrass herself. She moved to lie on her side next to Candace. "Should we slow down?"

"Las Vegas, remember?"

"Yes, but there's Las Vegas, and then there's drunk as hell in Las Vegas. You and me having sex less than twelve hours after our first honest conversation about our feelings is definitely drunk as hell."

"There's no one I'd rather get wasted with." Candace rolled toward her, ran her hand down Jenna's side, and grasped her hip. "But if you want to stop, we can."

"I don't want us to risk—"

"Jenna, I'm okay. Please. I can't go out there today without this."

Jenna understood. After all they'd been through, after what they'd seen here yesterday and what they were likely to see today, Candace needed to prove she was alive and well—that they both were. Jenna wanted that, too.

She glanced at the clock. "We have forty minutes, and then we need to be showering and getting ready to meet the others at the car. That'll be a bit of a hurry for me, but I'll give it a shot." Jenna winked.

"Oh, swoon. Finally, a girl with stamina." Candace laughed as she kissed Jenna again.

Had Candace been missing that with other women? They didn't talk specifically about their sex lives. She hadn't realized until now how firmly they'd planted that boundary between them. She talked to Everett about women she slept with, and she thought Candace talked to Sam. Had Candace put up that wall deliberately?

She didn't know what Candace liked in bed. Did she want to take control, or was she more comfortable in a submissive role? Apparently, she liked stamina, so Jenna should start there and figure out the rest as she went.

She pulled back, then met Candace's eyes. "You're my best friend, and that is not going to change no matter what happens here. So if you need something or decide to stop at any time, just tell me." She waited for Candace's nod of agreement, and when she got it, she slipped her hand under the front of Candace's shirt, stroking her fingers across Candace's flat stomach.

Candace sat up and lifted the shirt over her head, then lay back down. Her breasts were small and tipped with dusky-pink nipples. Jenna rested her hand on the center of Candace's stomach and met her eyes. Candace smiled, covered Jenna's hand, and slid it upward until she cupped her breast.

"Why don't we pick up where we left off?"

Jenna paused, waiting to see if touching Candace felt strange. But when Candace's nipple hardened against her hand, she felt only anticipation edged with arousal. She flashed back to that moment she'd thought was a dream. She bent and kissed Candace's chest just below her collarbone.

"If I'd been awake enough to realize what I was doing, who knows where that night might have led?"

"You would have freaked out, yanked your hand away, and maybe slept on the couch for the rest of the trip."

Jenna laughed against Candace's skin, and when Candace did, too, she felt the vibration beneath her lips. "You might be right. I never had as much game as you guys thought I did."

"Mm. You don't need it when you look like you do."

"But I'm here now. Not freaking out. And I really want to learn what drives you crazy."

She kissed a path to Candace's other nipple, then curled her tongue around it. It pebbled immediately, and Candace arched her back and moaned. *Sensitive.* Jenna filed that discovery away. She tested her teeth against it, lightly, and Candace sucked in a breath and laid her hand against Jenna's head. When she applied more pressure, Candace curled her fingers into Jenna's hair and gave a slight tug. She eased up and the tugging ceased.

She continued reading Candace's body, alternating kissing and biting, finding the spots where she liked the sharpness and where to soothe with her tongue.

"Please, Jenna." Writhing against her, Candace grabbed her wrist and pushed her hand under her pajama pants. "I need you to touch me."

Jenna's chest clutched, and she ached with the need to fulfill Candace's desire. God, she hadn't even realized she'd been missing this for so long. When she slipped her fingers between Candace's legs, heat flared between them, flashing, then settling into a glow that grew more intense as she stroked Candace.

Candace arched and whispered encouragement while Jenna soaked in every word as if Candace's pleasure—her approval—were the only thing she ever needed. Candace gripped the back of Jenna's arm, holding her there as she trembled and tightened, then thrust against her hand.

Jenna buried her face in Candace's neck, her own orgasm desperately close just from absorbing Candace's. As Candace's frenzy slowed, Jenna sucked her earlobe lightly, sending another shudder through her.

"I knew you'd be that good," Candace whispered with a chuckle.

"Oh, honey, we're not done yet. We still have fifteen minutes." Jenna rose to her knees and grabbed the waistband of Candace's pants. Once she'd removed them, she lowered herself between Candace's legs.

With several strokes of her tongue, she brought Candace back to the edge again.

"Oh, shit, not yet." Candace tried to pull away, but Jenna held her close and slowed her attention.

She followed Candace's pace, enjoying the way she pushed herself near orgasm, then backed off. Candace's muscles contracted and relaxed as she controlled her body, using deep breathing to keep herself from release. Watching Candace restrain herself this way had Jenna riding the line, too. She'd never been more turned on by her partner before. She needed to get off so badly, and she didn't have any self-discipline. She snuck her hand between her legs, under her silk shorts, and started rubbing her clit. Within seconds, she clenched her thighs around her hand, gasping against Candace.

Candace raised her head and their eyes met. Whatever Candace had been using to hold back slipped away, and she spasmed beneath Jenna. She dropped her head back and cried out.

"Damn you," she rasped as her motions quieted again.

"Me?" Jenna rested her head on Candace's thigh.

"Yes. I was good until I saw you coming all over your hand." Candace's stern voice dissolved into a quiet chuckle. "There's a sentence I never thought I'd say to my best friend."

Jenna laughed as she sat up. "You? At least you had yearnings. Imagine how I feel hearing it now."

"I had yearnings? I'm not some Victorian maiden."

"Victorian what? I'm sorry, babe. We don't have time for role-playing right now. We've got to get ready. But maybe later tonight." Jenna climbed out of bed, dodging Candace's attempt to slap her ass. She went into the bathroom and turned on the shower to start warming the water.

"Don't worry. I've got all kinds of plans for later tonight." Naked, Candace followed Jenna into the bathroom, and while Jenna was still undressing, she stepped into the shower.

"Hey. That was for me."

"You could join me, but then we'll be late," Candace called from the other side of the curtain. "Maybe you should find a way to amuse yourself until I'm done. You didn't seem to have a problem with that a moment ago."

Jenna loved the cocky edge to Candace's voice. She grabbed her toothbrush while she waited her turn in the shower, and while she brushed, she daydreamed about what Candace had planned for later.

❖

"Where did that come from?" Jenna asked as she flopped on the bed face-first.

They'd returned to the room after another full day and grabbed showers. But Jenna had barely toweled off when Candace had her on the bed on all fours.

"I've been thinking about that all day." Candace lay down, half on her and half beside her, still buzzing with the feel of Jenna squeezing around her fingers as she drove her to climax. She'd caught herself looking at Jenna during odd moments while they worked today, remembering the feel of her hands and mouth on her. Her only regret about this morning was that she hadn't made time to reciprocate.

This morning had been amazing. She'd been nervous about how they would be together, but she needn't have worried. At least not about that. They hadn't had time to talk afterward, or maybe they'd purposefully avoided serious conversation since they seemed to find time to continue flirting and trading promises about tonight. She was okay if they were still holding on to the premise that this couple of days was a vacation from real life.

She hadn't held anything back this morning. She didn't know what would happen when they returned to real life, but she was determined not to have any regrets. It would have been easy for her to shelter a part of her, out of self-preservation. But she very deliberately let down all her walls for Jenna, knowing that taking a chance could lead to devastation. Unless, as was her fervent hope, their experiment didn't end.

Jenna turned her head to the side. "Who are you, and what have you done with my friend?"

"I'm still me."

"Seriously? How come I didn't know you were amazing in bed? I mean, I assumed but—"

"That wasn't all me." Candace didn't have casual sex, so when she did, she was usually connected to the person. But this morning, and just now, had been on a whole other level. And, she realized as she idly painted a pattern on Jenna's lower back with her finger, she was ready to touch her and be touched by her again. "How's your shoulder?"

"Amazing." Jenna turned over onto her back.

Candace smiled. "I doubt that."

"Seriously. Although I can't really feel my body at all right now, so there's that."

Candace rolled to her stomach, laid her arm along Jenna's chest, and rested her chin on the back of her hand. "Do you want me to get you some ibuprofen, just in case?"

Jenna swept her arm out and curled it around Candace. "No. I'd really prefer you think of me as a lover who can handle anything than one who needs ibuprofen to get through an active night."

Candace pushed herself up on her elbows. "Would you rather I talk about how incredibly sexy you are?" She stroked a hand over Jenna's stomach.

"That's better. Tell me more."

"You have amazing hands—I knew you would. I've watched you use them to save lives. They're quick and confident." She threw a leg over Jenna's hip and sat up, straddling her. "What I didn't anticipate was that your mouth—the one that so often gets you in trouble—could also be so awesomely talented."

Jenna lifted her chin with a cocky grin. "Well, in case you think you're the one with all the good ideas, I want to tell you what I'm thinking about right now."

"Yes?"

"If you come up here, I could show you again how good I am with my mouth." Jenna grasped her thighs.

"Really?" Jenna had just found the one thing Candace had always wanted to try but never felt comfortable enough to.

"Oh, yeah."

Candace could now recognize the arousal transforming Jenna's features, darkening her eyes, and making her bite her lower lip. She dropped her gaze to Jenna's hardened nipples, several shades darker than her skin. She pinched one between her fingers, and Jenna thrust into her hips. Before Jenna could get enough friction, Candace moved into position over her mouth.

Five minutes later, satiated, Candace spooned Jenna, pressing closer and wrapping an arm around her middle.

"Everett is going to love this," Jenna said.

"Don't talk about Everett in my afterglow," she mumbled against Jenna's shoulder, then sighed. "Why is she going to love this?"

"Ever since Sam and Nicole got together, she's been wanting us to find someone, too. She's surprisingly obsessed with us all being happily paired off. I bet she never thought we might end up with each other."

"She could have an idea now. I sort of vented to them at bowling the other night."

"What?"

"Hey. You'd just tried to break up our partnership. I was distraught."

"You know I could never leave you—you're my ride or die."

"Really?"

"Yeah."

"I love that so much, I'm going to pretend we're hip enough for you to say it." Candace squeezed Jenna's hip.

"Are you hungry? Want room service?"

"Mm. I'm good for now." They'd last eaten around lunchtime. But Candace didn't want to move from her current position, and she definitely didn't want either of them putting clothes on to answer the door.

CHAPTER TEN

Have we left Las Vegas yet?" Jenna asked halfway through their drive home. The conversation had been light, if not flirty, for the first half of the trip. They'd just gotten on the road after stopping for a late breakfast.

"I suppose we have."

"Should we talk?"

"I've never seen you so eager to talk while in a relationship."

"You've got to stop comparing this to what you've seen with my previous girlfriends. I told you, you aren't just another woman. And I don't want what's between us to be like any of those situations."

"Okay. Let's talk."

"How are you feeling about what happened?" Jenna asked.

"Well, since I just referenced us being in a relationship, I'm hoping we're in the same place."

"You're my best friend—"

"Oh, no." She'd said she was okay with whatever happened after their Vegas vacation, but her heart sank when it seemed she'd be getting the we-should-just-be-friends speech.

"What?"

"Nothing. Go ahead." Determined to keep her promise, she tried to ignore the cracking in her chest. She would get over this—somehow.

"You're my best friend, and I can talk to you about pretty much anything. You were there for me when I got hurt, even when I didn't want to let you." Jenna glanced over at her, then back at the road. "I never thought we could improve on that. But what I've felt these past two days—I'm having a hard time finding the words."

Suddenly, Jenna pulled to the side of the interstate, near an exit ramp where she could get the rig far enough off the road to be safe.

"What are you doing?"

"I have to look at you when I say this." Jenna angled in her seat and took Candace's hand. "I love you."

Candace's heart soared before her head could intervene. But logic still managed to take control of her mouth. "We're friends. Of course you do."

"No. I mean, yeah, I love you as a friend. But this is more than that. I know we just opened ourselves to the possibilities the day before yesterday, and it seems too soon. But, Candace—" Jenna squeezed her hands. "I've known you more than long enough to realize this is true. I just needed to get to know myself better to believe it."

"I love you, too. And I just needed enough confidence to admit it."

"The fear of losing each other didn't hurt either."

"That, too."

Jenna half stood in her seat to get close enough to kiss her. "I want more than Las Vegas."

"I'm so happy to hear you say that."

Jenna parked next to Everett's SUV in the bowling-alley parking lot. As they got out, she saw Nicole's car nearby. They were the last to arrive. Nerves suddenly knotted in her stomach. They'd been back for several weeks, but between work and spending their evenings together, they hadn't seen their friends at all. They texted them some, and Candace had said that she told them they'd made up, but nothing more. Of course, they'd known they had this gathering coming up, but they hadn't talked about how to handle it. She'd been too busy exploring the new facets of their relationship—in every room of Candace's apartment.

Jenna held back, tugging Candace's hand to stop her for a second. "Let's not say anything to them for now."

"Why not?"

Jenna shrugged. "If things don't work out, it won't be as weird with them."

"It's been three weeks," Candace said, as if that were a lifetime. "Do you think it won't work out?"

"I think it will. But if not, I don't want them taking sides. I want us all to stay friends." She'd been friends with them first, so it would be natural for them to take her side in a split. They'd actually liked some of her exes, but none of them kept in touch with them after each breakup. Candace was different—for her, but also for her friends. She didn't think they'd abandon her, but she didn't want to take any chances.

"Okay." Candace deliberately dropped her hand. "Should I go in first, and you wait a few minutes so they don't get suspicious?"

"No. Your place is between mine and here. They won't think it's weird that we rode together."

The other four already had shoes on and had bowled a couple of warm-up frames. Jenna didn't mind, though, when she thought back to why they were late. They'd finally found Candace's discarded bra, which had fallen behind the sofa, where she'd flung it while Jenna took off her pants.

As they approached, conversation among their friends ceased suddenly. She glanced at Candace, who looked just as confused as she was. Had they been talking about them—possibly figured them out already? The idea didn't scare her at all.

"What's going on, ladies?" She glanced at each of their faces, mystified by their nervous expressions. If they were onto them, she'd hoped for happiness, maybe even some teasing, but they avoided eye contact and offered awkward greetings.

"Nice try. What were you talking about when we walked up?" Candace shoved her shoulders back and raised her chin, clearly ready for a confrontation. Jenna loved her protective instincts and had to stop herself from putting her hand on the small of her back in support.

They both waited while the other four had a silent conversation consisting of eye contact and small nods. Then Everett met Jenna's eyes, becoming the spokesman for the group.

"Sit down." She nodded toward an empty seat next to Claire.

Jenna wanted to insist Everett say her piece while she remained standing, but the others' expressions made her nervous enough to comply.

"I thought you might have heard already. Jared Ackerman pled guilty."

Now she was glad she'd sat down. The flash of rage at hearing his name mingled with a sharp, sick feeling in her stomach. But as she processed Everett's news, relief sanded the rough edges. She wouldn't have to endure watching a drawn-out trial covered from every angle by the media. Her name and profession wouldn't be broadcast next to those of the other victims.

"I didn't know."

Everett shifted her gaze to Claire, then back to Jenna. "Sentencing is next week, but the prosecutor isn't seeking the death penalty. They said that was probably part of the plea deal. But they expect he'll get life in prison."

Candace moved closer and rested a hand on her shoulder. Jenna smiled and covered it with hers.

"You okay?"

Jenna closed her eyes briefly, imagining that if they were alone Candace would slide down onto the seat beside her and enfold her in her arms. She was so much better than okay now. She nodded, and Candace squeezed her shoulder.

"I am." She suspected Candace needed to hear the words. The others still stared at her warily as well. "At least that part will be over and we can move on."

She couldn't say that all that had happened wouldn't still affect her. But she'd healed, mostly, and she had friends who cared. Enduring that day had made her realize her feelings for Candace and that time was too fragile to risk missing out on anything.

"I'm good, guys. Now let's bowl."

She and Candace exchanged one more meaningful look, with the silent promise to revisit these emotions later if they needed to. For now, she wanted to enjoy an evening with her friends. She debated spilling their secret but wanted to wait until it wouldn't live in the shadow of Everett's revelation.

She'd underestimated how difficult it would be to play it cool with their friends. She was pretty certain both Nicole and Claire had caught her winking at Candace. And when Candace bowled a strike, Jenna jumped up, ready to hug her, only to have Candace turn it into the most awkward fist bump ever. Jenna nodded as she turned away, feeling four pairs of curious eyes on them.

Then, after getting another round of drinks, Jenna set them down on the table, sat down next to Candace, and instinctively reached for

Candace's hand. But she caught herself mid-action and ended up giving her a pat on the knee instead.

She finally had to walk away, under the guise of going to the bar to order some chicken wings. But Everett jumped up and said she wanted some onion rings and followed her. As they leaned against the bar next to each other, Jenna stared up at the television behind the bartender.

"Why are you guys acting so weird?"

"We're not." Even to Jenna, her voice sounded unnaturally fast and high-pitched.

"Seriously? Is it because of what we told you when you came in?"

"No." Everett gave her a skeptical look, so she added, "I promise."

"Then what's going on with you two? You're being very attentive and strange at the same time."

Jenna glanced over her shoulder at their friends and caught a quick look from Candace, a moment so full of love she couldn't contain it anymore.

"If I tell you, you can't say anything to the others."

"Absolutely."

"Since we got back from Henry County, we've been seeing each other."

She didn't expect the judgment that clouded Everett's expression. "I don't know if that's a good idea."

"Why not?"

"She's just not the kind of woman you play with, Teele."

Then Jenna understood Everett's apprehension. "I know she told you guys about her feelings for me."

Everett didn't confirm or deny, but the tense press of her lips relaxed a little.

"I'm not playing around. I'm in love with her."

"Seriously?" Everett broke into a grin.

"Yeah."

Everett turned and headed straight for their lane, onion-ring order forgotten.

"Damn it." Jenna followed, knowing she wouldn't catch her in time.

She reached the group just in time to see Everett pull a twenty-dollar bill from her wallet and slap it on the scoring table in front of

Nicole. Nicole glanced at Jenna and Candace, then grinned and put it in her pocket without a word.

"No way," Sam said quietly.

Candace glanced at Jenna, but she looked away, already knowing what was about to happen but refusing to help accelerate it.

"What inside joke am I missing?" Candace asked.

"It seems that we're the ones left out of the loop." Everett gave her a smug grin, then shifted her eyes toward Jenna.

Candace swung an accusatory look at Jenna. "You told her."

"It slipped out." Jenna wondered if Candace would buy that explanation, and her uncertainty made her response sound more like a question.

"You're the one who said we shouldn't tell them yet."

"I know. I'm just so happy, I couldn't help it."

"So tell the rest of us. I need to officially hear it," Nicole said.

Candace looked at each of them, then at Jenna, her gaze seeking confirmation. Jenna gave her a small nod, hoping her own eyes relayed the confidence she felt in their relationship. These were their friends, family, really, after all. They should share in this major event, and she was wrong to think otherwise.

Jenna took Candace's hand and said, "Candace and I are dating—very seriously dating—exclusively—as in—"

"We get the idea," Claire said as she stood and approached them. "I'm so happy for you." She wrapped Candace in a hug, and Jenna couldn't hear what she whispered in her ear. But from the laughter they shared when Jenna responded, she suspected she'd been wrong, and she'd been talking to Claire about sex lately, not Sam.

After they all shared a round of hugs and congratulations, Jenna took Candace's hand, and when Candace squeezed hers, she remembered a moment, over four months ago, in the ambulance, as she lost her battle with consciousness and Candace's hand had been her anchor. She should have known then that Candace was the one person she needed in order to heal.

About the Author

Erin Dutton resides near Nashville, TN, with her wife. They enjoy traveling with their much doted-on dog. In 2007, she published her first book, *Sequestered Hearts*, and has kept writing since. She's a proud recipient of the 2011 Alice B. Readers Appreciation Medal for her body of work.

When not working or writing, she enjoys playing golf, photography, and spending time with friends and family.

Books Available From Bold Strokes Books

All the Paths to You by Morgan Lee Miller. High school sweethearts Quinn Hughes and Kennedy Reed reconnect five years after they break up and realize that their chemistry is all but over. (978-1-63555-662-9)

Arrested Pleasures by Nanisi Barrett D'Arnuck. When charged with a crime she didn't commit, Katherine Lowe faces the question: Which is harder, going to prison or falling in love? (978-1-63555-684-1)

Bonded Love by Renee Roman. Carpenter Blaze Carter suffers an injury that shatters her dreams, and ER nurse Trinity Greene hopes to show her that sometimes hope is worth fighting for. (978-1-63555-530-1)

Convergence by Jane C. Esther. With life as they know it on the line, can Aerin McLeary and Olivia Ando's love survive an otherworldly threat to humankind? (978-1-63555-488-5)

Coyote Blues by Karen F. Williams. Riley Dawson, psychotherapist and shape-shifter, has her world turned upside down when Fiona Bell, her one true love, returns. (978-1-63555-558-5)

Drawn by Carsen Taite. Will the clues lead Detective Claire Hanlon to the killer terrorizing Dallas, or will she merely lose her heart to person of interest urban artist Riley Flynn? (978-1-63555-644-5)

Lucky by Kris Bryant. Was Serena Evans's luck really about winning the lottery, or is she about to get even luckier in love? (978-1-63555-510-3)

The Last Days of Autumn by Donna K. Ford. Autumn and Caroline question the fairness of life, the cruelty of loss, and what it means to love as they navigate the complicated minefield of relationships, grief, and life-altering illness. (978-1-63555-672-8)

Three Alarm Response by Erin Dutton. In the midst of tragedy, can these first responders find love and healing? Three stories of courage, bravery, and passion. (978-1-63555-592-9)

Veterinary Partner by Nancy Wheelton. Callie and Lauren are determined to keep their hearts safe but find that taking a chance on love is the safest option of all. (978-1-63555-666-7)

Forging a Desire Line by Mary P. Burns. When Charley's ex-wife, Tricia, is diagnosed with inoperable cancer, the private duty nurse Tricia hires turns out to be the handsome and aloof Joanna, who ignites something inside Charley she isn't ready to face. (978-1-63555-665-0)

Journey to Cash by Ashley Bartlett. Cash Braddock thought everything was great, but it looks like her history is about to become her right now. Which is a real bummer. (978-1-63555-464-9)

Love on the Night Shift by Radclyffe. Between ruling the night shift in the ER at the Rivers and raising her teenage daughter, Blaise Richilieu has all the drama she needs in her life, until a dashing young attending appears on the scene and relentlessly pursues her. (978-1-63555-668-1)

Olivia's Awakening by Ronica Black. When the daring and dangerously gorgeous Eve Monroe is hired to get Olivia Savage into shape, a fierce passion ignites, causing both to question everything they've ever known about love. (978-1-63555-613-1)

The Duchess and the Dreamer by Jenny Frame. Clementine Fitzroy has lost her faith and love of life. Can dreamer Evan Fox make her believe in life and dream again? (978-1-63555-601-8)

The Road Home by Erin Zak. Hollywood actress Gwendolyn Carter is about to discover that losing someone you love sometimes means gaining someone to fall for. (978-1-63555-633-9)

Waiting for You by Elle Spencer. When passionate past-life lovers meet again in the present day, one remembers it vividly and the other isn't so sure. (978-1-63555-635-3)

While My Heart Beats by Erin McKenzie. Can a love born amidst the horrors of the Great War survive? (978-1-63555-589-9)

Face the Music by Ali Vali. Sweet music is the last thing that happens when Nashville music producer Mason Liner and daughter of country royalty Victoria Roddy are thrown together in an effort to save country star Sophie Roddy's career. (978-1-63555-532-5)

Flavor of the Month by Georgia Beers. What happens when baker Charlie and chef Emma realize their differing paths have led them right back to each other? (978-1-63555-616-2)

Mending Fences by Angie Williams. Rancher Bobbie Del Rey and veterinarian Grace Hammond are about to discover if heartbreaks of the past can ever truly be mended. (978-1-63555-708-4)

Silk and Leather: Lesbian Erotica with an Edge, edited by Victoria Villaseñor. This collection of stories by award-winning authors offers fantasies as soft as silk and tough as leather. The only question is: How far will you go to make your deepest desires come true? (978-1-63555-587-5)

The Last Place You Look by Aurora Rey. Dumped by her wife and looking for anything but love, Julia Pierce retreats to her hometown only to rediscover high school friend Taylor Winslow, who's secretly crushed on her for years. (978-1-63555-574-5)

The Mortician's Daughter by Nan Higgins. A singer on the verge of stardom discovers she must give up her dreams to live a life in service to ghosts. (978-1-63555-594-3)

The Real Thing by Laney Webber. When passion flares between actress Virginia Green and masseuse Allison McDonald, can they be sure it's the real thing? (978-1-63555-478-6)

What the Heart Remembers Most by M. Ullrich. For college sweethearts Jax Levine and Gretchen Mills, could an accident be the second chance neither knew they wanted? (978-1-63555-401-4)

White Horse Point by Andrews & Austin. Mystery writer Taylor James finds herself falling for the mysterious woman on White Horse Point who lives alone, protecting a secret she can't share about a murderer who walks among them. (978-1-63555-695-7)